CW00517307

DEATH HOUSE

BOOK ONE OF THE DEATH SERIES

CALLUM PEARCE   CHISTO HEALY   CHRIS HEWITT

DAVID GREEN   E L GILES   EVAN BAUGHFMAN

G ALLEN WILBANKS   GREGG CUNNINGHAM

HARI NAVARRO   JOHN H DROMEY   KIMBERLY REI

MICHELLE RIVER   NICOLE LITTLE   PETER J FOOTE

SCARLETT LAKE   SCOTT DYSON   SHAWN M KLIMEK

STEPHEN HERCZEG   TERRY MILLER

ALANNAH K PEARSON   ALEXANDRA HARPER

JADE CINDERS   MAGGIE D BRACE

NICHOLAS WILKINSON   PHILIP ROGERS

RACHEL C PENDRAGON

RAVEN & DRAKE PUBLISHING

Raven and Drake Publishing

Copyright © 2021 by Raven and Drake Publishing

This anthology is entirely a work of fiction. The names, characters and incidents
portrayed in it are the work of the author's imagination. Any resemblance to
actual persons, living or dead, events or localities is entirely coincidental.

Paperback ISBN: 978-1-914320-06-4
Hardback ISBN: 978-1-914320-07-1

First edition.

www.ravenanddrakepublishing.co.uk

ALSO BY RAVEN & DRAKE PUBLISHING

April Horrors

New Tales of Old (Out 2021)

Candy Capers - A charity anthology (Out 2021)

MORE IN THE DEATH SERIES COMING LATE 2021

Death House

Death Ship

Death Beyond

Ancient Death

We ask only to be reassured about the noises in the cellar and not the window that should not have been open.

T.S. Eliot

Thank you to our Buy Me A Coffee supporters,
including our members
Dean Jones & Zachary Hennis

To support us and indie authors,
or to join our membership please visit
https://www.buymeacoffee.com/ravenanddrake

CONTENTS

FOREWORD

Houses have always been synonymous with hauntings and horrors beyond the imagination. They are often seen in movies, explored in television shows and found sitting on the street three doors down. The one with the yellow police tape blocking off access as the coroners pull out several white bags and have something akin to an ancient Egyptian excavation site in the back yard. The one that has way too many bodies buried beneath the Earth.

Haunted houses and those steeped in horror that oozes out of every crevice are explored in this anthology by several talented authors. Each one taking us on a journey through those houses that bring nothing but fear and death to whoever crosses their threshold.

We hope you enjoy these haunting shorts and remember to keep the lights on. Oh, and best check to make sure you've locked the back door.

Wait... was that window open before?

WITCH HOUSE
BY E.L. GILES

*H*artford, Connecticut, 1958

"Admit it, Butch. We're lost," I said, stopping next to the same tree I was sure we had walked past at least two times in the last hour. We were going in circles and sinking deeper into the forest. "This shortcut leads nowhere. We should already have gotten to the main trail by now, don't you think?"

"I know exactly where we are!" shouted Butch, offended. He rounded his thick chest as if his muscles could help get us out of this maze of vegetation. I let him calm before asking him to have a look at the map again. He hesitated at first, but I insisted. Until he realised that he had no other choice but to unfold it before my careful gaze and try to locate where we were. I knew then, as his eyes grazed across the map, that we were totally lost. In fact, it appeared he didn't even know how to read the map. Once again, Butch's pride had overtaken his common sense. He should have told me. I would have taken up the task. But no! Butch was too proud to admit he couldn't do something. Result: we were lost somewhere on Talcott Mountain, our rations—as well as my patience—diminishing quickly. I was hungry. I was tired. Within me, a wave of unstoppable anger started to grow towards Butch. I tried to tamp it down but to no avail.

"Whatever," he said. "We keep walking straight ahead until we find a stream to follow, and voila! We'll be back to civilisation in no time."

"So, we're lost! Dammit. I knew it was a bad idea to trust you! I fucking knew it. Just by the way you told me that you knew exactly where we were going, that this *shortcut* would help us save hours of walking. I should have known then that you were shitting me, and you had no freaking clue how to read a bloody map. I should have stayed home. Oh, Lord, I should have."

"Remind me whose idea it was, this trek and this camping trip?" Butch pushed the crumpled map roughly into my chest and started to walk again—in the opposite direction of where, not a minute ago, he'd claimed we should go. I ran to catch him up. "We're just a bit off the trail. That's it. No biggie. There's no reason to overreact."

"No biggie? Overreact? We should already be on our way back home, Butch. I was supposed to take Maggy out on the town. So, tell me, how will we make it out?"

Butch shrugged. "We will. That's it."

The midday sun, high in the sky, shone blazing hot. The stifling heat of July hit the top of my head, making me want to plop down in front of any of the myriad trees and sleep in its shadow. But we couldn't. Not now. Not with this gnawing anxiety festering in my gut, constantly pushing me to keep going. We had to find the damn trail as soon as possible.

The heat and exhaustion soon overcame us. We stopped by a gigantic willow tree that stood in the middle of a clearing. It looked quite inviting—I would even venture as far as to say cosy. A gentle breeze rustled through the lazy branches, making them dance and sing a mournful madrigal of aerial voices. Butch hastened to drop his backpack onto the ground and open it. He took out two cans, placing one beside the other.

"Corned beef or devilled ham? Your call!"

I pointed at the corned beef. I much preferred beef over ham but highly doubted either of the choices could even be called meat. That was all we had left, so it was wise to make the best out of them. Butch fiddled with the can for a moment, trying to pry its lid open with his rusty utility knife, finally managing to get it. He picked up a fork and a piece of stale bread, handing them to me. I sighed. Our snack looked far from appetising. I nonetheless took the chunk of bread and dipped it into the can, hoping the salty, moist beef would alter its taste and soften it somewhat. I fantasised about all the better meals we could be having.

"I swear that the first thing I'll do when we get out of this forest is to stop by the closest fast-food joint and pick up a cheeseburger. No! Two cheeseburgers," I said.

"I'd go with an enchilada and a shitload of hot sauce and French fries," said Butch. We began to try to one-up each other with all the best meals we could think of until we had exhausted the possibilities. In the end, it only served to darken my mood and push my exasperation a little further. Looking at my piece of bread, a sudden fit of anger overtook me, and I swung my fork and chunk of bread as far as I could, letting myself fall back against the tree trunk.

"I'm sorry," Butch said. He patted my shoulder, but I said nothing. "I should have told you about the map. And I shouldn't have suggested the shortcut. The spot looked sick, you know, and I wanted some excitement. You know how I am. I'm impulsive, and I like to improvise. Maybe a hiking trip in the forest wasn't the best place to start improvising though."

"No, it wasn't."

Butch continued with his apologies. His babbling soon became background noise. There was something soothing about his voice, or perhaps it was the sound of the breeze and the chirping birds. After a moment, I gave up resisting the urge to let everything go and allowed my mind to fall into the limbo of slumber. It didn't take long until Butch's voice and the surrounding noises of the forest faded, and all I heard was the whoosh of blood in my head. My breathing slowed until darkness came to comfort me.

J didn't know how much time had passed when I opened my eyes. It took me a moment to assemble my thoughts and process them. I looked at my watch and then raised my head to verify that I was really reading 7 pm. This was confirmed with the descending course of the sun and the subtle chill permeating the air. The day was almost gone, and we had lost precious hours of walking. I jumped to my feet, adrenaline coursing through my veins.

"Damn, Butch. Get up. We fell asleep," I said, picking my backpack up and slinging it across my shoulders. Butch didn't answer. I turned to wake him, but he was nowhere to be seen. His backpack was right where he'd last left it, and I noticed as I gazed about the clearing, that he'd started erecting our tent at some point. He must have stopped and waited for me to wake up and help him finish the assembly, venturing out to look for wood for a campfire. "Butch? Butch, where are you?"

I waited in anticipation, listening for an answer, which didn't come. I called again and again, my voice disappearing into the vast forest. I decided to enter the underbrush by the nearest path, consisting of brambles that scratched my skin, even through my pants and shirt. I walked for about ten minutes before realising that I'd gotten turned around. I had returned almost exactly to the place from which I had started. Beside me, some yards away, was the willow tree, our backpacks, and the skeleton of the tent. How could that be? I hadn't even noticed I had diverted from the path. I left the camp again, this time marking my way as I went. My goal was to cover the largest area possible without moving too far from the camp. Butch couldn't have gone far. I mean, there were plenty of branches and tree limbs everywhere. Why go far?

He must have gotten himself lost. I almost laughed at the thought. But after a quick survey, I couldn't find any trace of him, and when I returned to the camp, he still wasn't there.

"I swear if you're messing with me, I will kill you straight off!" I yelled, sure now that he was about to prank me like he always loved to do. I headed toward the tent and began to finish erecting it. All the while looking over my shoulder, expecting Butch to jump out of the bushes at any moment. I spent the next half hour in such anticipation, ultimately being proved wrong. The tent was now up, our backpacks secured inside. I'd even piled up some branches and dead leaves, which I was about to light up. Butch's absence weighed on me. "Freaking idiot."

He had really gotten lost, and now I didn't find it hilarious. Not at all. What were the chances that Butch would get lost searching for firewood? It was beyond ironic that he would get lost while we were already lost in the woods.

The gloom was rapidly settling, and I grabbed the torch I carried in my backpack. I turned it on and shined its light down onto the ground, where I hoped to find Butch's footsteps. I didn't know why it had only struck me now to look for footprints, now that the sun was low, the visibility was poor, and my chances of finding him were thin. All I found were several layers of dead leaves, broken limbs, and branches. But there were no other options left. I had to find Butch. He couldn't have gone far, could he?

I quickly lost the notion of time. I couldn't tell if minutes or hours had passed since I left the tent in search of my friend. The night grew pitch black without me noticing. It seemed as quick as turning the light off. It was surprisingly cold and windy, considering the season.

The trees took on the form of mystical guardians, standing sentinel over their kingdom in anticipation of intruders like me. A sense of oppression grew inside of me, accompanied by a horrible loneliness. Occasionally, the moonlight pierced through the gathering of clouds overhead, allowing my tired eyes some respite, opening the way ahead. All of a sudden, a sheet of rain descended, hitting me with such intensity that I was forced to take shelter under one of the larger trees nearby.

I waited. And waited some more. Neither the rain nor the wind stopped or slowed down.

"Butch! Butch!" I cried restlessly; my voice drowned out by the storm. I nonetheless persisted. I couldn't stop. In fact, finding Butch—and the tent—was the only thing I could think about now. *Find Butch.*

Why had I stopped marking my way?

Idiot. Bloody idiot.

I was soaked and frozen, and I was terrified. Not only by the frightening darkness, the beam of my torch didn't suffice to tame, but by the thought that I would never see my friend again. That I, myself, might never exit this hellish, morbid forest that would drive even a man with the most sound of minds to madness. Desperation grew as I realised I might have left Maggy alone, and she might never know what had happened to us. Profound guilt prickled my mind from not reassuring Butch when he kept apologising.

My state of terror climbed up to a new level when cries elevated through the tempest—cries of utter pain and fear. Blood chilled in my veins. I was frozen, my feet nailed to the ground. I didn't dare advance toward the sound.

"Help!" I heard Butch yelling. That sufficed to trigger the courage to leave my shelter. Head down, I ran through the trees and through the sheets of silver rain in the direction I thought the voice had come from.

"I'm coming! Hold on!" I kept repeating. I hoped Butch would do the same, keep screaming so I could pinpoint his position. But something else caught my attention. Something that sent such chill through my body that it forced me to stop. I ducked behind the closest tree, a slender maple whose naked branches hung dully like devitalised.

Flames flickered in the darkness, bobbing as their bearers moved across the uneven ground. Voices elevated, but I couldn't quite decipher what was being said. There seemed to be at least about twenty of them, maybe more. Were they hikers just like us? Were they rescuers? I started to run in their direction, crying out for help, when my foot got stuck in the mud, and I fell facedown onto the ground. When I got up again, my eyes couldn't catch sight of the flames again. They had disappeared. But another vision replaced this one, one that left me baffled.

A house...

It seemed so incongruous to find a house that hadn't been there few minutes before. A house, here in the middle of this forest, atop the mountain, isolated. What the hell was this? Was I being tricked by my brain? Had I hurt my head when I fell? Or was I simply becoming delirious, falling prey to a fever I didn't know I had?

I hesitated for a long moment before I started to walk toward the tall building—I wanted to make sure I wasn't hallucinating. But then, just as my feet penetrated the vast shadow of the house, the storm that had gone on hiatus resumed, raging more intensely than before. This alerted my most basic instincts of survival, and I ran for it, passing through the front door, ignoring the fact that the structure might collapse at any moment. Forgetting momentarily about Butch or the group of hikers. I slammed the door closed behind me and angled the light of my torch all around me, illuminating the hall in which I stood. A smell hit me, acrid and pestiferous assaulting my nostrils like an unwelcome visitor. Malign, I would even dare say, for there floated an aura I couldn't explain. It was like the house had been waiting for me, and I was now trapped inside a prison I couldn't escape. I shook the idea out of my head.

"Butch?" I said, walking a few steps and stopping by the central staircase. Could he have found the house and sheltered here? I waited, listening intently and twisting my head slightly so I could catch the sound of his voice. But I heard nothing, and the eerie silence started to play on my nerves. It was all nonsense. "Butch, are you here? Please, tell me you're here."

Whimpers filled the void, subtle but real, traversing the hall like an ephemeral breeze. The whimpers grew into sobs that shared no similarities with Butch's voice. No, it was a woman I heard.

"Is there anybody here?" I called. "I'm lost and looking for my friend. He's tall and blond; named Butch. Have you seen him around?"

"You!" I seemed I hear as if it was coming from the depths of the house itself. The word—as benign as it seemed—as well as the voice which spoke it, stirred something inside of me. A sensation I could neither explain nor ignore. I felt accused of something. But what? "Avery!"

Upon hearing my name, a sudden dread washed over me. It resonated inside, harming me in some inexplicable way. And this, more than the fact I was hearing a totally random voice in the most isolated of places, shook me to my core.

"I'm...I'm leaving." I would have liked to just do that: leave. Leave this place behind, despite whatever awaited me outside. But the moment my hand touched the door, I found it locked, and an inextricable pain surged through my arm and my head. Like I'd been put in the middle of ardent flames, it burned. When I looked at my hand, I saw nothing. No marks, no reddening.

"What do you want?" I screamed, rubbing the ghost of pain out of my aching arm. "Who are you?"

Now that I demanded answers, I received nothing but bloodcurdling laughter; demonic and bone-chilling. And then I heard him, Butch, crying and begging and mumbling.

"Hold on, buddy! I'm coming."

I turned around and ran across the main floor of the house, stopping at every room only to find darkness and emptiness. It soon began to weigh so heavily on me that I had to stop to catch my breath.

"Butch, I beg you, answer me. Where are you?"

Butch's voice had died as simply as a radio being turned off. Loneliness once again made itself felt, heavy and full. Loneliness, and nothing else but this decrepit house.

I sat on the cold and dusty floor, trying to gather my wits. All of this was nonsensical. Butch had disappeared. I had heard him cry, and then...nothing. As if he wasn't here at all. There were people in the woods, walking with torches, who had disappeared in the blink of an eye. And there was this house, which had materialised without warning. Then there was the woman's voice. I started to doubt my sanity for a moment. Was this house real? I punched the floor and listened to the thumping it produced, feeling the throbbing and aching spread up to my elbow. That voice, it seemed real... *so* real. How could it be fake? And what about Butch?

I leaned forward and rested my blisteringly hot forehead onto the cold of the ground, hoping this would mitigate the growing migraine. Jolts started to invade my body. I knew they would turn into sobs, and then I'd start crying. I was desperate. I didn't see an end to this nightmare. And yet, I couldn't sit around and do nothing. Butch was somewhere here. I'd heard him... I'd felt his presence, and I refused to believe it had been a trick.

I raised my head and noticed that the room was dimly lit by candles held in lanterns hanging on the walls. I blinked and rubbed my eyes to be sure I wasn't mistaken. Every time my eyes fell on my surroundings, everything remained the same, and it left me baffled. From what I could see, there was nothing modern about this house. Rough wooden planks and beams comprised a major part of the walls, flooring and ceiling. There were no switches, no electricity that I could see, no modern conveniences. The staircase was narrow and roughly built, without any finish work to it. There was no paint or wallpaper whatsoever. No carpet or decorations. Only the bare essentials. And what little furniture populated the room seemed to have come from another era.

Where in the hell am I?

I could hear the voice of the woman once again. She was singing softly. I listened more intently, trying to decipher the bizarre words that were being recited like an antique nursery rhyme. One I had never heard before.

Three Blinde Mice,
Three Blinde Mice,
Dame Iulian,
Dame Iulian,
The Miller and his merry olde Wife,
She scrapte her tripe licke thou the knife

Something followed. Something that made a chill crawl up my spine. A series of words, possibly Latin, assembled into a sort of... I don't know, *incantation?* A baby cried, wailing harshly and then coughing before crying again more forcefully. The candles flickered and died before lighting up again as if reacting to the baby's pain.

A presence grew behind me. Faint at first, but unmistakably there. I twisted my head, and there appeared a... *shadow*, for lack of a better word to express the apparition. This manifestation that grew before my frightened eyes. It crawled over the ceiling like a pestilent plague attracted by the sight of fresh souls to torture. I watched as it passed over my head and climbed the stairs. The demonic mass seeming to have spotted its next victim. My heart raced, and, not knowing why, I followed the shadow. I climbed the steps, one by one, attracted by this *thing*, ignoring the threat it might represent. Was Butch up there?

"You'll be fine. Sleep well, my little angel," the woman murmured, her voice echoing back to me in a muffled whisper. The baby instantly calmed. I continued to follow the black mass across the narrow corridor to a door, which the shadow smashed open. "If you touch him, I swear I'm going to kill you."

I hastened my pace and barely had time to glimpse inside of the room before the door slammed in my face. I gripped the handle, turning it frantically when I heard the lock engage. I tried to force it open, but to no avail. It was like trying to demolish a brick wall with my bare hands. I placed my ear against the door and listened, hearing someone breathing quickly, as if terrified. Then footsteps walking across the room, resonating through the floor and making it vibrate under my feet.

"Please," begged the woman, "William's sick. I only made him a concoct—"

There was a loud thump. The woman had fallen to the floor and was now sobbing hysterically.

"You are poisoning our son, you witch," accused a male voice, sinister and devoid of any humanity.

"No... no," the woman began. All the strength with which she'd confronted the man seconds ago seemed to have evaporated, leaving her weakened, terrified. "No, it's not. I... I'm trying to save our son. They're just plants and—"

"And words spoken to worship Satan and give him our son's soul."

"Of course not. I—"

"Enough." I heard another thud, and the woman's voice broke off. The heavy footsteps resonated behind the door; he was closing the distance between us. I moved back and cleared the way for the tall figure, short-haired and broad-shouldered, who slammed the door open. He strolled down the hallway, his shadow following behind like a black, misty fog, floating inches above the ground.

I was frozen in place, staring at the dark figure in the door. I was unable to decide if I should enter the room or follow the shadow. What kind of hallucination was this? Was the woman still inside? Or would I find Butch? Putting aside all the peculiar manifestations I'd witnessed, I tried to convince myself that it was all in my head, that there was nothing to be afraid of. I stretched out my hand, holding it a few inches over the door handle. The memory of the burning still lived within my muscles, making my fingers twitch. I inhaled deeply, and after a moment, I decided to open the door enough to peek into the room.

"Butch, are you in there?"

No one answered. I felt the cold breath of desperation on my neck. The room was empty. There was no one in there. Where the hell was my friend?

I could have turned around and inspected the other rooms of the house, opened every door and tried to find a way out of this place. But I didn't. *This* room called me inside of its purulent womb. I tried to resist. Something was crying at me to turn back, as if there was a lurking danger inhabiting the room.

Why didn't I trust my instincts?

Why couldn't I resist this attraction?

*T*he hardest part was to get one leg inside the room, letting it brave the unknown, face whatever might be hiding behind the darkness. Once that was done, I penetrated the room fully. The room was small in size, about a hundred square feet perhaps. A seizing coldness, the origin of which I could not quite determine, reigned. I didn't like the dread it filled me with, the pestilent smell of morbid terror. It was like death itself inhabited this place, like this was its kingdom.

The window was closed. Though had it been wide open, I don't think it would have changed anything. Such frigidity was more psychological than physical. More ominous than anything. It was a sensation rather than an annoyance.

In the middle of the room was an antique wooden cradle. I approached it as there was nothing else deserving of my attention. It was moving slightly, swaying gently and creaking like an old rocking chair. I placed my hand on it and stopped its motion, trying to reach out with my senses. Could the cradle tell me something? Could it help me understand the reason for my presence here, or Butch's disappearance?

I closed my eyes and breathed deeply. At first, all was black. But just then, light crawled through as if I was opening my eyelids. But I wasn't. I was... I was seeing through someone else's eyes. From *her* eyes?

A fire crackled within the fireplace. But despite the comforting warmth that filled the room, a glacial atmosphere still permeated my skin. My chest felt constricted, and my heartbeat erratic. Breathing became difficult. I moved toward the cradle and leaned over it, noticing that it was empty but for a crucifix in the middle of the pillow—an omen.

"No!" I heard myself cry. "You bastard!"

I crossed the room and strolled down the corridor, kicking every door open only to find the same heavy emptiness behind each and every one. Vacant rooms, devoid of anything. There was a single crucifix hanging on the wall in the hallway opposite the doors, like an inquisitive witness. The sight of it nauseated me, and I fell to my knees, hands pressed onto my thighs as I tried to collect my wits.

"Where have you taken him?" I heard myself yell. "I swear that God himself won't stop me from getting my baby back. *My baby!*"

Suddenly, a thought crossed my troubled mind. Something that would condemn me to a lifetime of wandering this vast world, with no friends to help me but my own will to survive. Such notions filled me with such a surge of longing for this future, this freedom, that I ran toward the last remaining door. With a maniacal determination to end his life, I raised my head. The first thing that fell upon my eyes was a poker, leaning against the mantel as if it had been placed there just for me, to inspire me, to help me reach my freedom. I ran across the room, picked up the simple object—which, in my hands, turned into a weapon—and ran back into the corridor and down the stairs.

Everything turned black again—a deep, abysmal black. A loud thud, like the sound of a body slumping onto the floor, tore me out of this otherworldly vision and brought me back to reality. The silence was stifling, and I knew instantly by the awful smell that I was myself again. I was Bobby Avery. And my friend Butch was missing.

After a long moment, during which I tested my brain and memory to be sure I wasn't being tricked again, I dared open my eyes. I still held the cradle, but now with white knuckles. Releasing it, I became aware of the painful throbbing in my hands. For one moment—one futile moment—my eyes slipped over the inside of the cradle, as if expecting to see the baby boy or the crucifix. But what I found there sufficed to convince me of the evil nature of the house and its inhabitants.

Spread inside the cradle like a quilt was a red shirt—Butch's red shirt!

"Butch! Butch answer me! I know you're here."

I ran across the room, as if expecting that he might pop out in front of my eyes at any moment. In a few short paces, I had explored the whole room, finding nothing other than the path in the dust I'd created—the floating particles dancing in the air in the flashlight's beam.

"Help!" I heard Butch crying. Finally!

"Help! Bobby..."

His voice seemed to come from far away, like he was outside the house, lost among the crowded, tenebrous trees. I didn't know what to do, break the glass of the window and jump down into whatever lay beneath? There must be about twenty feet separating the ground from the window. I'd surely break a leg. Or worse. But there was the front door. I must get it open! I must be able to endure the pain it will inflict me to save my friend.

I must try.

I must.

*F*lashbacks assaulted me as I ran out of the room. Along the narrow, poorly lit hallway, I seemed to see the shadow of the woman holding the poker in her hand, ready to swing it. The steps I descended seemed to resonate with the echoes of screams of agony. During the time it took me to reach the main floor, my brain was attacked from all sides at once with sounds and visions, each gloomier and more confusing than the last. Through the windows, I noticed the halos of flickering flames moving around the house. The smell of smoke tickled my nose, becoming suffocating as the heat grew in the house. The walls were burning. Smoke rose from the floor. The structure of the house was cracking and crumbling in a deafening cacophony. There rose the screams of a baby in terrible pain, and then nothing.

My feet had landed on firm ground. But the pain that suddenly shot through my body made me wince and lose my balance. I fell onto the burning ground, and it was as if millions of ardent shards were piercing my body simultaneously.

The front door was right there, a few feet away, but still so far away, unreachable.

"How does it feel, Bobby?" asked the woman's voice, her eerie whisper tormenting me. "Does it hurt? Do you want it to stop?"

"Yes, please," I begged. "Make it stop. Make... it... stop."

A peal of terrible, deep laughter filled every corner of the house. Tremors crossed the floor under me like it was about to be torn open. I hadn't thought it possible, but the pain stepped up to another level, and now it was as if I were being burned alive.

"Burn in hell," she said mockingly. "That's what he said, Charles Avery, before setting the stake ablaze."

Witch! Witch! Witch at the stake! Came a strange chorus from outside.

The pain subsided significantly, leaving in its place an awful dread as I caught sight of bobbing torches through the dusty window.

I got up, with the strange sensation that I was once again inhabiting the body of the woman—or rather that *she* lived inside of me. I saw everything through her eyes as well as mine, and the merging was so flawless and absolute that I could not tell if what I was seeing and feeling was real or not; mine or hers. Everything around me, the house and its furniture, appeared in their former glory. Yet, there remained a certain vacancy to them, an aura that seemed dead. As if the soul of the house, or simply the souls of its inhabitants, were already ashes.

Witch. Witch. Witch. Witch at the stake!

The voices grew heavier and fuller.

Witch. Witch. Witch. Witch at the stake!

Each second that passed brought them closer to the house. I could now hear the muffled noise of discussion among the gathering and the thumping of their feet on the porch. I couldn't catch what was being said, but I felt deep down in my gut that I needed to hide.

Was it my idea or hers to use the trapdoor dissimulated in the floor? Everything happened with such haste that I barely had time to process it. I was already hidden, the trapdoor closed behind me, and the smell of rot and earth surrounding me, when the front door of the house slammed open. The pounding of a dozen of pairs of boots echoed throughout the house. They kept a brisk, heavy pace as they covered every inch of the bottom story. The light of their torches flickered through the cracks in the floor. I held my breath and slapped my hands over my mouth, trying to block the screams that were building in my throat.

Go away. Go away, I thought.

"She must not be far away. Find her," someone said—a man with a low, guttural voice that instantly sent a chill crawling up my spine.

A strange smell began to tickle my nose. The acrid stench quickly became unbearable. I was suffocating. When I raised my head and approached the closest crack in the floor to breathe in some fresher air, the trapdoor opened. I hadn't been aware that someone was spying on me.

"I got her," said a woman, her face emaciated with starvation, her teeth black and repulsive. Someone gripped my shoulder and locked my arms behind my back.

"Here she is. The witch! The murderer! Satan's whore!"

"Witch. Witch. Witch at the stake!" Everyone chanted, brandishing their torches.

Internally, I fought to separate myself from this nightmare, to bring myself back into my own era, my own time. In this goddamn forest, this freaking house, where there was nothing else other than gloom floating over my head. But how could one separate himself from such a mystical grip? I tried to think of my family, my friends, my girlfriend, Butch... Nothing helped.

"Burn down the house!" yelled the man with the low voice. And I finally met his gaze. His eyes were dark and emotionless, as if the life had left them long ago. He grinned at me—*her*—and my stomach twisted. The tangle of emotions running through me finally converged into the realisation that this was my end —our end.

Two men grabbed me and took me out of the house, avoiding my stare and trying to ignore the flow of bizarre things that the woman vomited with my own mouth. I didn't have enough will to express anything with my own voice. I was at their mercy— the woman as well as these people. Had this been Butch's fate? Had he been captured and led through the dark woods to some unknown destination, accused of crimes he hadn't committed? This was all such nonsense! I couldn't bring myself to believe it was real. It couldn't be. It must be a nightmare. A nightmare from which I couldn't awaken. A nightmare that made me want to die right now in order to avoid what was to come.

I took one last troubled glance behind me at the house, which was burning at a stunning pace. Its roof slowly collapsing, glowing so vividly it almost felt like we were in total daylight. This troubled me even more than before. In what kind of parallel universe had I landed to enter a house that had been burned down decades before?

If only that was the strangest thing occurring...

We were walking through the forest, rounding the sentinel trees and their deep shadows when I heard him, his voice coming from *somewhere else*, distorted and unclear. But I recognised him. Butch!

I glimpsed his shadowy silhouette, seated under a tree at the foot of a steep cliff. He whined as he held his bleeding leg. A thick branch had pierced it. I could read his expression across the flickering glow of the flames, and I regarded the fear, desperation, and pain that contorted his face.

"Butch!" I cried, but to no avail. My voice seemed to remain trapped between the ridges of the warping realities. That or *she* blocked it out completely. Either way, Butch didn't see me. He didn't hear me or the freaks that escorted me, pikes and forks in hand.

"Bobby," I heard Butch murmuring. "Help me!"

Butch, too, knew that he was about to die in this abominable forest. His death would be one of atrocious agony and desperation. What would mine be made of?

We walked for what seemed like forever. Finally crossing through the open field with the willow tree, the one where Butch had erected our tent. The tent wasn't there, but the willow tree was, small and puny.

How does it feel? asked the woman as we finally exited the forest, her voice tormenting my very soul. *How does it feel to be back home?*

I looked around me but couldn't recognise anything I might associate with home. The main dirt road didn't trigger my memory whatsoever. The sight of the town we entered wasn't familiar, but for a few antique buildings, I thought I remembered, though seeing them in their former youth made the experience hard to believe.

Yes, Bobby. It's Hartford. Your home. My home. The pestilent wound that contaminated the entire country with its war against what they called witchcraft.

The woman burst out laughing. A spectral cackle. One devoid of joy but inspired by unbounded rage, hatred and sadistic pleasure. I now noticed the source of her sudden fit of madness. Before us was the wooden stake and the many spectators.

"Witch! Witch! Witch at the stake!" The chant resumed, echoing eerily through the otherwise calm night.

"No! No!" I implored, fighting as much as I could. It was useless, though, and only helped exacerbate their cruelty. Thrown pebbles. Punches and kicks. Pikes and forks and knives cutting me without no remorse. My strength and will to live quickly succumbed to the pain, and the drowsiness overcame me.

I didn't fight when I was pulled atop the pile of wooden logs and attached to the stiff stake. I couldn't quite comprehend or believe what was going to happen. My brain couldn't process things amidst such suffering. It was only when four figures approached the stake with their torches, heads masked with thick burlap tarps, that I came to realise I wasn't going to wake up.

"Mary Hobbs, you are charged with the murder of your husband, John Corey, and the crime of witchcraft. You are therefore condemned to die by immolation."

Once again, strange words exited my mouth, as if the woman was chanting a curse. The words weren't in English, but Latin, and were spat with such vehemence that it drove the closest figure to gag me and then blindfold me.

"I, the honourable Charles Avery, condemn you to death. Burn in Hell!" said the man with the low voice. Charles Avery. My ancestor.

"How ironic," said the woman. She wasn't in my head anymore but stood beside me and murmured in my ear, her lips tickling my lobe as they moved. "That *your* own ancestor is going to murder you. I told him I wouldn't rest until the very last Avery was extinguished from the face of the earth. Burn in Hell!"

E.L. GILES
ABOUT THE AUTHOR

My name is Eric Labrie Giles. I am a dreamer, a passionate about art, a restless worker and a bit of a weird human. I started my artistic journey as a music composer until the need to put my thoughts and stories down on paper grew too strong for me to resist it any longer. I live in the French Province of Quebec, Canada, with my girlfriend and my two sons.

www.elgilesauthor.com
www.facebook.com/elgilesauthor

CUT CORNERS
BY CHRIS HEWITT

"*Y*ou're late," said Amelia, staring at her watch as the three men fell out of the pickup truck.

"Yeah, sorry, love. Had to pick up some bits and pieces," said Bob, checking his phone.

Amelia crossed her arms. "You should have been here yesterday!"

"Ah yea, about that. We had a problem with another job. Couldn't have been avoided."

Bob's phone rang. "Ah, shoot, I got to take this. Sorry."

Amelia watched in stunned amazement as Bob walked away, talking on his phone. She'd got his voicemail twenty times yesterday. But today, right now, he took calls? Amelia's hands balled into fists, her gaze turning to the smirking men unloading plasterboard. Jack and Ed didn't even try to hide their amusement, no strangers to Bob's customer management techniques.

Amelia's fingernails bit into her palms, and with a shake of her head, she stormed off into her half-finished home, slamming the front door behind her.

She'd bought the property cheap at auction three months

ago, with the last of the money her parents had left. There were no other bidders for the out of the way ramshackle house. She'd known it was the right house for her the moment she saw it, in part because it needed so much work. Ever since her parents' passing, she'd been looking for a project she could sink her teeth into.

S he ran her hands under the cold tap, watching the water wash away the blood.

"Sorry about that. Things are crazy at the moment. Good news is we've got the plasterboard to finish the back bedroom. The guys are going to be on it all day."

"You should have finished a week ago," hissed Amelia, rubbing her palm.

"Sorry, love? Didn't catch that."

"I said you should have finished a week ago."

She spat each word as she turned to face him, drying her hands.

"Yeah, well, that was before the dry rot in the dining room and the…"

"What? What's the next excuse? Nothing is finished around here. Even the bloody front door is still sticking."

Bob held up his hands. "I get it. It's far from ideal."

"Ideal?"

"Look, love, we're doing the best we can. This job is costing me money now. Two guys. An extra five days. I'm gonna be out of pocket."

Amelia laughed. "Out of pocket! I've given you half up front, and you're not getting anything else until I see something fixed. As for your *guys*. They've only been here three days in the last week, and even then, they were sat on their arses."

"What do you want me to do? Cut corners?"

Amelia stared at the builder, the anger draining from her face, replaced by a cold conciliatory smile. "You're right. I'm sure you're doing the best job you can."

Bob gave an uneasy nod and retreated from the kitchen. "Good. We'll, err, crack on then."

She watched him leave, watched him swirl his index finger around his ear, eliciting laughs from Ed and Jack as they carried through the plasterboard.

*A*melia felt a pang of guilt as she climbed the stairs, balancing the tray of mugs. A feat even the nimblest of acrobats might struggle with on the treacherous staircase. The creaking, broken stairs, another thing on Bob's long list of tasks. Another job no nearer to completion. She found Ed and Jack in the back bedroom and, pushing the door aside with her foot, entered the almost but never quite finished guest room.

"I thought you might like a cup of tea. Couple of digestives there as well."

Ed busied himself fixing a floorboard under the window. Jack read a newspaper giving no hint of having done, or planning to do, any work. But in a rare demonstration of effort, leant across to snatch a mug and a biscuit.

"Red one, two sugars, right?"

"Right, nice one. Just what the doctor ordered."

Amelia placed another mug down beside Ed. The last thing she wanted was to give him an excuse to stop working.

"Thanks, love. I'm parched."

"You're welcome, one sugar," she said, staring around the room. "Where's the boss?"

Mouth full, Jack pointed to the ceiling.

"He's sorting out the electrics for the lights," Ed added, the thud of the nail gun punctuating his sentence.

The electrics? Bob appeared to be a master of all trades, carpenter, plumber, plasterer and now electrician, to name only a few of the jobs she'd seen him turn his hand to over the last six weeks. All up to scratch and specification, she had little doubt. After all, it wasn't like Bob to cut corners.

In the hallway, she stood at the bottom of the step ladder and hollered up into the loft hatch. "Tea!"

A rumble of movement and Bob appeared, beaming down at her.

"Ah, grand," he said with a wink. "Shove it on the top step, and I'll grab it a minute."

He vanished back into the loft space, and she reached up to balance the steaming mug of tea on the narrow top step. "Of course, there you go. Enjoy."

"Thanks, love."

Amelia ground her teeth. Love? They bandied the word around like they knew what it meant. Her mother used to call her love. The word had meaning then. She felt it, warm and comforting. Every time she heard the word now, she felt nothing but bitter anger.

She turned at the sound of a thud and a crash from the bedroom and peered around the door. Jack lay on his back, mug by his side, eyes staring up at the unpainted ceiling. Ed appeared slumped against the wall, still knelt where he'd been fixing the floorboard.

A glance back at the loft hatch, she saw a fumbling hand reach down to pick up the mug as she slipped into the back bedroom. She tip-toed over to Ed and, seeing his half-empty mug, gave a sigh of relief before jumping back as the labourer groaned. Amelia's heart froze as she reached out a hand to touch his shoulder. Ed twisted and fell, his back to the wall, his legs unable to take his weight. He stared up at her, eyes dilated, tea trickling down his chin.

"W... What have you done, you bitch?"

Amelia glanced back to the door, concerned Bob had heard the commotion. When she turned back around, Ed held out his arm, a nail gun in his shaking hand. *Thud! Thud!* Two large nails poked through the tea tray she'd instinctively held up to cover her face, one nail for each eye. She peeked around the tray as Ed's arm slumped to his side, and he gurgled a foam-infused curse. Amelia lowered the tray as Ed's accusing stare wandered, his head slumping onto his chest. The tea tray slipped from her trembling hand with a crash, and she turned to find Bob standing in the doorway, surveying her handy work.

Their eyes met for a moment before Bob bolted. Amelia looked around and, snatching up a hammer, took off in pursuit. A glance up the hallway revealed Bob's mug shattered, tea splashed across the unfinished floorboards.

She heard the big man stumbling down the stairs, then a loud crack, followed by a rumble of thunder. When she reached the landing, she found Bob groaning, lying face down at the bottom of the staircase. She descended the stairs, stepping over a now broken step. Bob glanced up at her and, and with one look at the hammer, started for the front door, blood pouring from a gash on his forehead.

For a moment, Amelia thought he might escape, but reaching the foot of the stairs, she laughed, watching him frantically tugging at the unyielding door. "See, I told you."

Before he could react, she seized her chance and leapt across the hall, bringing the hammer down on the back of his head with a sickening thud. The big man slid down the door and onto the floor, arms and legs twitching as Amelia stood over him, blood dripping from the hammer.

"I told you. It keeps sticking."

*A*melia lit up another cigarette and took a long drag; her hands no longer trembling. It had taken all her strength to drag Bob's heavy body onto the sofa. Along with the chair she sat in and the scratched coffee table, the tatty sofa was the only furniture in the property, remnants of the previous occupants. With a cough and a splutter, Bob returned to the living.

"Good. I thought I might have killed you," said Amelia.

"What the fuck," said Bob, struggling, only to find himself wrapped tight in coils of electrical cable. The empty wheel sat on the table beside a nail gun and a jerry can. Realising his predicament, Bob shook his head and laughed. "Alright, alright, I get it. It's a joke. They put you up to this. Cheeky bastards. Ed, Jack, yeah, you got me. Come on now, love. Let me loose."

Amelia took another long drag on her cigarette, smoke twirling in the single sunbeam that divided the gloomy room. Bob tried to stand, only to howl out in agony, staring at his feet, two pulped bloody porcupines pinned to the floor.

"Sorry, I've never used a nail gun before. It took a few practice shots," said Amelia, picking a fleck of tobacco from her tongue.

"L... l... look, love. I'm sure this is all a big misunderstanding. Nothing I'm sure we can't sort out."

"Of course. That's what you do, isn't it? Sort things out. A proper handyman."

Bob nodded. "Sure. Sure. Whatever you want."

"Well, Bob, I'll tell you what I want. I want my parents back. My mother and my father. Can you do that? Can you bring them back?"

Bob stared at her, his face a mask of confusion, and under her intense gaze, he shook his head.

"No. I didn't think so."

Amelia stood, leaned across the table and picked up the jerry can, cigarette hanging from her lips as she poured the contents over the screaming squirming builder. Fumes burning her eyes, she threw the empty can aside.

"You know what I think about most. Were they awake? Or did you kill them in their sleep?"

"What? I've never killed anyone," spluttered Bob, choking on the fumes.

Amelia grinned. "Oh, no, Bob, you killed them. It was your sub-standard wiring that sparked and set light to the cheap non-regulation lagging you installed. You built their funeral pyre with the money you fleeced from them."

"I swear it wasn't me."

"It was you, Bob. You might not remember me, but I remember you. I bought you tea. Three sugars, right?"

Bob gasped as Amelia flicked the cigarette in his lap, wriggling to escape a conflagration that never came. The glowing tip of the cigarette faded, extinguished by the dampness of the gasoline. The cowboy builder laughed, big manic belly laughs until his eyes met Amelia's.

She grinned at him. "Tsk tsk, that wouldn't be a fitting end for a master electrician, now would it."

She turned and walked to the wall, and Bob's eyes followed the path of the extension cable snaking across the floor, the plug lying beside a wall socket.

"No, you'll go the same way my parents went, with a spark."

Amelia picked up the plug and jammed it in the socket, finger poised over the switch as she glanced back at the murderer. The dodgy electrician stared down at the other end of the cable. Two bare wires wrapped around a nail sat in his petrol drenched lap. His pleading gaze met Amelia's as she flipped the switch.

*I*t had taken minutes for the old wooden house to be ablaze. Amelia had watched it laid on the bonnet of Bob's pickup truck. Maybe if his work had been up to scratch, the house might have lasted a little longer. It didn't matter; no one would come to put out the flames this far off the beaten path. It had taken an age to find just the right property. Tomorrow, she'd make a well-practised panicked phone, but tonight her vengeance would keep her warm.

CHRIS HEWITT
ABOUT THE AUTHOR

Chris resides in the beautiful garden of England, and in the odd moments that he isn't dog walking he pursues his passion for all things horror, fantasy, and science-fiction.

Facebook: https://www.facebook.com/chris.hewitt.writer
Blog: https://mused.blog
Twitter: @i_mused_blog

FUNNY AND SAD
BY SHAWN KLIMEK

"The house has fangs now," Misty observed as they turned into the driveway of her childhood home. Veronica had to lean over the steering wheel and crane her neck to see where her friend was pointing. A pair of long icicles bracketed the main entrance, descended from the snow-covered eves.

"Ooh, how appropriately sinister," she agreed.

Veronica parked the car, turned off the engine and radio, and then both young women sat in silence for as long as Misty needed to work up the nerve to get out of the car. This was the same house in which Misty had made a lifetime of happy memories. Her late parent's house had recently become her inheritance—too soon, now that she despised it; and too late, now that those memories had been displaced by nightmares. This was the house where her father had murdered her mother before killing himself.

Misty's grip hesitated on the passenger-side door handle. She glanced back at her friend, and the two exchanged nervous laughs. Steeling herself with a sigh, she exited the car and headed across the snowy yard. Something caught her eye as she neared the porch. "What are those yellow spots?" she asked over her shoulder.

Veronica needed to circle around the car before she could venture an opinion. "Bits of torn police tape?" she suggested as she approached. "The police must have kept the stuff in place with staples and then ripped it all down once their investigation was closed."

Misty scoffed. "Ha! What was there to investigate? When they found Dad with his brains blown out, the gun that he used to kill Mom was still in his hand. It makes no sense that I had to wait a month to collect my things. The only question unanswered is why he did it, and Dad made damned sure no one could ever ask him!"

"Insanity," Veronica reminded her with a sympathetic shrug.

"Yeah," Misty agreed, sadly.

"A month isn't so long if you consider that someone needed to clean up all the blood," Veronica reasoned.

"I suppose so," said Misty uneasily, then tested the doorknob before reaching into her purse for the house keys. There was still an evidence tag on them, labelled with the case number. Right beside the keys, a banner displayed on the face of her smartphone signalling a missed call. She recognised the number as belonging to Homicide Detective Bill Harris, the same officer who had overseen the murder investigation. Resentful, she pretended not to have seen it yet and closed the purse. After unlocking the door, she held it open wide to let her friend enter first. Her father had taught her those manners.

Both women strolled into the darkened living room, their exhalations fogging the air. Obviously, the heat had been shut off. Much of the furniture, including the brown couch and wooden end tables, seemed to have been pushed towards the walls, creating an unexpected pathway leading conspicuously toward the kitchen, toward the crime scene. No doubt, this had been a practical choice for the cleaners. Still, the rearrangement felt like a needless trespass, adding to Misty's annoyance. More troubling, however, was the creepy way the pathway seemed to beckon. Misty had come with no intention of visiting the macabre spot where her parents had died. She had only come to pick out a few personal items from her childhood bedroom and maybe some keepsake from amongst her mother's possessions. After that, she preferred that the estate resellers dispose of everything.

"Hey, I remember that bumpy old couch," Veronica remarked. "Folds out into a bed, right? We watched TV there during our sleepovers."

"Same couch. I wouldn't be surprised if there's still some of that popcorn you spilt between the cushions if you're hungry."

Veronica laughed. "What? Like your mother never cleaned?"

The mental image of her late mother cleaning struck Misty with an unexpected twinge of emotion. It was a reminder of how much unresolved grief lay beneath her cavalier façade, like something buried in a shallow grave. Forcing a laugh, she rubbed her eyes and shook off the sadness. Pushing a dining room chair out of the way, she headed for the stairs. "Come on. Let's get this over with, Ronnie. I want to get some things from my bedroom first," she said.

"Right behind you," said Veronica. "I can't wait to see if those 'One Direction' posters are still on the wall!" she teased.

"Haha," said Misty. "If they are, you can take whatever you want."

The house's upper story consisted of two bedrooms and a bathroom, connected by a hallway. Misty's old bedroom was the first door on the right. Her mother's sewing machine now occupied her old homework desk. A pile of clothing and some odd bolts of fabric lay strewn across the bed, but aside from these intrusions, little had changed. Her childhood teen-idols even still smiled down at them from the walls.

"Hello, Harry darling," said Veronica, lovingly caressing one of the posters and pretending to give it a kiss. "Misty said you're mine now."

"They're all yours," said Misty, laughing. She began opening and closing drawers, looking for her old diary and sketchbooks. Because their contents were innocent, it was silly to worry about their exposure to strangers. On the other hand, she valued her privacy. It was a fact that she would feel much safer taking personal responsibility for their destruction. The drawer where she remembered having last seen them was now filled with scissors, thread and other sewing stuff. Closing that drawer, she shifted her search to the closet, where ten minutes later, she discovered them in a shoebox for men's shoes.

"Found them," she announced, raising them like a prize.

"Great. Hey, come check this out!" Veronica was standing at the window which faced the front yard.

"What is it?"

"There's a police car outside."

Misty glanced out at it, remembering the message on her phone. Could the message have been about something urgent? Or was this a routine follow-up of some kind?

"I guess we'd better go see," she said.

"I'm right behind you," said Veronica, grinning. "I just want to grab this one poster."

Misty contemplated checking the message now, but her hands were full, and someone was already knocking on the door as she reached the bottom of the stairs. Through the curtained windows, she could see a partial profile of a female police officer, which seemed to make the message moot.

Crossing the living room, she dumped her things on an end table and opened the door.

"Hello, officer."

"Misty Thayer?"

"That's me."

"I'm Officer Owens—one of the regular patrol officers for

this neighbourhood. Detective Harris asked me to do a drive-by and check up on you."

"So that's what his message was about!" Misty did a quick eye-roll. "Well, that's very friendly of you both. Anything else?"

Officer Owens glanced briefly back at her squad car before replying. "The thing is... Have you seen anything suspicious since you've been here?

"What do you mean by 'suspicious?'"

"Open windows? Broken locks? Suspicious strangers checking out the property?" Owens appeared to be trying to see past her into the house.

"Well, the truth is, we only got here an hour ago," said Misty. "Except for the living room, we've only been in one room upstairs so far."

"And the upstairs bathroom," Veronica volunteered, walking up behind Misty and peering over her shoulder. "The plumbing works," she whispered into Misty's ear.

"Good day, Miss," said Officer Owens politely. "Are you a friend of Miss Thayer's?"

"I'm a dirty old squatter," Veronica replied.

"That's my friend, Veronica," said Misty sheepishly. "She's kind of a smart-ass."

"I see," said Officer Owens, smiling.

"Do you think burglars might have hit the place since the investigation?" Misty asked. "It has been vacant a while."

"There's always a possibility. Would you like me to have a look around?" asked the officer, shifting her stance.

Misty held up an arresting palm.

"There's plenty of snow everywhere," she said. "A burglar would have left footprints, wouldn't they? Why don't you have a look around the exterior, Officer. We'll check around inside."

Officer Owens seemed to hesitate. "Yes, I can do that, Miss Thayer," she said, thoughtfully. "I'll come right back and let you know if I've found anything. Meanwhile, if you see or hear anything suspicious, give me a loud shout."

Misty's eyebrows arched. "Alright, Officer. Will do." She shut the door. "What was *that* about?"

Veronica gently struck her friends elbow with a rolled-up poster. "You were kind of rude to her."

Misty was defensive. "Me? That's hilarious coming from you, *squatter!* The police have had access to this place for a month while I've been kept away. Doesn't it seem strange to you that, one day after I finally get the keys, they suddenly want back inside? Why didn't they check for burglars on Monday?"

Veronica smirked. "Maybe one of the investigators accidentally left something personal behind, like their badge or wallet, and sent Officer Owens to sneak back and get it."

"Yeah, that sounds about right." Misty chuckled as she turned towards the stairs. "Come on, let's finish up before she gets back. I just need to hit my parent's bedroom real quick, and then we can both get out of here."

"Alrighty." Veronica dropped her poster on the same end table where Misty had deposited her things and then followed her up the stairs.

Veronica was on her heels when Misty stopped short of entering her parent's bedroom to stare at some yellow police tape and a sheet of notebook paper taped to the door. Scrawled in crayon on the makeshift sign were the words, "Darrin's Room. Keep Out!"

"Who the fuck is Darrin?" she pondered aloud.

"You've been at college. Maybe your parents adopted."

"Not likely. Even if they did. They would have given the new kid my old room, not their own bedroom."

"They always loved Darrin best."

"Weirdo!" Misty gave her a sharp elbow, then ripped down the tape and paper, crumpling the mess into a wad before tossing it into the hallway.

"Hey! Have a little respect," said Veronica. "Darrin probably worked hard on that!"

Misty pushed open the door to her parent's bedroom, confronting unexpected darkness. A faint, rectangular halo of indirect sunlight outlined where the edges of the window were masked by curtains.

Misty's hand fumbled against the wall, seeking the light switch. Finding, it she flicked it on and off, to no avail.

"Just perfect," she said. "The bulb's gone out."

"Maybe Darrin doesn't like the light."

"Ronnie!" Misty admonished, "You're supposed to be my emotional support. Quit saying such creepy things."

"Sorry. I'll go open the curtains," she replied, venturing into the room following her outstretched arm. "Hey, seriously, for a minute. What if your Dad was going crazy and started calling himself Darrin?—Hey, what's that!" she exclaimed excitedly.

"What's what?"

"I think something just ran over my foot."

"Like what? Use the flashlight app on your phone, dummy!"

"Good idea!"

Intending to do the same, Misty reached for her own phone, only to realise she didn't have it.

"Damn! I left my phone downstairs," she said.

In no time, Veronica had flipped on a bright beam. She scanned the room, pausing on some beady eyes. "A rat," she said contemptuously. Using the light, she was able to safely navigate to the window without further incident. Grabbing the curtain fabric with one hand, she tugged one panel aside until a narrow gap of blinding sunlight appeared. A second yank on the opposite panel drenched the whole bedroom in sunlight.

"Run and hide, rat."

The Thayer's queen-sized bed lay unmade, which Misty considered an unusual state, and dust motes swirled in the glare. In other respects, her parents' bedroom remained much as she remembered it.

"Now that's better," said Veronica. "What are we looking for?"

"My mother's jewellery, mainly," said Misty, pulling open drawers. "It's probably in one of the nightstands or dresser drawers. There's a hat pin that belonged to my grandmother that was going to be passed down to me, plus I want to pick out something personal of Moms as a memento. She didn't own anything fancy and had horrible taste anyway, so I'll just have to pick something out when I see it."

"What did you do with your mother's wedding ring?"

"Same thing I did with my father's. I sold both to the nearest gold dealer the same day they were handed over to me. Never even touched the metal. The thought of those cursed things binding my parents' ghosts to the material plane would have haunted me."

"I thought you didn't believe in ghosts!"

"Bad mojo, whatever," Misty said. I'm not really superstitious, but better safe than sorry."

"You better hope your Mom's *not* a ghost, or else she just heard you say she had horrible taste in jewellery."

Misty cupped a hand beside her mouth. "No offence, Mom!"

A noisy disturbance downstairs startled both women. Seeing the look on each other's faces broke the tension.

"Oh shit! I think she heard you!" said Veronica, giggling.

"It's more likely Officer Owens decided to let herself in," said Misty, sourly, but then softened. "Hell. Maybe she tried to text me but got worried when I didn't answer."

Veronica withdrew a flat wooden box from the nearest nightstand and shook it in front of her. "Hey, I think I found it."

"Great. Hand it here. Let's get out of here before whoever Darrin is gets back," said Misty with a smirk.

Veronica followed, their conversation continuing as they

headed downstairs. "I know, right? What did you think about my theory about it being your Dad?"

"Going crazy and calling himself Darrin?" Misty shrugged, shook her head. "A good as any theory. But why did Mom never tell me if he had begun behaving strangely? That poor, lonesome woman."

As they reached the living room, Misty thought she heard a noise in the kitchen. "Officer Owens? We're in the living room!"

To the astonishment of both women, Officer Owens suddenly pushed open the front door, responding, "Thank you! I was just about to ring the doorbell. You haven't been answering your texts."

Confronting Misty's shocked expression and frantic gestures towards the kitchen put Officer Owens immediately on her guard. Her right hand slipped down to her gun. After waving the women back with her free hand, she squared her shoulders towards the hypothetical presence and raised her voice. "This is the police! Whoever's in the kitchen, come on out!" she commanded.

After a silent pause, she repeated her commands with the same result. After a second pause, she glanced back at Misty, who admitted in a whisper, "It might be just rats. We found one upstairs."

"I'd better check it out to be safe," Owens said quietly. "Have you spoken to Detective Harris?"

"Not yet; why?"

Keeping her shoulders squared towards the kitchen, Officer Owens lowered her gun and took a few careful steps backwards to facilitate their hushed conversation.

"You should check your texts, Miss Thayer!" she scolded. "He has a new theory about your parents' deaths."

"What? Not a murder-suicide?" Misty hurried to the end table and picked it her phone. She swiped it open and activated the messaging app. Detective Harris' messages spoke

of a rash of suspiciously similar murder-suicides, implying a
serial killer familiar to his victims. Her back had only been
turned for half a moment when her attention was distracted by
a flash of scarlet out of the corner of her eye and the
deafening *Pow-Pow* of Officer Owen's service weapon firing
twice into the ceiling. Dropping her phone in shock, she
turned around in time to meet a fever-hot splash of blood
across her face, arcing in long gouts out of the places in
Owen's neck where Veronica appeared to have repeatedly
plunged a pair of sewing scissors. Misty watched in shocked
horror as her childhood friend stabbed a third and fourth time.
Owens let go of the gun in a desperate effort to protect her
neck, but lacking the life force to complete the motion,
crumbled instead to the blood-splattered carpet, flailing in
vain. Blood masked her face and painted her uniform fire truck
red while continuing to spurt from her neck in increasingly
small arcs until the dwindling fountain was the only part of
her still moving.

Misty trembled, and her face was pale beneath the red.
"What the hell happened, Ronnie?!"

Veronica's wild eyes turned to meet those of her childhood
friend. "I have my own theory about your parents' deaths, Misty.
Do you want to hear my theory?"

"Did you do it?"

"Darrin did it."

"Do you mean my Dad?"

Veronica laughed and took a careful step over the sticky-slick
corpse of Officer Owens.

"Darrin is not your Dad, Misty. That was a joke. Darrin is an
avenging angel only I can see. He appeared to me the night your
Dad molested me during one of our sleepovers."

"He did what! You never told me that, Veronica!"

"No need. I had Darrin. Darrin promised me that when I was
older, he would give me justice. Well, he finally did, didn't he!"

"Why did you kill my mother? Why did you kill Officer Owens?"

Veronica looked down at the floor and at her bloody hands. "Oh, her? Bloodlust, I suppose. Darrin gets excited and can't seem to stop. He says that's okay, though, because everybody's a little bit guilty. Even you, Misty."

Misty staggered backwards, bumping the end table. One hand reached back and gripped the edge, while the other lifted to fend off an imminent stabbing attack.

"Me? I'm your best friend!'

"That is funny and sad, Misty. Darrin always says that comedy and tragedy are two sides of the same coin."

"What does that even mean, Ronnie? Stop! Stop! Put down the scissors! I'm sorry my Dad hurt you but tell Darrin to stop now."

"I can't stop now, Misty!" said Veronica.

In a flash, Misty spun around, pulling the end table between them. Veronica swung her scissors but missed as her knees collided with the wooden object. Seeing the door, Misty made a run for it while tipping the end table between them but lost her balance on the blood-slicked floor, falling short. Seeing her prey escaping, Veronica leapt to cut off her friend's path, but stumbling over Owens' corpse, she also fell. As both women righted themselves, panting, charged with adrenaline, their wide eyes met, mere yards apart. The murderess planted one foot on top of the dead officer and, twisting it back and forth, wiped the bottom of one shoe.

"Wrong shoes for this!" she said with a grin. "Girl shoes!"

Misty could hardly believe what was happening. She was still grieving over her parents, and now this. "Please don't do this!" she begged. "I've never been anything but your friend!"

"Some friend! Luring an innocent child into your perverted father's lair!"

"I didn't know anything about that, Ronnie! I was just as

innocent as you!"

Veronica shook with righteous rage. "Your father's blood is your blood!" she shrieked.

Out of the corner of one eye, Misty spotted her phone, where she had dropped it earlier. If she could grab it and then somehow race upstairs, she thought, she might be able to lock herself in a room and then call 911. Afraid to take her eyes off Veronica's raised weapon, she took baby side steps, attempting surreptitiously to locate the phone with her foot.

"Ronnie, listen," she stalled.

"It's Darrin!" snarled Veronica, lifting the scissors. "Darrin, the blood-thirsty avenger of evil!"

"Stop! Listen to me! Darrin needs to leave now! His work is finished!"

Veronica stopped suddenly, the rage leaving her face. She frowned and knitted her eyebrows as though considering these words. Her head turned slowly as she scanned the room. "Wow. The cleaners will probably close down the house for another month," she said.

A sudden clatter came from the kitchen as a cereal box tumbled mysteriously from the top of the refrigerator. Both women turned toward the serendipitous distraction, but only Misty had a vantage into the kitchen from where she stood.

"Oh hey, Officer Harris!" she bluffed.

Veronica's eyes narrowed warily. "You're trying to trick me!" she accused, her anger returning. "That was probably a rat!"

Misty doubled down on her new gambit, even lowering her hands to feign conviction. "Don't just stand there!" she said as though to someone just out of view while pointing nonchalantly to the dead policewoman. "Officer Owens needs an ambulance!"

"You're such a bad liar!" said Veronica, with rising venom. Aiming her bloody scissors, she advanced menacingly yet betrayed enough reservation to stretch her neck in hopes of a better view of the kitchen. Misty rocked slightly on the balls of her feet, ready to dodge. When she decided that Veronica had come too near, she bolted to a new position. Then to a second as the murderess gave chase, hoping that if she could not reach the door, she could at least put the couch between them. Her manoeuvre took her directly over Officer Owen's outstretched arm, which she was mindful to avoid tripping over. Her foot struck something hard and unseen, foiling her purpose and causing her to stumble. The officer's service revolver, hidden where it had fallen under the dead woman's arm, skittered into the kitchen, spinning out red droplets.

Two startled rats scampered suddenly into the living room, running in tandem, following the baseboard to the door which led to the basement, before squeezing underneath through the gap. Veronica seemed momentarily stunned for a second time before realising that Misty now intended to reach for the pistol. The chaos had evened the odds.

"It's over for you, girlfriend!" she taunted, then charged, shrieking with rage and committing herself to the bloodbath that was to follow.

Misty had successfully reached the kitchen, but ungracefully, and further panicked by Veronica's battle cry, fumbled to get a grip on the blood-slicked gun. She answered the shriek with her own screams and had just managed to raise the pistol when Veronica tackled her, hacking madly. Both women fell, tumbling over spilt cereal, grappling frantically for the upper hand.

"Ronnie! Ronnie! Stop!" Misty pleaded as she felt the scissors plunge into her. She clawed her friend's face and somehow managed to fire the gun.

It took less than an hour for Detective Harris to reach the Thayer residence after finishing the last of his business at another crime scene. Arriving at last, he and another officer, Brown, had discovered the three bloody corpses in two rooms, merged by a gooey red carpet of blood. Small paw prints crisscrossed the stains, and there were signs that Officer Owen's fingers had been nibbled. A crime scene photographer arrived and began quietly taking pictures.

Noticing a fallen smartphone, Harris tested a hunch by sending it another text message. When it vibrated, as expected, he reached for it with a gloved hand and dropped it into an evidence bag. Seeing the band poster, partially unfurled during the mayhem, he stooped to peek inside but didn't move it. Instead, he began browsing through the sketchbooks on the table, flipping through them.

"Good God," he muttered aloud. "What a nightmarish childhood that poor girl must have had."

Officer Brown looked up from the jewellery box, distractedly turning over a hairpin in his hand, before sliding it discreetly into his pocket.

"I have a theory," said Harris.

"What's that, sir?"

"Well, I'm no psychologist, but Jacobs once showed me something similar in a case he was working on once. This girl was probably abused by her father. There's your likely motive, Brown."

"Huh. Fits. Owen's gun was still in her hand. Case closed, sir?"

"Looking that way. The girl clutching the scissors that killed Owens must have been an accomplice; the two of them working together."

"Maybe one of them felt guilty at the end," Brown suggested. "That would explain the bullet under the chin."

"Huh. Murder-suicide… Ironic," Harris agreed.

SHAWN M. KLIMEK
ABOUT THE AUTHOR

Shawn M. Klimek is the middle child of seven creative siblings, a globetrotting, U.S. military spouse, a multi-genre short-story writer, poet, and butler to a Maltese. He also is the author of 'Hungry Thing", an illustrated, dark fantasy tale told in five poems. More than two hundred of his works have been published to date in e-zines and anthologies, including three best-of collections.

Blog: jotinthedark.blogspot.com
Facebook: shawnmklimekauthor
Twitter: @shawnmklimek
Amazon:www.amazon.com/Shawn-Klimek/e/B07MYMBJKS

THE HOUSE OF CRANE
BY ALEXANDRA HARPER

1

818.

Justin Crane surveys the scene around him. He sees the people watching him. He hears the rope creek on the wooden beam as he feels it tighten around his neck. He feels his lungs tighten as he looks around the house as everything goes black.

1819.

Eton Bailey draws his last breath, eyes lifeless, as he lays at the bottom of the stairwell with a broken neck.

1839.

Julliette Briande stares up blankly through the clear bath water, silently watching as a bubble rose to the surface, the last of her air.

1902.

Rachel Combes heard the creak and splinter of wood as the chandelier broke free from its fitting and plummeted onto her head.

1951.

Rosamund Clay smelt nothing as she struck a match that ignited the gas that eviscerated her.

1999.

Jenny Swan gasped out her last terrified breath mid-fall due to a balcony railing failure.

2021.

Mark Scallion feels the last wild beats of his heart as the electricity ploughs through his body, his eyes slowly falling shut for the last time.

2021.

Justin Crane thinks back to the day he died. Or rather, the day his soul had been forced out of his body when they had hung him. But then, instead of blackness, he was everywhere, in the windows, the doors, the roof, in the very walls of the house itself, in fact, he was the house.

He smiles then. After all, no-one suspects a house of being a serial killer.

ALEXANDRA HARPER
ABOUT THE AUTHOR

Alex resides in Hertfordshire, UK. When not writing she spends her time reading, taking photographs, travelling and hiking whenever she can. She completed a Bachelor of Arts in photography, film and writing at Edith Cowan University. An occupational therapist by day and film reviewer/writer by night, she loves writing or reading stories about injustice and inequality. She has had her stories published in a museum exhibition and another anthology, April Horrors.

THE HAND THAT ROCKS THE CRADLE
BY CALLUM PEARCE

*J*ohn hated the way the social workers looked at him. They both glared as though they were peeling away his defences and peering into his soul. He had always felt that as a gay couple fostering a child, that good enough wasn't quite good enough. He felt that he and his husband had to be perfect in every way. When John spoke to the social workers, they always made him feel like a kid himself. He felt as though they were waiting to jump on any perceived failing. This wasn't fair on himself or the social workers. He knew that they only had his son's best interests at heart. Still, when he had to talk to them about problems or issues that came up, he felt as though he was being judged.

"The psychologists said that this was something he would have grown out of by now," he mumbled, wishing he could shrink inside his clothes and hide from their eyes. "They said that by the time he started nursery and interacted with other children, that imaginary friends would be replaced by real friends. Well, he's been through the nursery, and now he's in school, and he still talks to her."

"I think it's different for all children. Some will see the lack of confirmation from their friends and let go of such things. Others may go on believing in things like that for much longer. I wouldn't worry about it too much," Susan said, looking through his son's file on the desk in front of her.

"So, I should just ignore it then?" John asked.

"Not exactly ignore it," Susan replied. "Take it as an opportunity to talk to him. He may be using this as a way to explore his anxieties and fears."

"It seems to me," the male social worker chimed in. "That he's created a sort of mother figure to replace the mother he lost. It's unlikely that he can remember his own mum. Perhaps he is just creating a female role model to fill that space."

"He has plenty of women in his life. He has aunts, and we have lots of female friends," John was getting more irritated; he didn't know this other social worker. Susan was his main caseworker. This new one seemed to be shadowing her to learn his role.

"I... I didn't mean to imply anything. Just trying to explore all possibilities," the other social worker stammered.

"The thing is," Susan interrupted. "He seems perfectly happy. He has made friends in school and seems to be enjoying it. I wouldn't worry about it all too much."

"Last time you spoke to him, she was still being nice. He would tell us that she read him stories and was always kind to him, but now he says that she's scaring him. Telling him that he is going to be taken away and she's acting strange and saying upsetting things," John spoke quickly, trying to get everything out that he needed to say.

"Have you noticed that you talk about her as if she's real?" the man started.

"In a way, she is. She's been around for as long as Michael has. Ever since he could talk, he has spoken about her."

"Is it not possible then that you are inadvertently confirming his belief in this character," the stranger looked quite pleased with himself. "If he is saying that she tells him he will be taken away, then surely that is just a manifestation of his own insecurity. It can be very difficult for kids in care. Worse when their parents are no longer with us, or they're unable to have contact for some other reason."

"I suppose that could be it," John knew the man was making a reasonable point; he just hated the smug way he made it.

"We're due to have a home visit in a couple of weeks anyway. We can have a chat with him then and see how things are going," Susan suggested. "I wouldn't worry about it all too much. Just reassure him when he talks about his fears."

John felt a little better as the meeting was ending. Just being out of the house made him feel a lot lighter. He used to love their home, but lately, perhaps because of the things Michael was saying, the place seemed dark and suffocating. Every noise would put him on edge. Sometimes he felt as though Michael's imaginary friend was standing over him watching everything he did. He knew that was ridiculous, but he found it hard to shake off when he was alone in the house. He was glad that Jason, his husband, and Michael would be home by the time he returned.

When John arrived home, he could hear the clattering of pots and pans, meaning that Jason had started making dinner. The sounds of Michael's favourite toy robot suggested that he was playing in the dining room.

"How was the meeting?" Jason asked when he got to the kitchen.

"It was okay," John replied. "They don't seem too worried about it. I suppose they see a lot of this kind of thing."

"And worse things, I imagine," Jason sighed. "I'm sure he will grow out of it eventually."

"They said to take the opportunity to talk to him about his fears when he brings her up," John explained.

"Sounds like a very social worker thing to say," Jason laughed. "He's a five-year-old kid with an active imagination."

"I'll go and say hello; he mustn't have heard me come in."

When John stepped into the dining room, he didn't see Michael at first. He didn't see the dining room that he expected to see. Feeling confused and dizzy, his eyes struggled to focus. The walls around him looked blackened, and there was a strong smell of smoke in the air. The dining table looked burnt and charred. In the corner of the room was something that looked like a burned mannequin until its eyes flicked open. Suddenly, something grabbed him around the waist. As he was about to scream and shake it off, his real dining room came into view, and he saw that what had grabbed him was Michael coming in for a hug.

"We're having spaghetti tonight," he said excitedly.

"Oh, your favourite, fab. Who doesn't love a bit of spaghetti?" The dizziness was leaving him now, and he rubbed his eyes. The room seemed perfectly normal again, and Michael's excitement helped him to push the images out of his mind. "Well, you. Let me go now, and I'll go and see if your dad needs any help with dinner. We can't have him ruining your favourite, can we?"

"No way," Michael seemed genuinely worried about the idea.

"It's okay. I'm on it." John laughed, rubbing Michael's hair so that he pulled away, trying to tidy it again.

Returning to the kitchen, he sat on a stool at the breakfast bar and watched Jason happily working away preparing the dinner.

"So, spaghetti, is it?" John laughed. "Trying to work your way into the position of favourite dad there."

"Well, we both know it's about the only thing I can cook

that's half decent." Jason giggled whilst carrying on with his work.

"It's nice to see him so happy," John said. "Did he seem okay when you picked him up from school?"

"Yeah, he seemed quite pleased with himself. One of his pictures made it onto the wall. I'll let him tell you about that over dinner."

"Ooh, our son the artist. Did he mention her at all?" John tensed up as he waited for a reply.

"No, not a word. It's playing on your mind still, isn't it?"

"It never bothered me until recently. Seeing how upset he was the other night... I don't know; it just doesn't seem as harmless now," John explained. He thought about telling Jason about the strange vision he had had in the dining room but decided not to worry him. It was bad enough with one person in the family seeing things that weren't there.

"We just have to keep reassuring him that he isn't going anywhere. If she keeps scaring him, we'll get an exorcist round."

John knew that Jason was joking, but the idea had occurred to him a few times over the years. Not because he truly believed in ghosts, more as a performance for Michael. Of course, he realised that this would probably be more frightening for their child than anything his imaginary friend could do. When he was a baby, he had always acted as though he was with someone else. Sometimes the small cradle they had would rock by itself whilst he lay inside it. He would always happily chatter and mumble to himself as though playing with someone. When he first started talking about Old Mary, he said that she would sit with him at night and read him stories or sing songs to him until he went to sleep. If he didn't see her for a few nights, he would ask where she was and when she was coming back. At first, they had laughed it off as the strange things children would say.

As time went on, they had started to worry more that he

wasn't growing out of it. Then there had been strange things, like the time Jason went to check on him and his cot was in pieces in a neat pile on the floor. Michael was sat happily in the middle of the room, surrounded by his toys, chatting away to himself. Other times, they would find him playing with a toy that they were sure had been out of reach on a shelf. Most of these things they laughed off. The toys could be put down to absentmindedness on their part. The cot was an old hand-me-down and probably quite easy to break as he was getting bigger.

"In a dream world there, John Boy?" Jason interrupted his thoughts.

"Just thinking over some things," John replied.

"Try to put it out of your mind. He hasn't mentioned her so far today. Maybe if we put her out of our mind, he will too."

He knew that Jason was right. Michael probably picked up on their stress and tension more than they realised sometimes. He decided to focus on a nice relaxing evening and an early night for everyone.

Michael chatted happily through dinner without a single mention of Mary. He talked about his friends in school and the artwork that had been displayed in the classroom. It was only when it was time to go to bed that he looked slightly reticent. As though he was nervous about going to his bedroom. He said nothing and clomped his way up the stairs, though.

"Did you see that?" John asked Jason. "He didn't want to go to his bedroom."

"What five-year-old ever wants to go to bed on time?" Jason laughed.

"It was different; he was scared to go up there," John continued. "Same when I came home before, he had brought his toys downstairs to play with them in the dining room rather than stay up there with them."

"You're probably reading too much into it. He must have

wanted to be close to the smell of my gorgeous cooking. I don't blame the boy."

"Probably," John sighed. "I might get an early night myself if you don't mind."

"Yeah, get some rest. I won't be far behind you."

John walked slowly up the stairs. He stopped at Michael's bedroom door and listened for a moment, but everything seemed quiet. He carried on to his own room. It took him a while to get to sleep. The meeting with the social workers kept playing over and over in his head. Flashes of the horrible scene he had imagined in the dining room earlier kept interrupting his thoughts. He kept seeing the burnt thing in the corner opening its eyes and staring at him. By the time he did fall asleep, Jason was still downstairs watching something on TV.

John woke in the middle of the night, wet with sweat. As he tried to sit up, he found that he couldn't move any part of his body. His eyes slowly adjusted to being open and awake. He could see an old woman standing over his bed. He lay staring at her, unable to move and unable to fully understand what he was seeing in his half-awake state. She seemed to be singing under her breath and staring at him. She held a large pillow in her hands.

"Hush little baby, don't say a word," she sang gently.

John tried desperately to move any part of his body. He wanted to open his mouth to shout, but his jaw was frozen shut. He attempted to make sense of things in his mind, reassure himself that he was dreaming and that he would wake any minute now. She just carried on singing as she lifted the pillow over him, letting it hover over his face for a moment. After what seemed like an age, she brought the pillow down over his face. John could still hear her singing as he felt the pressure of her hands behind the pillow. His throat and then lungs felt as though he was inhaling the feathers. A burning pain spread from his lungs through the rest of his body, and his head swam.

Far too slowly, everything started to go black, and the pain stopped.

"John sit up!" Jason was shaking him awake panicked.

John sat up in bed, coughing and spluttering, then gasping for air.

"I thought you were going to choke to death," Jason said, still shaking from shock.

"What happened? Where's Mary?" John's head wasn't fully awake yet.

"You just started gasping for air like you were choking. I couldn't wake you up."

"I was having a nightmare, I think," John mumbled. "It was her. It was Mary."

"It was just a dream."

"I saw something earlier too. When I was awake." He remembered the eyes on the burnt thing well. He hadn't noticed at the time because of the shock, but he was staring into those eyes now. Full of concern for him. "I'm just being silly." He couldn't tell Jason what he had imagined earlier. "I think I'm still half asleep."

"It's probably because of the meeting," Jason said softly. "It's all been causing you a lot of stress."

"Yeah, I think so. I just need to get back to sleep."

"Make sure you lay on your side. You scared the life out of me there," Jason sounded a little relieved, but his voice still had an edge of concern. He was speaking to John more like a patient than a husband.

He woke the next day, unaware of whether or not he had dreamed more. He could hear Jason and Michael downstairs chatting to each other as Jason was most likely preparing breakfast. In his mind, he saw Mary's face staring at him as she stood over him last night. They often joked about the ghost in the house when Michael was out of earshot and strange things had happened. Neither he nor Jason had ever really believed in her, or any other ghosts for that matter. It was always easier to find a rational explanation for anything that happened that was out of the ordinary. The smells in the dining room and the heat from the smouldering wood had been so real. He had felt himself die last night as the old woman had suffocated him. He could still remember the weight of her behind the pillow. The way his lungs had struggled for oxygen and burned in agony when it was denied. What had been a bit of a concern but largely a family joke now felt very real and very dangerous.

"How are my boys this morning?" John asked, taking a stool at the breakfast bar next to Michael.

"Good," they both said together.

"Did you have a good sleep? No nightmares?" He asked Michael.

"No. Mary didn't come and see me."

"You don't see her every night, do you?" John asked

"No, but she was here last night; she just didn't visit me." Michael seemed quite upset. "I could hear her singing in the other room."

Johns body felt suddenly cold, yet beads of sweat appeared on his forehead. He remembered the sound of the old woman singing as she had lowered the pillow over his face.

"You don't look well at all," Jason said, joining them at the breakfast bar. "Do you think you're coming down with something? You look really pale."

"Just a bit tired, I think," John mumbled.

"Good job, you have a few days off. Maybe you should take yourself back to bed for a bit when I take Mikey to school."

"I promised I'd go and see Lisa today. Just a coffee and catch up whilst I'm off." John answered. "I'll be back before you two get home."

"It'll probably do you some good to have a bit of time away from the house. Give her hugs from us," Jason said happily.

When they had finished breakfast, they had both left for

school and work. John dragged himself upstairs to shower and get ready to go out.

When he got out of the shower, he could hear a faint noise outside the bathroom. It sounded as though something was being dragged slowly along the floor. Every so often, he would hear a gentle thud and then the dragging noise would start again. He dried his ears, determined to believe that it was just the water sloshing about in there, playing tricks with his mind. He got dressed slowly; he was dreading opening the door to the bathroom.

When he couldn't delay it any longer, he swung the door open and stepped out into a small office. Instead of the landing of his home, he was in a small room with a large desk in the middle and shelves filled with books all around it. A nameplate on the desk said Mary O'Dowd, and papers were scattered all over the floor. It was as though somebody had swept things from the desk in a fit of rage. His eyes were drawn beyond the desk to the wall behind it. He wished he hadn't looked that way. On the floor at the back of the room were what looked like four small bodies wrapped in blankets. He couldn't bear to witness what he was seeing. Flames started to appear, eating through the cloth. One of the small bodies sat up and started to scream. John turned and ran from the room back into the bathroom he had come from and slammed the door shut behind him. He sat on the edge of the bath whilst he waited for his head to stop spinning. The screaming stopped, and he sat in silence for a few moments, not daring to open the door again just yet. He must have sat there for ten minutes before finally forcing himself to check what was out there. When he opened the door, he saw nothing unusual. Just his own home and the sunlight beaming in from outside. He got his things together and set off to visit his friend.

He breathed a huge sigh of relief as he locked the door to his home behind him.

"*G*od, you look shattered!" Lisa exclaimed as she opened the door to John.

"Thanks, you always know how to cheer me up."

"Sorry, but it looks like your eye bags are carrying luggage," Lisa laughed. She stepped back to let him into the house then lead him through to the kitchen. The coffee machine was already bubbling away. "Oh you had that social worker meeting, didn't you? Have they been stressing you out?"

"Not just them, it's all this stuff with Michael," John began.

"Still seeing ghosts?" Lisa asked

"Don't you start with all the ghost nonsense. It's just a kid's overactive imagination."

"Sounds like you're trying to convince yourself there, not me," Lisa replied. "I've always told you. That house creeps me out."

"You also told me that rock hanging around your neck cures depression," John snapped. "I think we can accept that we have very different beliefs."

"Well, someone got out of the wrong side of the bed this morning." Lisa seemed hurt by his comments.

"I'm sorry, I just slept badly last night," John mumbled. "I think all of this stuff is starting to drive me a bit mad."

"I'll forgive you this once," Lisa laughed. She poured them both a coffee and then led John into the living room.

"So, what did the social workers have to say?" She asked, taking a seat facing him.

"Same old stuff. Mother figure blah blah, separation anxiety blah."

"They haven't got a clue," Lisa sighed.

"It's not just Michael, though." He didn't want to say the words. He could feel them trying to force their way out of his mouth in response to Lisa's concerned attention. "I've been seeing things myself." Lisa leaned forward; both hands gripped around her large coffee cup. "It's like I go somewhere else for a moment, but everything seems completely real. Too real. I can smell everything and feel things that aren't there."

"Stress can do funny things to the mind." John could tell Lisa was trying hard not to look too concerned. She was failing miserably, but he appreciated the effort.

"I know it sounds mad, but she feels more real all of a sudden." He spoke quickly, knowing that if he didn't say all that he had to say, he may never tell anyone. "I had a dream last night. Well, not a dream. It was something else, like a sleep paralysis episode."

"Have you ever had anything like that before?" Lisa asked.

"Never," John answered. "It was really scary. She was there. Old Mary."

"Oh, that's creepy," Lisa shuddered. "It could be all the talk from our Mikey. Don't bite my head off, but... It could be that there is more to it than a kid's imaginary friend."

"I'll be honest with you. I don't know what to think anymore," John sighed. "Everything seems to have stepped up a gear from harmless fantasies to something truly sinister."

"Mary O'Dowd," John blurted out, remembering the sign on the desk. "Can I use your laptop?"

"Of course, you can," Lisa said, looking concerned. She pointed to the desk in the corner of the room. "It's over there. I'm already signed in."

John rushed over to the computer and tried searching for death records for anyone called Mary O'Dowd in their local area. There were hundreds and nothing to give him a clue if any of them could be related to his current problems. There had been nothing in the office to give away the period. He had no other clues about what to look for. He kept scrolling, hoping something would jump out at him, but he didn't know what else to look for.

"My mum used to study the history of this place. I could give her a call and see if she knows anything," Lisa said as John pushed the chair away from the computer deflated.

"It's just dreams. I'm starting to act like it's all real," John was feeling stupid. "Just forget about it and tell me what you've been up to lately."

"I'll ask her. I'm phoning her later anyway." Lisa declared.

"Watch what you say, though. I don't want her thinking I've lost my mind."

"I won't even mention you," she replied. "Just pick her brains a bit and see what she knows. Probably won't come to anything, but it's worth a try."

They left the subject of Mary there. They chatted for the rest of the day about work and Lisa's intriguing and busy love life. John was aware that he had stretched the visit longer than usual. He found himself not wanting to return to the house when he knew that he would be alone there. But they were having fun chatting, and it was nice to have different things to think about. By the time he left, he knew that he would be getting home just before the other two got back.

*A*fter dinner that evening, John's phone started to ring. Jason picked it up to pass it to him.

"Lisa? Did you two not talk enough all day?" he laughed, passing John his phone as he went back into the kitchen to clean the dishes.

"Hello..." John began.

"Oh my god, John. You are not going to believe this." Lisa sounded like she had just run a marathon. She was panting excitedly, and her voice was shaking. "I've just got off the phone with my mum. Turns out she knew plenty about a certain Mary

O'Dowd. She was surprised that we hadn't heard the story ourselves, considering where you live."

"What do you mean, considering where I live?" John asked, his stomach filling with butterflies.

"She said it was quite a famous story around here. There used to be an orphanage where your house is now." As she spoke, John pictured the small bodies wrapped in blankets. "Mary O'Dowd was the woman that ran it for the last five years," she paused. John was sure this was for dramatic effect. "Before it burned down."

"You're making this up." John didn't want to believe what he was hearing, but he remembered the burnt room and the strong smell of smoke from yesterday.

"She couldn't remember how long ago it all was. It was ages ago, but it was talked about for years afterwards. She's going to look through some of her old files and see if she can find out more," Lisa continued. "So anyway, this Mary took over the place for the last five years. Everybody loved her. The kids seemed happy and healthy, so she was practically seen as a saint in the local community. Then the place burned down, killing everyone inside. Well, obviously everybody assumed it was a terrible accident at first." She paused again.

"At first?" John asked, mostly to encourage her to carry on.

"It turned out they had been planning to close the place down, and Mary just flipped out. They found the bodies of some of the children piled up in her office. F..."

"Four of them," John interrupted. "She suffocated them."

"How do you know that?" Lisa sounded concerned and less excited than she had been when she started the story.

"I saw it, "John replied. That was all he could say. Words seemed to evaporate in his mouth when he tried to say more. The story mirrored their experience with Old Mary too closely. Five years of her seeming to be a kind presence, suddenly changing into something more sinister.

"You need to get away from that house," Lisa insisted. "Why don't you come and stay with me for a bit, at least until we can find out more. I can squeeze you all in here for a few days."

"Thanks, but it's just dreams. I need to process all of this. I. must have heard the story myself, especially if it's so famous. Maybe somebody in school told Michael about it too."

"Or maybe there is something creepier going on. You've got to admit this is all a bit weird," Lisa continued. "Just sleep on it tonight and then think about coming to stay with me, for a few days at least."

"I'll call you in the morning; try not to worry."

"Stay safe, all of you," Lisa replied before John hung up.

John decided not to mention any of this to Jason until he had a chance to find out more. He knew that Jason would worry that he was losing the plot. The idea of convincing him that this was real was an even worse prospect. He didn't want Jason to feel as scared and confused as he had been lately. He kept thinking about everything he had heard and connected the story with their own experiences.

That night, John dreamed that he was walking around the old orphanage. At first, all he could hear was the sound of children playing, but the laughter and songs soon turned to screams. The walls blackened around him. Flames started to climb over everything, and a cloud of thick, dark smoke filled the corridor that he was walking down. Wherever he turned, he saw only the thick, black smoke and heard the sound of screaming, crying children. He covered his mouth and nose and tried to push through to find an escape. His eyes burned and watered so that he could barely see anything. He started crawling along the floor, trying to keep the smoke above him, but it seemed to follow him down. He slipped and took his hand away from his face, and the smoke forced its way into his lungs. Gasping and coughing, he sat up in his bed, woken by the phone beside him.

He could still taste the smoke at the back of his throat even though he was awake. The burning feeling stayed in his nose. Looking at his phone, he saw that he had a couple of missed calls from Lisa and a text message.

I don't want to scare you... The message read... Mum got back to me. She said the anniversary of the fire was tonight...

John dropped the phone. Not from the shock of the message but from the realisation that the smell and taste of smoke weren't from his dream. He could see it now curling under the door of his bedroom. He turned to wake Jason, but he was alone in bed. John ran from the room and along the landing to Michael's bedroom. The smoke was gushing up the stairs, and he could feel the heat from below him. Michael's bed was empty. He ran back out and down the stairs into the heat and choking fumes.

He tried to open the dining-room door, but the handle burned his flesh, and the door seemed to be swelling inside the frame. The living room door was open, and he heard Michael shouting for him. John pushed through the smoke pulling his T-shirt over his mouth and squinting to try and see anything. The far side of the living room and the back of the house looked like a wall of flames. He stumbled and fell forward but kept crawling towards the sound of Michael's voice. It seemed that the house was stretching away from him as he moved forward. He could see the old woman through the smoke; she was dragging Michael toward the flames at the back. He forced himself to his feet and ran forward until he had hold of Michael's hand. The woman turned and hissed at him, but he managed to pull Michael away from her.

He picked him up, pulling his face close to his chest to try to keep the smoke out, and ran to the front door of the house. At first, the door wouldn't open. After a few tries, he felt it shift and the rush of cool air from outside. The flames seemed to chase him from the building, rushing up behind him as he threw himself and Michael on to the damp grass outside.

The neighbours must have seen what was happening and gathered around in front of the house. People were fussing around him and his son. He pushed away from the people that fussed around him and tried to run back into the house. Flames filled the entrance to his home, and parts of the building were already starting to collapse. Somebody held him from behind and tried as hard as they could to pull him back towards the others.

"Jason is still in there!" he screamed, fighting with the neighbour who was trying to save his life.

"He might have made it out the back of the house. There's no way you can go back in there now."

More people came to pull him away from the burning building, and he fell onto the grass sobbing. People tried to reassure him that his husband could have made it outside or may even have gone for a walk. All John could think of was the burnt thing that had stared at him with his husband's beautiful blue eyes the other day.

"He was in the dining room," he sobbed. "I couldn't get in."

The sound of sirens filled the air whilst the flames destroyed his home. Somebody brought Michael over to him, and they sat, holding each other crying, whilst people tried to fight the fire.

Jason was beyond his help. Now he just had to look after Michael.

CALLUM PEARCE

ABOUT THE AUTHOR

Callum Pearce is a Dutch storyteller, originally from Liverpool.
He is a fiction writer published multiple times across a variety of
platforms. A Lover of the magical as well as the macabre. He
lives in a foggy old fishing town in the Netherlands with his
husband and a couple of cat shaped sprites.
Featured in lots of drabble collections and anthologies or online.
He has also written factual articles for an LGBTQ+ lifestyle
website.

See his website for things that are available now, coming soon or
free to read online.
Callumpearcestoryteller.com
twitter.com/Aladdinsane79

THE HOUSE OF BONES
BY MAGGIE D. BRACE

*T*he house and I have cordially settled on our tacit understanding. For the shelter and safety provided by its dilapidated, cavernous hulk, I must dutifully fulfil my part of the bargain.

The two of us have a long history of co-operation. As a troubled teen, I sought solace in its empty bowels from the wretch who sired me and thus claimed free rein to abuse and torture the humanity out of me.

After I grew strong enough to fight back, each of his drunken rages would erupt into an all-out brawl. I would shelter in this lonely, abandoned house, nursing my wounds and vowing vengeance.

Our clever plan fleshed itself out slowly. Luring my father into the house proved easy. A casual tale of hidden riches brought him snooping. Then my faithful shelter provided the easy means of his disposal through termite ridden floorboards.

Thus, began our partnership. The house required its homage, I provided its victims.

MAGGIE D. BRACE
ABOUT THE AUTHOR

Maggie D Brace, a life-long denizen of Maryland, teacher, gardener, basketball player and author attended St. Mary's College, where she met her soulmate, and Loyola University, Maryland. She has written *'Tis Himself: The Tale of Finn MacCool* and *Grammy's Glasses*, and has multiple short works and poems in various anthologies. She remains a humble scrivener and avid reader.

PERRY LANE

BY TERRY MILLER

Old houses come with legends, especially those which have sat empty for some time. So was the case with the last house on Perry Lane. Boarded windows and doors only served to increase the mystery of what lay just beyond. "The house of the witch," some would say. Rumours were that her spirit still roamed the house. Others insisted that bizarre rituals took place in the basement. This or that person died there! The stories were endless. It sat a couple of acres from the previous house, and the property was at a dead end. The thick woods separating it from the other houses on the street provided onlookers with next to no view through the barrage of trees.

Sometimes during a stormy night, the people down the lane could hear the cries of children carried along the wind. Their whimpers begged for someone to help them. If the voices were to be believed, they were somehow trapped within the house. Police, on several occasions, explored the property to no avail and insisted there was no one there. Yet, the voices came in the night, beckoning. Some residents wore earplugs in order to rid themselves of the haunting voices that rang out in the pouring rain. Some thought themselves mad but received solace in neighbours' accounts of witnessing the same sounds.

David Morris, who owned the last house before the woods, came home from work one night. The fog was thick, and out of it, as he was turning into his driveway, a ghostly old woman came running toward him before simply disappearing. He told no one of that night. Many of the neighbours kept experiences to themselves. One of the things they all agreed upon was to never go past the woods. Something wasn't right there, no matter what the cops say. There was evil in that house, and it, or something else within, longed to get out.

"Hey, Ricky!" The voice startled young Ricky Covington. He was a timid, scrawny little boy with thrift store clothes and hand-me-downs from his older brother Larry.

"Hey, Sarah," Ricky returned. Sarah had been his friend since the first grade, and now that they were in the fifth, he developed a bit of a crush on her. The whole idea escaped Sarah as she knew Ricky as her best friend. If she had a brother, she wanted it to be him.

"Where are you riding to?"

Ricky was on his bicycle. It was a rare thing to see in the age of video games and computers. Kids nowadays mostly had their noses stuck in the tube or their cell phones. Yes, kids with cell phones. The perfect tool for a predator.

"I'm just going around. I had to get out of the house. Mom and Dad are fighting again."

Ricky's parents *always* fought. They were both drunks who got into knockdown, drag-out fights without a thought to the young boy in his room with the pillow to his ears trying to drown out the noise.

"Oh. Can I come?" Sarah asked with that smile he loved. It was times like this that he wanted to just be by himself, but how could he resist Sarah Clevinger?

He smiled. "If you want to."

They rode down by Morrison pond and skipped rocks across the water. Most of the time, they were silent. Sarah knew Ricky was thinking about his parents. Hers would argue at times as well, but neither of them drank or did drugs; it was just normal lover's spats. Ricky just sat, staring at the water for some time. Sarah found a nice, flat rock and handed it to him, and he moved it around with his fingers before plunging it toward the water. It skipped three times. A record!

"Come on! Let's ride some more!" Sarah insisted.

They got on their bikes and continued on down Morrison Road. They came to the corner of Morrison and Perry. Sarah's face lit up with a devilish grin.

"Hey, I got an idea!" She looked over at Ricky, and his eyes widened.

"No. There's no way, Sarah!"

They both knew the rumours of the Perry Lane house. Sarah's dad was adamant that everyone on the street had gone and lost their minds. After all, the cops already extinguished all the ridiculous rumours.

"What's wrong, Ricky? You chicken?"

No one calls Ricky Covington a chicken!

"Fine. Let's go!"

They pulled into the yard of the abandoned house. They sat and stared at the windows and door. The boards on the door had a space just wide enough for them to slip through. Their hearts raced.

"Um, this was your idea. You go first, Sarah."

She gave him a stern look, jumped off her bike, and walked to the foot of the steps.

"You coming?" She stalled.

"Right behind you!"

He wasn't *right behind* her. He was still on his bike and ready to flee at the first sign of a monster.

"Then get off your bike and come on, chicken!"

I'm not a chicken!

That did it. He joined her at her side. They walked up the steps together. Sarah went in, followed by Ricky.

The house smelled. It was still filled with furniture draped with yellowing sheets. The floors were caked in dust and creaked with their every step. They walked from room to room on the first floor.

"See? It's just a house. My dad tells us that all the time, remember?"

He did remember, but it didn't calm his nerves any. He watched plenty of horror movies to know that things aren't always what they seem. But Sarah had a point. The house was quiet, deserted. It was obvious no one had been there for some time.

"Let's go to the basement!" Sarah got a sudden burst of excitement.

"There's no way, Sarah! Look. I came with you, and we're inside. I proved I wasn't a chicken. Now let's go!" He was scared, but it was also getting late. Losing time with Sarah was easy to do. There's was no way he wanted to lose track of time and be in that house after dark!

She stared at him with a smile. She got a kick out of his reluctance. She knew she could get under his skin, though.

"So...bock, bock, bock!" She made chicken noises while flapping her folded arms like wings.

Ricky huffed. "Let's go."

The basement door's rusted hinges pierced the silence. Ricky found a light switch just above the first step and switched it on. A light in the basement flickered then shone bright. *Maybe this won't be so bad*, he thought.

They stepped off the last step onto the concrete floor. It was damp down there, damp and cold. Behind the steps was another door. It stood open with a crack. Sarah slowly opened it the rest of the way. It was so dark inside. The basement light only shined so far. The cold that emanated from the darkroom filled the rest of the basement. They heard a creak upstairs.

"Shhhh!" Ricky said, even though Sarah wasn't saying anything. They listened. The creak came again. They stood frozen. Nothing. Their imaginations were getting the best of them, they decided.

Sarah wished she'd brought a flashlight, but she didn't leave the house with the intention of going there. *Maybe tomorrow.*

"Where have you been?" Mr Covington interrogated immediately upon Ricky walking in the door. He was in his favourite chair with a beer and some Cheetos.

"Riding bikes with Sarah."

"Sarah." His dad huffed. "You need some guy friends, boy. Hanging out with that girl all the time is going to turn you into one!"

Ricky ignored him and marched to his room. His dad never had a good thing to say about anyone. Sarah was the only friend he ever had. The other boys picked on him. He was the boy with the weird clothes that never fit him because they were either too big or too tight. His shoes weren't Nikes. The trip to the pencil sharpener at school was always the walk of shame. Everybody judged him. He knew it, too. Sarah never cared about any of that. She just liked hanging out with him. Of course, it helped that she was pretty much able to get him to do anything she wanted.

Ricky lay in bed, thinking about the house. It hadn't been that scary, not really. Besides, he couldn't have a pretty girl like

Sarah thinking he was a chicken! He thought of her. He knew she didn't feel the same way about him as he did about her. It didn't matter, though. He got to spend time with her, and that was good enough.

☠

Sarah read. It was one of the old Boxcar Mysteries in her mom's collection. It was Mrs Clevinger's favourite series when she was a girl, so she kept it in the event that she had a child. The collection now sat on a shelf in Sarah's room above her headboard. It quickly became her favourite series as well. Her mom loved that her daughter liked to read. She was a bright child and definitely had a strong mind of her own, not too unlike her mother at that age.

She closed the book after chapter four. Reading at night was always the sure way to bring about sleep. She turned off the lamp on the bedside table and crawled under the covers. It wasn't long before sleep overtook.

☠

The next day was Saturday. Ricky loved the weekends. He'd get up early, hop on his bike, and ride before his parents were even awake. It was the only way to ensure his day didn't begin with hearing one of them calling the other a bitch or a dickhead. Most of the time, they wouldn't even notice he was gone until he came in for lunch. Often, Sarah would be with him. If not, he was with her at her house. Sarah's mom loved Ricky. She thought he was a sweet boy. She felt sorry for him since she knew a lot of what went on from Sarah. If she were a man, she'd go over and beat some sense into both of them. Mr Clevinger took a different angle to the whole situation, though. "It's none of our business," he would always say. He was right.

She knew it. But, damn it, they still needed a good whack upside their heads.

Ricky rode past Sarah's house right as she stepped out the front door. It seemed they were always on the same wave. She met him at the end of her driveway and rode off toward the pond.

"You know, Sarah. The house wasn't scary at all." He was proud of himself. He'd shown her. He was brave.

"I told you! We should go there again! I'll take my dad's flashlight with us!"

Ricky hesitated. "Not right now," he replied. "Let's sit here for a bit. I want to watch the fish jump." If they didn't skip rocks, they'd occasionally catch a glimpse of one of the fish jumping out of the water. The rocks would just scare the fish, and they'd stay closer to the bottom of the pond.

"How about tonight? We can sneak out." Sarah's devilish grin came again.

"Sarah." Ricky didn't want to. Not at night. That was just taking it too far.

"Come on, Ricky! It'll be fun! Besides, we saw yesterday that there wasn't anything to it. It's all in people's heads like Dad says."

He didn't argue with her point. The house was empty. He bit his bottom lip.

"You'll bring the flashlight?"

"I told you I will! Please?"

There it was. He couldn't resist, and so he agreed. Sarah jumped up and hopped on her bike.

"Come on!" She beckoned him with her hand. "Let's go to the shop down the road and get a soda!"

He found it odd that she called it *soda*. To him, it was *pop*. She'd argue that it sounds like you're talking to your dad by calling it that. *Who calls their dad pop?* He didn't know. Nevertheless, he was game.

*T*he evening sun began to set beyond the horizon. Sarah and Ricky were both in their rooms. His parents were already drunk and passed out. They would never have a clue. He opened his window and climbed out. He had left his bike at the side of the house. He got on and rode toward Sarah's.

Sarah came out the front door, got on her bike, and met him at the road.

"How did you just walk out the door?" He was impressed.

"Mom and Dad have some friends over. They won't even notice I'm gone."

Ricky nodded his understanding. They peddled toward the house.

In the fading light, the house stood more ominous. Ricky felt the lump grow in his throat and quickly swallowed it back down. *Show no fear, you chicken!* They went inside. Sarah's flashlight was bright. Everything appeared as it did the day before. Ricky felt himself calm. He felt silly. They went into the basement and opened the other door. The flashlight shined upon a brick wall just ten feet inside the door. They went in. Thunder roared in the distance.

The cold made them wish they had worn jackets, but the thought escaped them on such a hot July night. The thunder grew closer. The creaking noises from upstairs came again. Then the main basement door blew shut.

They both jumped then laughed. They looked around for a light switch but found none. The flashlight would have to do. Rain began pouring as the wind outside picked up speed. The flashlight flickered and went out. Sarah hit it a couple of times against her hand before it came back on. A shadow moved in front of them. Sarah didn't see it, but Ricky felt himself tremble.

"Did you see that?"

"Yes, I saw it. I'm holding it, remember?" She sounded agitated.

"No, not the light. Something in here moved."

"There's nothing in here but us, Ricky!"

He reckoned she was right. His paranoia could sure get the best of him. Then he heard her gasp.

"What is it?" He jumped.

"Over there!" She pointed to the corner. Something stood there, dark and without eyes. It vanished into the darkness away from the light.

"Help us!" Voices came at them from all sides, growing louder.

They huddled together and swung around with the light, but there was nothing to be seen except for the bricks of the wall. Thunder cracked again. They ran out of the room, but the electricity in the house was completely out. The faint light illuminated what it could in the basement, and what it did, struck terror in the two children's eyes. Two shadow-like figures stood between them and the staircase.

"Help us, please!" The figures implored.

Ricky and Sarah couldn't speak. The flashlight shook in Sarah's tiny hand. All they could do is stand there, frozen.

"We were your age once. But then she trapped us here, the old lady with the wrinkled and trembling hands. We haven't been able to leave for years. Help us!"

Laughter bellowed down the stairs.

"Oh no! She's found us again!"

The shadows wept as the basement began to fill with water. The overhead light flickered and came back on. The shadows disappeared.

"Let's get out of here!" Sarah insisted. Ricky agreed. They ran up the stairs and out into the living room. There to meet them once more were the shadows.

"Why won't you help us?" The voices spoke at a lower pitch this time but were still childlike. "Please, before she comes back!"

Ricky had to be the man.

"What do you want?"

"Ah, the boy speaks." One figure announced. It's long, dark, but ghostly arm reached out, beckoning him to come closer. "Let me have a better look at you."

Ricky shook his head, Sarah followed suit.

The figures laughed, then circled around the two of them. After years of captivity, the soul changes grows dark, restless. Neither of the children dared to speak as they fought the tears in their eyes. *Why were they so stupid?*

"They can still help us." One of the two spoke up.

"We're not helping you with anything!" Sarah scolded with a shaky voice.

"Oh, but you are! You don't have a say in the matter, I'm afraid." They drew closer. The flashlight went out for good. The house shook and filled with the sound of pictures crashing to the floor. The old witch was returning.

Ricky and Sarah screamed.

*T*he storm raged. The children were soaked as they stood in the living room of the Covington house. Mr and Mrs Covington asked where they had been but got no answer. Ricky and Sarah were expressionless as they stared on like they were daydreaming.

"Damn it, boy. Your mother and I asked you a question, and you best be answering."

Still, they said nothing. "I said answer me, you no good little shit! Where were you all hours of the night?"

Finally, the children smiled. It was what happened next that disturbed the parents more. The kids faced one another, stripped each other of their clothes and began to scratch at each other's flesh. Strips fell and hung. Blood poured from bizarre symbols they etched in each other as the thunder once again began to roar furiously. The lightning flashed as if the night was angry.

"Help us. Help us!" the children said in unison. "Help us, please!"

Ricky and Sarah scratched and scratched until they both collapsed in a pool of their own blood on the floor. Two dark shadows rose from their bodies and passed through the walls to the outside.

*K*nock! Knock!
        David Morris woke to the knocking at his front door. The clock said midnight, and he, begrudgingly, got out of bed and put on his robe.

"Where are you going?" Mrs Morris asked, still half asleep.

"Some dumbass is knocking at the door, Rachel. Just go back to sleep."

"What? What time is it?"

"Midnight."

He put on his slippers, exited the bedroom, and descended the stairs. The knocks came again, this time a little louder.

"Okay, okay. I heard ya. I'm coming! Hold your britches!"

He opened the door, and lightning flashed behind a lone figure on his porch. His mouth began to tremble. The figure emanated a freezing cold he could feel in his soul.

A pale old woman stared into Mr Morris' eyes. Her clothes were ragged and dated.

"Have you seen my children, kind sir?"

TERRY MILLER
ABOUT THE AUTHOR

Terry Miller is an author and poet residing in Portsmouth, Ohio, a small city in the southernmost part of the state bordering the Ohio River. His work has been featured in various publications, print and online, from around the world. He received a nomination for the 2017 Rhysling Award from the Science Fiction and Fantasy Poetry Association which garnered him a spot in their annual Rhysling Anthology for his nominated poem "Salome's New King". He has a split collection, with author Stephen J. Semones, called "MONSTERS" available on Amazon. Terry continues to pursue his writing in hopes of writing his first novella within the next year.

amazon.com/author/millerterryl

PARADISE IN THE STORM
BY STEPHEN HERCZEG

*B*rendan gunned the Oldsmobile Super 88 through the darkening gloom that heralded the oncoming storm. The three hundred cubic inch V8 engine roared through the early evening, the white-walled tyres spitting gravel as it rounded another bend.

"Do you think we'll reach Vicksburg before this storm hits?" asked Jean.

Brendan ducked his head down and peered up at the sky. Broiling clouds and thunderheads blocked the last of the day's light from view. He hoped there was a chance. He wasn't familiar with the roads and wished he'd never decided on the short cut through the back roads from Darnell.

It had been Lou's suggestion. Brendan had finished playing in the early afternoon, and they had left Mer Rouge not long after. Brendan hadn't wanted to go with the others on the team bus. He'd preferred to take Jean on a road trip.

You couldn't tell what might happen on the road. There might be a nice place for a picnic along the way, and you never knew where that might lead. Lou had suggested the road from Darnell to Alsatia. It wound along the Macon bayou, where there were lots of picnic spots. You just had to look out for gators.

They had managed to find a nice secluded spot along the Macon, but in hindsight, had lingered a lot longer than they should have. When Brendan had seen the dark clouds gathering on the horizon, he'd made the quick decision to high-tail it out of there in the hopes of skirting the storm altogether.

As the first spot of rain hit the windscreen, his hopes were dashed. He turned on the wipers; they squealed as they were dragged across the thin layer of dust, smearing thin lines with each new drop.

"Doesn't look like it," he said.

"Damn."

Dozens of drops followed the first spot. Within moments the windscreen wipers struggled to clear enough water for Brendan to even see the road ahead. He slowed a little, but only enough until his confidence grew again. He drove on, hoping that the car would stay on the road and the rain would settle down quickly.

Neither happened.

The back roads of Louisiana are anything but smooth. The Oldsmobile ran into a deep pothole and let out a groaning squeal of broken metal as the front passenger-side leaf-spring assembly sheared from its mounting. The car slewed to one side; Brendan wrenched at the wheel, only managing to keep control through sheer willpower.

He stabbed the brakes and skidded sideways onto the verge, bringing the hulking great car to a stop. Jean squealed and threw her hands up over her face as she was thrown against the passenger's door.

Brendan's heart pounded in his chest. His hands gripped the wheel so tight his knuckles were white in the gloom. The glow of the dashboard threw a sickly yellow pallor across his face, hiding the sickly green pallor that he felt must be there. He drew several deep breaths then turned to check on Jean.

Like him, she was terrified out of her wits and simply stared through the front windscreen and held her shoulder with her left hand.

He reached out and touched her on the left shoulder.

"You okay?"

She slowly turned, a tear caught in the corner of one eyelet go and slid down her cheek.

"I hurt my arm," she said.

"I'm sorry. Stupid pothole," he said rage against the road building inside him. He turned away and thumped the steering wheel. "Stupid short cut. I could have got us killed."

It was Jean's turn to reach out to him.

"Can we keep going?" she asked.

"I don't think so. That noise sounded pretty bad," he said. "But I'll try."

Without looking back, he started the car and slammed it into gear. As the car moved forward, it lurched and threatened to drag them further off the road.

"What's wrong?" asked Jean.

He killed the motor and dropped his head onto the wheel.

"Suspension's broken," he said through his folded arms. "This old girl's going nowhere."

"What should we do?"

Brendan shrugged off the inner feeling of being a total loser and peered through the windscreen again.

"We can stay here until morning," he said.

Jean's face dropped in shock. She pulled her cardigan around her shoulders.

"It's getting cold, and your heater's broken, isn't it?" she asked.

He nodded. He loved his car, but she was almost on her last legs. The broken suspension might be her death knell.

"Yeah," he mumbled.

The rain had diminished to a few spots.

"It's clearing up," he said. "Darnell was about ten miles back; we could make for the town. I've got an umbrella in the trunk. We can use the picnic blanket to keep dry as well."

Jean didn't look convinced, but she didn't like the thought of staying in the car for another ten hours or so.

"Did you see any houses or farms around?" she asked hopefully.

"I thought I saw lights a couple of miles back," he said. "We can head for there. Might have a telephone we can use."

Jean brightened a little.

"At least it should be dry."

Brendan nodded. He reached into the back seat, grabbed his jacket and gave it to Jean.

"Here, put this around you. It should be a little warmer than that flimsy thing," he said, indicating her light cardigan. "I'll get the umbrella and blanket." He opened the door and was gone before she could reply.

The sounds of Brendan opening the trunk and rummaging around echoed through the car as Jean pulled the jacket around her. She had just finished when her door was wrenched open, and she found Brendan standing before her, shielding them from the rain with a flimsy umbrella. He was wrapped in the picnic blanket, but she could tell he was still suffering as the wind whipped between the folds of material.

She stepped out and closed the door behind her. The night was the blackest she had ever seen. The clouds blocking out any moonlight or stars, the lack of streetlights and houses adding to the abject darkness.

The rain lightly pattered down on the umbrella as they headed off towards Darnell. The wind smacked into them with enough force to hinder their progress and slow them to a stumbling walk. The thick hedge beside them provided no cover, forcing them to face the wind.

"Should we go the other way? This could take hours," Jean asked.

Brendan's face screwed up in contemplation.

"Alsatia's about fifteen miles in the other direction, Darnell's only ten."

"The wind will make it feel like twenty."

Brendan spied a break in the hedge and nodded towards it. They ducked inside the gap and realised it was a broken and rutted gravel driveway that led off into the gloom. They sheltered behind the hedge and sighed in relief.

"This isn't a happening thing, is it?" said Brendan, his determination waning under the assault of the wind and rain.

"Nope. I'm sorry. We would have been better off in the car," said Jean.

They both looked back in the direction they had come. Now that they had found a small oasis of comfort, neither wanted to face the elements any further.

"We can't stay here," Brendan said. "May as well head back."

A sudden flash of lightning lit up the entire area. Brendan saw the house out of the corner of his eye. He turned and peered down the dark driveway.

"Did you see that?" he asked.

Jean, huddled into Brendan's chest to avoid the cold, looked up. "What?"

"There's a house. Down there," he said, indicating the dark tunnel ahead of them.

Jean peered into the deep dark but could only see black.

"You sure?" she asked.

"No, but what have we got to lose?"

Jean thought for a few moments. The prospect of a possible dry house versus the certainty of a cramped, cold car won out.

"Not a lot," she said.

$\mathcal{T}$he rain picked up as they made their way down the long, dark driveway. They could barely hear the crunching of gravel over the howling of the wind through the nearby trees and the pattering of steady drops on the umbrella.

Finally, after what seemed an aeon, they stood before the front steps of the house.

In the dim light, they could tell it was two storeys high. A veranda ran along the entire front of the house, the paint peeling and gone from several of the posts. At the far corner, it had given way to time and rot and collapsed under its own weight. The windows were all dark, but the glass was mostly intact, with only a few panes broken or cracked.

Brendan tested the porch steps and ascended to the front door. He stopped and looked back at Jean.

"Should I knock?" he asked.

"I really don't think there's anybody here," she said.

He managed to turn the handle but found the door stuck fast. Using his best football experience, he dropped his shoulder and charged the door. On the third try, it burst open with a loud crack.

He stepped inside, with Jean huddled close behind.

They both looked wide-eyed around the entrance. A deep layer of dust covered every surface, and thick cobwebs crowded in the eaves and corners.

"This place hasn't been used for decades," said Jean.

"Should we move in?" Brendan said, his mood lightening now they had somewhere dry to wait out the storm.

"Well, it needs a bit of fixing up, but maybe," joked Jean, relief flooding her senses. It was old, dusty and gross, but a slice of paradise compared to the storm outside.

Another bolt of lightning sent a flash through the front rooms. Brendan spied a candle in a holder not far away. He made for it and brought out his Zippo lighter. Within seconds a small circle of light played out around them.

They were standing in a small entranceway. A staircase to one side led up to the first floor, a narrow corridor beside it went into the bowels of the ground floor. A doorway to one side led into a parlour. In the low-light, Brendan spied a large fireplace. He moved towards it.

"Hey, we might be able to light a fire," he said.

Brendan hunkered down near the hearth and found a pile of kindling and logs. A small mound of ashes in the chimney were congealed into a solid mess from years of damp. He picked up some logs and felt for dampness. Satisfied, he laid them in the driest part of the fire and added some small sticks of kindling. He turned to Jean.

"You got any paper on you?" he asked.

She shook her head, then looked around. An old book sat on the floor. It seemed to have fallen from the arm of a nearby chair. She didn't think the owner was going to be finishing it any time soon. Picturing the stern gaze of the school librarian in her mind, she tore several pages from the book and handed them to Brendan.

"Will this work?" she asked.

Brendan smiled as he looked at the typed pages.

"Best use of a book I've ever seen," he chuckled, quickly screwing them into balls and laying them around the kindling. Using his Zippo, he set the balls of ancient paper alight and watched as they were quickly engulfed and took the kindling with them. Within a few moments, the hearth was home to a small fire for the first time in years.

Jean sloughed off the wet jacket and dropped it onto a chair. She moved up next to Brendan and soaked in the warm glow of the fire.

"Good job. My mother always said to find a man that could

provide," she said with a grin. He stood up and put an arm around her, bathing in the warmth of the flames.

The flickering fire played across the glass of a large portrait hung above the fireplace. It showed a tall man with a long dark beard and a shorter woman sitting beside him. The style was very nineteenth century.

Jean nodded at the painting, "Do you think that's the owners?"

Brendan nodded, "Yeah, I wonder what happened to them."

After a few moments, Jean broke away from Brendan's embrace. "We might be here all night, may as well be comfortable."

She moved around the room and found more candles. Once lit, the room took on a more homely charm. The fire flickered off the glass of several portraits of sailing ships adorning the wall opposite. They were all three-masted clippers and reminded her of pirate ships she'd seen in old children's books. She leaned in and read the name.

The Fontine. Curious name.

She moved to one of the stuffed chairs and patted the cushion, immediately coughing as her mouth filled with dust.

"Damn, idiot," she said to herself.

She pushed a couple of chairs across in front of the fireplace. Brendan placed two straight back chairs, from the nearby dining table, on the edge of the firelight and hung the picnic blanket over them to dry.

As Jean stood with her back to the fire, warming her rear, her eyes peered off towards the room opposite. Movement caught her attention. She concentrated harder but, when nothing else appeared, put it down to the storm raging outside.

As she turned to sit, she saw a flash of white pass across the doorway. She yelped in surprise.

"What?" asked Brendan, seeing her face drop in shock and turning his head in the same direction.

"I think there's someone here," she said.

"Can't be. This place has been deserted for decades," he said, a slight chill running up his spine.

He looked around and grabbed a brass poker from the set next to the fireplace. He picked up a candle, walked into the hallway and through into the room beyond. He searched the room and found that one of the windows had a small crack that let in the wind from outside. A moth-eaten, mould ridden curtain blew in the breeze.

"It's just a curtain," he shouted back. When there was no reply, he looked towards the other room and saw Jean framed in the doorway. She stood, her mouth open in shock, her eyes staring wide at something he couldn't see.

"What's wrong?" he said, running back to her. As he turned to face the object of her horror, he dropped the poker and almost screamed.

At the far end of the room, a translucent figure hovered several feet above the floor.

"Jesus Christ," he blurted out, trying to drag his eyes away from the spectre, but finding his feet rooted to the spot.

The apparition looked familiar. The clothing was ancient, like something his grandmother would wear to church on Sunday. The face was etched with deep lines and wrinkles —the eyes, merely hollow sockets bereft of any sight. A cascade of wispy hair fell down beneath a crocheted lace bonnet. The figure held out a wasted hand towards the couple and pointed a slender meatless finger at them. The spirit silently spoke, mouthing words that neither could hear.

Jean broke first and grabbed Brendan, pushing him towards the entrance.

"We need to get out of here now," she said.

"The blanket, umbrella, we'll get soaked," Brendan said as they burst into the entranceway.

Jean's face was incredulous. "I don't care. We stay here; we're dead."

Brendan nodded and reached for the front doorknob. As he grabbed for it, a luminous white claw appeared through the wood and clutched at his hand. He screamed and pulled away. The dry withered face pushed through the door, mouthing words at them. Jean seized Brendan's shoulder and dragged him away from the horrid countenance, dragging him into the room opposite the parlour.

"What the hell do we do now?" he yelled, peering around the room. The only obvious exits were the one they had come through and a small doorway that led to the back of the house. He grabbed a small side table and hefted it above his head.

"I can break through the window," he yelled.

As he stepped towards the front of the room, the spectral shape appeared to block his path.

Brendan dropped the table. The top broke off and skittered across the floor. The apparition floated towards them. Its mouth opening and closing, revealing crooked teeth through the drawn back lips.

Brendan stood transfixed for a moment, staring at the wasted features of the hovering spectre.

Jean shouted, "What are you doing? We've got to get out of here."

"It looks familiar," he said as Jean yanked him backwards.

They ran through the rear door and found themselves in a hallway that connected the rooms at the back of the house. Jean turned left and bolted. Brendan took one last look at the ghost before following.

His last glimpse was the spirit simply hovering at the windows. It watched them escape but made no attempt to follow.

Brendan headed down the corridor and found Jean in a small

kitchen area. His immediate thought was to try the door that lead out the back of the house.

The wood had swollen over the years and was stuck fast in the jam. Brendon tried the knob, it turned, but the door wouldn't budge. He dropped his shoulder and rammed it. The result was a sore arm and a closed door.

"Damn, this thing's stuck fast," he said.

Jean looked around the room; the only other exit was a solid door nestled between two cupboards. She pulled at the handle and managed to wrench the door open, revealing a yawning pit of black beyond.

"The cellar?" she asked out loud.

Brendan joined her and stared into the dark recess. He pulled out his Zippo and ignited a flame.

"There might be a window leading out. Might not be swollen shut, or at least we can break it open," he said.

They carefully picked their way down the steep staircase. The ancient steps creaked beneath their feet. The treads breaking under their weight filled Jean with dread. She kept to the sides, the strongest part of the stair.

With relief, they soon reached the dirt floor at the bottom of the flight. Brendan moved into the dark, searching for anything that could provide more light. Jean gripped the post at the bottom of the flimsy balustrade. In the dark, she reasoned, knowing where the staircase was might be their only hope of escape.

Brendan dropped to his knees to examine a small wooden crate. He flinched and dropped the hot lighter to the ground. It went out, plunging them into a pit of darkness.

"Shit," he said, groping around for the lighter.

"I'm over here. Follow my voice; we'll go back up," Jean said.

She heard Brendan stand and shuffle across to her.

Suddenly, they were bathed in a soft, cool white glow. The

luminescence bathed their terrified faces in its radiance as they looked up and saw the spectre hovering before them.

She hung quietly in the air with her dress and hair animated by a gentle spectral wind. Her eyeless sockets stared at the two of them, her thin lips drawn back from yellowed teeth giving her a joyless rictus grin.

Her right arm rose slowly, the index finger extending and pointing towards them. She mouthed the same sentence over and over.

Jean's terror subsided as her curiosity grew. She studied the ghost and realised where she had seen her before.

"It's the woman from the painting," she said.

"That's it; I knew I'd seen her before," said Brendan.

Jean studied the spirit and began to comprehend.

"I don't think she wants to hurt us," she said.

She pushed Brendan away and stepped to the side. The apparition's hand remained pointing in the same direction. Jean turned and glanced behind them.

The phantasm's glow petered out after a few yards, but it reflected off something just out of reach.

"There's something back there," she said.

Brendan looked down and saw his lighter lying next to the crate he had been rooting through. He was surprised to see several candles inside the box. He snatched one up and lit it with the lighter. The dull glow sent shock waves through both of them as it illuminated the object of the ghost's attention.

Hanging from a roughly made noose was the desiccated body of an adult woman. Even from that distance, they both realised it was the body of the ghostly apparition. The woman's dress was ravaged by time and mould and hung from her withered frame in rags. Her skin was stretched taut over a skeleton devoid of muscles that had rotted away decades previously. The white glow filled the empty eye sockets with shadows. The rotten teeth smiled through peeled back lips as if mocking them.

"Good Lord," said Jean.

"It's her," said Brendan. "The woman from the painting."

He turned. The ghost still hovered behind them. Its arm resting at its side.

"Why?" asked Brendan innocently. "Why did you kill yourself?"

It dropped its gaze towards the teenagers and raised its hand again. The finger pointed off to the side.

Jean stepped across and found a piece of mouldering paper lying on the ground. She motioned to Brendan. He brought the candle over, and they dropped to their knees. The note was written in an elegant script, she read the words, and it all began to make sense.

Dearest Jonathon,

It has been twelve months since last I received word from you. The authorities cannot tell me the whereabouts of The Fontine. They claim that you are lost at sea or have put to an unknown port with no way of contacting me.

I have lived these last few months full of hope and fear. I hope that you live and will return. Fear that you are already gone. The last few weeks have been the worst so far. I have now lost all hope, and I fear I cannot go on. I truly believe that you have passed, and I will never see you again on this Earth. My only hope now is to join you in heaven so that we can be together forever as it should be. If I am mistaken, please forgive me; I believe it is for the best.

I will see you again.

Yours forever

Mary

Jean turned and stepped towards the floating spectre, concern rife on her face.

"You poor woman," she said.

The apparition dropped its hand to its side once more and gazed at the teenager.

"No one should live in such fear. No one should die alone like you," she said, turning back towards the corpse. "We need to make sure she is buried properly. We need to tell the Police. We need to find out what happened to her husband. Only then will she be able to rest," she said to Brendan.

"How?" he asked.

"I don't know. I don't really care. I just know that it is something we need to do," she said, turning back to the spectre. She looked up at the ravaged face. "Will that give you closure? Will that let you rest?"

The spirit nodded and faded from view, leaving them with only the pale-yellow light of the candle.

Brendan's voice broke the silence. "You do realise we are stuck out here with no car in the middle of a storm, don't you?"

Jean held up a finger. "Listen."

They both stood still. The sounds of the storm had ceased. Outside the house, all was quiet.

"The storm brought us here for a reason. Now it wants us to leave. We have a duty to this woman," she said, indicating the hanging corpse. "She will not rest until we finish."

STEPHEN HERCZEG
ABOUT THE AUTHOR

Stephen Herczeg is an IT Geek, writer, actor, film maker and Taekwondo Black Belt from Canberra, Australia, who has been writing for well over twenty years, with sixteen completed feature length screenplays, and numerous short and micro-fiction stories. Stephen's scripts, TITAN, Dark are the Woods, Control and Death Spores have found success in international screenwriting competitions with a win, two runner-up and two top ten finishes.

He has had over a hundred short stories and micro-fiction drabbles published through Hunter Anthologies; Things In the Well; Blood Song Books; Dragon Soul Press; Oscillate Wildly Press; Black Hare Press; Monnath Books; Battle Goddess Productions; Fantasia Divinity; The Great Void Books; DeadSet Press; Belanger Books and MX Publishing.

Later this year, his collection of stories – The Curious Cases of Sherlock Holmes will be published through MX Publishing.

He lives by the creed Just Finish It, and his Mum is his biggest fan.

Stephen's Amazon author page can be found here: https://www.amazon.com/-/e/B07916SQQS

You can catch Stephen at his Facebook page: https://www.facebook.com/stephenherczegauthor

LONG DEAD
BY JADE CINDERS

*J*t's funny to think how it used to be a home. That at some point in time, after an evening of conversation and laughter in the family room, a mother tucked her child into bed in the upstairs bedroom.

Those days are long dead now. As dead as the family that once lived there. The family that still haunts those halls, scraping their fingernails down the walls as they shuffle aimlessly from filthy room to filthy room. I know because I've seen them.

I've seen their gaunt faces staring from the windowless window frames. Inky blackness filling the voids of their eye sockets as they look beyond the confines of their prison. A part of me wants to feel sympathy for them, knowing the horror of their story (a whole family massacred in their own home), but then I think of what they did to Chuck... Oh god!

I see him too sometimes. He was my best friend.

Every time I walk by at night, I see them; beckoning. I'm so scared that one day they're going to figure out a way to entice me in.

Wait! Is that my sister Lucy walking up the steps?
Oh god…

JADE CINDERS
ABOUT THE AUTHOR

Jade Cinders is a writer of all genres and the founder of the popular Facebook writing support group, Writing Bad. She has lived many places, and so often struggles with the seemingly innocent question, "where are you from?" Being lost herself, Jade connects best with other lost souls and finds herself most comfortable in strange places with strange people.

Due to her continued disconnection from reality, Jade has a fondness for all things fictional. She has lined her walls with bookshelves full of books of all sorts, to which she enjoys spending her time with more than anything or anybody else in the world, with just four exceptions: her fiancé, her two feline companions, and her son.

For more information about Jade, please visit JadeCinders.com where you can read all her latest news & updates. Links to Jade's social media pages are also accessible from her author page.

HOUSE OF SHADOWS
BY DAVID GREEN

*E*ach time I close my eyes, I see it—that house. The state of it that morning when they came for me. In my mind, the vision pulls backwards; I stand outside, looking in from the path; its doors wide, welcoming. Crimson rivers rush through its maw, like carpets of red for me to tread on. From the time Mary disappeared, I knew my path would cross that place. I saw it in my dreams. A townhouse—as normal as any other—wrapped in black shadows, a menace lurking behind it. A threat, just out of sight, but its presence felt. Did she send me those visions, somehow? Did she give them to me so that I may discover the truth or as a warning?

Afterwards, they asked me if I regretted my actions. If I felt remorse. I did not. What I did, I would do again. Until the truth of those people who lurk in the dark corners of the earth are exposed. Until those I sought were brought into the light.

For Mary.

People say I am damned. That Thomas Howard Jefferson is as deranged as the lunatics screaming for salvation in their cells around me. Worse, even. Arkham Sanitarium is home to those deemed criminally insane by the state of Massachusetts.

Another house, though of a different kind; impossible to escape from, though many have tried. I hope it is just as difficult to break in. The orderlies, so vicious with the depraved inmates, leave me alone, save for the sorry excuse of what they call food they push beneath the iron door to my cell. I have a reputation. *The Boston Herald* claimed the world had not seen such horror since the Great War. For once, the press does not exaggerate. I am here by design, safe in my cell—from *them*.

Innocent, they called those 'people.' A family slaughtered in their home. No. I know the human body, alive or dead. My former employment as a pathologist at the Arkham mortuary meant I am well versed in the latter. Familiar with how small and shrunken we are in death. If only I'd known how insignificant. Hopeless.

My fiancé, Mary, had been missing for weeks. A budding journalist, she had been investigating a spate of disappearances which afflicted neighbouring Dunwich and Innsmouth for months. Her findings convinced her that black arts were involved—cults. The word sent a shiver down my spine when she uttered it. I knew Arkham, with its lurid and unholy past, would not be spared. I begged her to leave her findings hidden. Burn the evidence, anything but publish what she knew. My sweet Mary. Her face is etched in exquisite detail in my mind. My memory forever remembering her touch.

Since she left, I dreamt of that house. I saw it beyond my sleep, waking visions of that shadowy place. It lay there, just behind my eyelids, always on the edges of my vision—the lights behind the windows swallowed by the darkness.

On the night I uncovered the truth, the Police informed me they had found Mary.

Dead.

They would deliver her lifeless body to me at the mortuary. In shaking hands, I grasped the locket I gifted Mary on her 18th birthday. I discovered it on my doorstep following her disappearance. Lost in thoughts of the house that seemed more real, more solid in my mind than ever before. I jerked with surprise when my assistant, accompanied by the tall, jowly Police Inspector Francis John Marlow, wheeled the cadaver into my lab, slamming through the double doors. Marlow claimed to have happened upon Mary's corpse, so felt duty-bound to report his findings to me, as Arkham's mortician, no matter my personal attachments. A conflict of interest, yes, but I would trust the autopsy to no one else.

"Where do you want her?" Karl, my assistant, asked, not meeting my eyes. Many refused to do that of late. I knew a fever burned behind them; perhaps it shone through.

I glanced at Marlow, his face in shadows. Just like the ones that clung to the house in my dreams. I signalled to the workstation closest to me. "That one, please. Now leave me; I wish for solitude."

The men glanced at each other before hefting Mary's body. They turned, passed through the double doors. Beyond it lay the house. I blinked, and the vision passed, the dark corridors returning. My shaking hands gripped Mary's locket tighter as if it could lend me the strength I desired as if it could chase the visions of that house away. I'd find myself there soon; the images came with alarming speed, more real than before. A reckoning awaited.

Filling my lungs with air, I uncovered Mary's corpse. Tears leaked from my eyes as I examined her, falling on the lifeless body. To the smallest detail, it looked like Mary. But no. The thing before me felt alien. My skin crept in the husk's presence.

"No," I mumbled, wiping away the tears from my cheeks. "It is anxiety getting the better of me. Too many sleepless nights."

The house flashed in my mind as I closed my eyes to steady myself. I forced the vision away and looked on Mary's unblemished face one last time before I began my work. Her raven hair framed skin as white as a bridal veil.

The sensation wouldn't leave me; instead, it grew!

"It's so like her," I murmured, running a trembling finger across her jaw. "But it feels so... inhuman. Like no corpse I have studied before."

The mockery appeared perfect; anyone else would view it and see Mary. But I knew it. The dim light of the room seemed to shrink as my unease heightened. My jaw locked; my mouth ran as dry as a pioneer. My neck and head muscles became tight, tighter still, as though they sought to protect my fragile spine and grey matter from a sudden, vicious attack. Despite the chill air, I broke into a feverish sweat—my palms so damp, my loves locket, which I still held as if it would ward away evil, fell from my grip, shattering on the floor.

"What? No!" I bent to gather the shards of the locket to see they'd fallen in the perfect shape of the house in my visions. "What are you? What are you trying to tell me?"

I saw myself standing outside the building, a presence beside me. It urged me to look at it, but I knew if I did, the madness that threatened to take me would devour my mind. I squeezed my eyes shut as my head throbbed. Raising my hands, I cradled my skull as I felt sure it would pop.

A cough. "Mr Jefferson?"

The pressure building ebbed away. I glanced toward the double doors to find Karl waiting.

"Yes?" I croaked, glancing at the floor. The locket lay there, intact. I gathered it with care and placed it in my waistcoat's pocket.

"Do you require my help, sir? This cannot be easy; the strain weighs heavy."

I watched, forcing myself to my feet. Could he not feel it? The strangeness surrounding the husk that looked like Mary. I pointed at it.

"Who is this?"

"Your fiancé, sir. If you wish, I could carry out the—"

"Leave." Karl didn't move. "Leave!"

My growl chased him from the room, the slam of the doors echoing. A stray laugh bubbled from my lips. Though even now, I fail to see what amused me.

"This is not Mary," I whispered, laying my autopsy tools out on the tray. "It cannot be."

Uncertainty and fear grew hand in hand as I began the examination. A heart I found. Lungs, stomach, liver. I had carried out countless autopsies and knew one thing to be true. There is always a trace of the soul left behind. Some hint of the person departed, but this demon bore none. I spent hours pouring over the body, sweat cascading from my pores as I left no inch undisturbed in my quest, finding no obvious signs of death. It led me to one conclusion—some*thing* wore skin to resemble hers.

Had she died? Replaced by this creature for reasons I could not comprehend? Or did she live still? As my mind turned the questions over in my mind, my instincts urged me to flee that place, lest I succumb to the same fate as my beloved. I remember my assistant, Karl, disobeying my wishes for solitude. His desire to assist with the autopsy recalled the looks he shared with Police Inspector Marlow. I pondered the house from my visions and how that place played into all this. With frantic fingers, I packed away my carry case and escaped to the lobby.

To find Marlow waiting.

I saw it then, a brief glance in the corner of my eye. I saw the Police Inspector for *what* he was. As I did, a vast fear overwhelmed me. I knew if I gazed upon it, madness would take me. This thing in front of me represented something Old, unknowable. It demanded that I supplant myself in front of what it represented, to swear off my God for its worthier vessel. The terror reached its pinnacle. Just as my mind begged me to give in, for sweet oblivion, to stare at the inkling lurking at the corner of my vision—the moment passed. A wrinkle in reality sealed, but a slither remained open. A horror lingered out of sight. I knew it for what it was.

The creature inhabiting Marlow's body was one of *them*. The real Police Inspector taken and replaced, just as my fiancé. Mary's studies into the occult had led her to the same two words time and again—*Dagon. Cthulhu.* This unspeakable evil in front of me was an acolyte of this depraved cult. Creatures come to enslave humanity or wipe it away. It did not matter. *We* did not matter. Had Mary called them upon us through her investigations, or is it our time to be erased, like the extinct species before us?

"You know the truth of it, Thomas?" the thing asked in Marlow's mock-kind voice.

"Truth?" I stuttered. The body, I thought, he must mean the body. "Truth. Yes. Laudanum poisoning, I am sure. She suffered terrible headaches, became too fond of the drug. I warned her."

"My condolences," the entity wearing Marlow's skin replied, fake tenderness in its eyes. "If there is anything I can do? You must call upon my home, at least. I am sure we can ignore the prohibition in such circumstances. My position comes with *some* perks."

Home. The visions slammed into my mind. The house, wrapped in shadow, a presence by my side as I lingered. Marlow. Yes, he waits with me. The doors open, red carpets of blood welcoming me into the belly of the beast.

"It is not too late?" I asked, a plan hatching in my mind. The monster did not know that it was revealed to me; I would use that.

"Not at all, my friend," Marlow replied, a heavy hand falling on my shoulder as we walked. My very bones crawled at its touch. "My home isn't too far from here; you know where it is. You must pass it on your way to work, yes? A nightcap will do us both the world of good."

A usually busy town, I remember finding it unusual to see

Arkham's streets deserted as we headed for Marlow's home. Not a soul braved the mist which hung upon the place that night. The cobblestoned streets seemed to ooze dampness as if the ground itself felt unease at the disquiet. We arrived at our destination, the stately home wrapped in shadow despite the lanterns adorning it. Icy fingers clasped my heart; Marlow's house and the one from my visions were the same. A presence lurked inside there, something not of this world. Something evil. Would I find some clue there? Some hint as to Mary's fate?

"Your wife and children?" I enquired, hesitating outside. I half expected the doors to fly open, for rivers of crimson to cascade out.

"In bed by this time," the thing resembling Marlow replied, unlocking the door. It swung open, revealing a modest home inside. Ordinary, so mundane. Yet the *feeling*! I wanted to wail, snarl, gnash my teeth, run into the night. The thing ushered me inside and closed the door behind me. It saw me eye the heavy bolts as it fastened the locks. "Cannot be too sure, times as they are."

I held my equipment case against my waist. The unspeakable fear which assailed me at the mortuary had returned. I had entered their lair, locked in with the beasts. Or were they sealed in with me?

The house staff found me the next morning. As the creature inside Marlow led me into his study, I acted, a scalpel to the throat. As it bled out, gargling blood as it attempted in vain to hold its life-source in its windpipe, I had endeavoured to find some clues in the nightmare's body. As it died and grew still, I delved into the corpse for some facts to expose the creature but discovered nothing to assist me. Marlow's body appeared so human. But not, *I knew it!* Driven, I widened my search to the former Police Inspectors family.

Even the children emitted the same sense of wrongness.

As I worked, I realised why the visions of the house came to me. This night's importance had become my destiny. I scoured their bodies, investigated every nook and cranny of that alien home. With its evil lurking behind the mundane normality of it all—and understood my life had built to my meeting with the house. Perhaps these creatures themselves had killed my Mary, between those very walls, and my acts were that of pure vengeance? No. Science, understanding. Knowledge. That's what drove me, that's what set me gibbering and screaming as the night drew on and a faint light rose through the windows. I failed.

I found nothing tangible. The family's blood congealed to slime as I worked through the evening. Some dripped from the bedroom floorboards into the lobby and continued to do so after I moved the terror's lifeless shells there one by one to conduct my work. The light flowed better, so many windows to the outside world. The help discovered me as they returned the next morning, restraining me as I sought to work on the creatures some more. The place resembled an abattoir, and I the butcher. 'The Slaughter House' is what they call it now. They do not understand the danger Arkham is in, cannot fathom my attempts to reveal it all to them. The house stands as a testament to my work. As a warning to those of the cult Marlow and his family belonged to.

An alienist, Dr Henry Collins, visited me in prison as I awaited trial, and we spoke of the house. How it came to me, how I knew my path led there. Collins seemed to believe me, urging me to tell him everything. I did; I told him how I wept when I murdered the children, how I howled when I ended Mrs Marlow's life.

At my trial, he informed the judge and jury that grief had broken my mind. I could not process Mary's disappearance, let alone her dead body being wheeled in for me to take apart piece by piece. His professional view, he stated, was that I was thoroughly insane. That I blamed the Police for their role in not locating Mary, becoming fixed on Marlow's home as I passed it each morning and night. That I'd grown paranoid. Rambling about secret societies, Old Ones returning. Of inhuman *things* wearing people's skin. The traitor. Though a thought occurred to me, and I smiled as I listened. Oh, I knew him, too.

So, I played up to Collins' prognosis. How far did this foul cult reach? How many had they replaced? The alienist, for sure.

I had taken four of them, the trial laying my secrets bare. My actions placed a target on my back. I pleaded not guilty, for you cannot kill something that is not one of God's creatures. I howled with laughter as the witnesses described what they found in Marlow's home that bloody morning. Or perhaps I cried. My memory fails me.

My cell is the safest place for me to wait out what is coming. I am here for the rest of my days. Until all life is gone, and they find their way in. My fellow inmates continue to wail, to cry out and gnash their teeth. Their screams have become more urgent. Frenzied. Something is coming.

They are coming.

DAVID GREEN
ABOUT THE AUTHOR

David Green is a writer based in Co Galway, Ireland. Growing up between there and Manchester, UK meant David rarely saw sunlight in his childhood, which has no doubt had an effect on his dark writings. Published with Black Ink Fiction, Red Cape Publishing and Eerie River Publishing, David has been nominated for the Pushcart Prize 2020 and his dark fantasy series Empire of Ruin launches in June 2021 with "In Solitude's Shadow."

Website: www.davidgreenwriter.com
Newsletter: https://tinyurl.com/y6ah8brp
Twitter: @davidgreenwrite

A VIEW FROM WITHIN
BY MICHELLE RIVER

*J*t started at the base of my neck. It wasn't a thing you'd really notice until something happened to draw your attention to it, but a small numb spot had developed almost between my shoulders. I don't think I realised it was there at first, so I'm not sure how long it had been there before things got bad. All I know is, it all started after we moved into our dream house and found that little doll in the room behind the walls.

The two-story Victorian was magnificent. We'd fallen in love with it the moment we'd seen it; the long dirt driveway, the giant pines giving way to the old farmhouse with its wild, expansive garden, and two giant bay windows to take it all in. The realtor said it had been vacant for five years due to an issue with finding the executor of the estate. We put an offer in that day, and it was accepted by the end of the night.

We planned on a few renovations to make it our own —a change of tile here and painting there—but six months into what should have been a three-month renovation, we found something strange.

The plan was to expand the small *en-suite* bathroom by taking down the adjoining wall between it and the linen closet in the hall so we could extend the vanity countertop. But, when we broke through the wall, we found a completely different space—a room between the walls.

Ryan poked his head inside and gave a long whistle. "Jade, come check this out."

I turned on my phone's flash and squeezed through a narrow gap between the exposed studs to investigate. Although the room was small, it was very cozy—just wide enough to turn around in with my arms outstretched and long enough to lay down. A large, comfy pillow was in the corner, propped against the wall with a quilted blanket and surrounded by scattered and forgotten art supplies.

"You have to see this," I called to Ryan over my shoulder, admiring what had to have been someone's private art studio.

The inner walls were a tapestry of crayon and charcoal. Bright stick figures and awkward butterflies hovered near the floor in crayon while everything between the floor and ceiling grew in skill and detail, culminating in the masterpiece above the pillow: a stallion running wild in an open field. A perfect moment of freedom and wonder captured in black and white charcoal. It was magnificent, and I wondered if there was a way we could preserve it somewhere else in the house.

"Wow, that is impressive," Ryan said as he surveyed the room from the bathroom. "What's up with the creepy doll, though?"

"What doll?"

"Right over there, under the blanket."

Tucked between the folds of the quilt sat an antique porcelain doll. I took care to remove her from the old blanket, smoothing out the soft linen of her dress and brushing away the dust.

She was beautiful. Perfect but for a fine crack upon her rosy cheek. Her deep brown eyes were framed by light blonde hair and soft, pale skin. I gently ran my fingers through her hair. It didn't feel like the plastic dolls of my childhood. It was smooth and silky, like it had been freshly washed. I wondered how it could still feel so clean and soft after all these years and how old it must be to have used real (or what I assumed was real) hair.

Her realistic glass eyes stared back at me with an intelligence I almost believed was real.

The effect was strange because it felt like I was holding a very tiny person in my hands, someone who knew and understood the world around them. It reminded me of when I was little, and I'd believe my toys were alive and listening.

"We'll find you a nice new home once we get the house finished," I whispered to her. A chill washed over me but was gone as I turned toward Ryan, still peering through the hole we had made. "This is perfect! Look at all the extra room we have now. We don't even have to get rid of the linen closet!"

I set the doll in a box marked for donation, along with all the other small items we'd found forgotten and left behind by the old owners.

A week later, the house was finally finished. The last of the paint had dried, and the new ceramic tiles were set. We could finally relax and enjoy our dream home.

Some nights later, as I lay wrapped in Ryan's warm arms, I finally took note of it: the lack of feeling. I thought little of it at the time, of the tingling whisper of sensation wrapped around a perimeter of nothingness, but a few days later, I realised it had grown to the size of my palm, and I worried. Shortly after that, it had spread across the breadth of my back, an ever-present void just behind me, and Ryan pushed me to see a doctor.

It took a few anxious days to get my medical records transferred, and I worried I'd lose more sensation the longer it took, but within the week I had booked an appointment with our new doctor.

The clinic was located just off of Main Street, a small building attached between a bakery and the pawnshop. In the waiting room were three plastic chairs and a small coffee table facing a large cork-board, which consumed one of the walls. It proudly displayed faded pictures of a young doctor cheerfully posing with babies and children. I recognised the same man in each photo, ageing throughout the collage of thank-you cards and birth announcements as his hair eventually went grey and thin, but his smile stayed just as brilliant. It was a comforting smile.

When the plump receptionist called my name, I followed her into the only examination room and took a seat on the old exam table. When the door opened again, I was greeted with the same smile I had seen plastered on the photos in the waiting room, and immediately felt at ease.

He assessed my back, walking his fingers up the base of my spine towards my neck.

"Can you feel that?" he asked as his fingers moved into the dead zone.

"No. Where are you touching me?"

"Along the eighth thoracic vertebra," he said, leaning around me and using his index finger to mark a spot on my chest. "It is the same level as your chest bone, right here. And you say there is no pain? No stiffness or loss of movement in your shoulders or neck?"

"Not at all. Occasionally I'll feel a tingle like when your leg falls asleep, only obviously it's on my back, and some pressure. It'll be like that for hours, then fade away, and I won't feel anything anymore. I'm numb by morning."

"Nothing else?"

"No. Well, yes, maybe. I don't know how to describe it, but my chest feels heavy, almost full. I can sometimes feel the beat of my heart, or my lungs feel like they're pushing against something."

"Do you have a cough? Anything chronic?" I heard him pop the cap off of a pen. Using his fingers as a guide, he outlined the encroaching numbness on my back, mapping out the dead zone like water damage on the ceiling.

"No. No cough, nothing like that."

"Hm." He looked at me for a moment, his blue eyes pondering me like a puzzle with no end pieces. "The good news is your lungs and heart sound perfectly healthy, so I wouldn't worry about that. But, while I can't say for certain, I don't believe the numbness you are describing is neurological. I'll refer you to a colleague of mine in the city just to rule everything out, but I believe this is most likely caused by a pinched nerve."

He smiled at my relief as I let go of a breath I didn't know I was holding.

"You've been cleaning up and renovating that old farmhouse out on McGarry Road, right?"

My heart fluttered in surprise. I felt put on the spot when I answered. "Yes. We took possession about six months back and just finished the renovation a week ago."

"It is such a shame what happened to them, the Murrays. I knew them well. Such a tragic accident," he said, shaking his head as he sat down with a *humph*. I quickly realised I had found the town gossip, and he was waiting for me to ask for more. Normally I wouldn't pry, but I was curious about the family that had lived in our new home.

"What happened to the Murrays?" I prompted. "We were told there was an issue finding the executor of the estate, but nothing else."

"It was just the two of them in that big old house," he said. "Dan and Mary never had any children. Well, that isn't true. They did have a little girl way back when, but she was born wrong and too early. The little darling passed just before her first birthday. But the accident happened only five years ago. All we know is, Dan was the one driving when they crashed head-on into a semi just up on Highway 6. They think he may have fallen asleep at the wheel because there weren't any signs of him trying to avoid it. Neither of them made it to the hospital."

"That is just awful," I said, my heart sinking.

"Well, I am glad someone finally moved in," he said, smacking his knee as he stood up. "A house like that needs someone to take care of it."

"We're trying to. The house has been empty for... well, since the accident I guess, so there were a few surprise challenges. Like getting all the rodents out of the attic, and kitchen cupboards for one," I laughed.

"Well, good luck." He shook his head. "Unfortunately, there isn't much you can do once they're inside. They only need a little space to squeeze into. Once they're in, you'll never get them out. Vermin are persistent little buggers. Get yourself a cat or two. That should keep the population down, at least."

He moved to the cabinet in the corner of the room and pulled out an old binder. Flipping halfway through, he removed a business card.

"This is the neurologist I'd like you to see," he said, passing me business card. "It takes a month or so for new patients to get in, so make the appointment when you get home. In the meantime, I want you to take it easy. Get a massage. Don't do any heavy lifting. Monitor the numbness; it could take a couple weeks for the inflammation to go down. If you notice any pain, or if things change drastically, head over to the hospital in Mansburge; they have an MRI and could probably get you in for an emergency scan if needed."

I thanked the doctor for his time and booked an appointment with a masseuse when I got home.

*T*he masseuse arrived the next afternoon, carrying a bulky massage table and a Bluetooth speaker into the newly renovated den. I quickly moved the box of forgotten donations to the mantle over the fireplace and moved the small coffee table so she could set up. She motioned for me to lie down once the table was prepped. The sound of babbling water poured from the speaker.

It reminded me of a cheesy scene from an old *Friends* episode, and I stopped myself from making an inappropriate joke.

She massaged my feet with oil, easing me into the sensation of touch. I couldn't stifle a groan when she moved up to my calves. The last six months had left my body tired and sore, and her strong hands plied my aching muscles until they were putty.

"I'm moving to your upper back now," she said after a while. "I'll be gentle around your spine, but sometimes a pinched nerve can send a sharp sensation when stimulated, so please let me know if you experience any discomfort."

"OK," I said, trying not to let anticipation ruin the good she'd already done.

Her fingers quickly disappeared into the void of my back, her strokes imperceptible but for the way my body rocked under the pressure: rolling like flotsam on an invisible ocean. It was soothing in a way.

"Can you feel this?" Her voice startled me.

"No. No, sorry. I fell asleep for a moment. This is very relaxing."

"No problem at all. I'm glad you're enjoying it. I just wanted to check in, make sure you aren't uncomfortable. I'm just massaging lightly around your spine, about three inches below the mark on your back."

"Wait." A lance of panic pierced me. "You're below the line

the doctor drew?" I twisted around, straining to see where she was touching me.

Her hands were just above my hips. Well below the line the doctor had drawn yesterday. My heart was racing as I lay back down, using the mirror over the fireplace to watch her.

How had it progressed so far so fast?

The vacant eyes of the porcelain doll peered over the edge of the donation box, watching as the masseuse continued her way up my spine.

"I wouldn't worry too much," she said as she moved toward my dead neck. "These things happen. I haven't seen a case this severe before, but loss of feeling is really common. I'm sure once we get your spine healthy again, you'll be back to normal."

I knew she meant well, but I was too numb to receive any comfort. All I could focus on was the tingling around my shoulders and controlling my anxiety as she pressed her hands against me. The pins and needles gave way under her fingers and almost made me gasp in surprise, but then there was nothing.

More nothing.

I could no longer feel the top of my arms.

I called the neurologist after the masseuse left and tried not to cry when the receptionist gave me a date three weeks out. I didn't have three weeks, I told her, still fighting down the panic. She put me on the emergency call list, and when I hung up, I sincerely prayed for a cancellation.

The next few days were terrifying as the encroaching numbness encased my arms and legs at an alarming rate. When I woke up to find it had spread below my elbow, Ryan rushed me to the hospital, demanding every test we could think of before it was too late.

The nurse who took my vitals was patient and sympathetic.

"When did it start?" She looked up from the computer, watching me as she waited for an answer.

"About three weeks ago, I guess." I worried at my lip.

She tapped a few keys. "Any loss of bodily functions?"

"Thankfully no. No issues in the bathroom yet. I just can't feel anything."

"Any loss of motor control, or decreased strength?"

"No."

"Jade," Ryan said softly. "What about at night?"

I looked up at him, confused. "What do you mean 'at night'?"

"This has happened a few times. After you fall asleep, you wave your hands around. You've hit me a few times. When I asked, you said it was night terrors."

"What are you talking about? I don't have night terrors." I tried to keep the panic from my voice.

"Yes, you do. Like last night. We were on the couch watching Netflix. You fell asleep and started jerking your arms around, then hit the coffee table. That's how you got that bruise." He pointed to a dark shadow of purple and black on my left arm. The concern in his eyes as he searched my face for something I couldn't give him broke my heart. "You woke up and said how much it hurt before falling back to sleep."

A chill crashed over me. I had no memory of that happening. Last night, or any other night for that matter. And what he said was impossible, anyway. I couldn't have felt the pain last night because that arm had already lost sensation.

Hours later, after all the tests were complete, we left the hospital to await the results. I didn't want to stay there any longer than I had to. I was losing touch with my body, and I didn't want the last things I felt to be scratchy bed sheets, cold floors, and IV needles. I cried silently in the car, hot tears disappearing into the void of my numb cheeks.

Ryan carried me to the couch, moving the porcelain doll out of the way and onto the coffee table. He surrounded me with pillows and soft blankets, embracing me in warmth only he could feel. We stayed like that for hours, just holding each other, my head tucked underneath his chin just so. He stroked my hair like he used to, back in the old apartment before all of this happened.

"I am so sorry, Ryan. This isn't fair to you," I whispered, and he kissed my forehead as I said, "I love you."

"I love you too," he said as I drifted off, and the numbness finally took over.

I awoke suddenly to the sensation of falling. It was light outside, and to my surprise and confusion, I was standing in the kitchen, making a pot of coffee in my housecoat. Like I do every morning. But something was wrong. I wasn't doing this.

Am I sleepwalking?

I watched as I scooped the dark grounds into the filter, humming a tune I didn't recognise. Try as I might, I couldn't get my body to respond to my commands. I was locked inside, unable to control or affect anything.

What the fuck! I tried to scream, but no sound came out.

Ryan came around the corner looking tired, his hair still wet from the shower. "Morning, love," he said, embracing me in a hug I couldn't feel.

My body groaned. It leaned in toward him. I watched my hands caress his arms, bringing them in tighter.

He laughed, his lips so close I could hear his breath quicken. "Someone's feeling good this morning."

My body turned around and sighed, my hands moving up his chest, over his blue work shirt to grip the back of his neck. His arms curled around me tightly as his lips met fiercely with mine. I watched through hooded lids as he backed me into the counter, lifted me onto the ledge, and placed himself between my legs. Confused, but also eager, he pulled away ever so slightly. We hadn't been intimate in so long. I knew he wanted this. He needed me to want this.

"Don't stop," my body panted. "I want to feel this."

I watched myself pull him closer, my legs wrapping around his waist.

I watched as he took me on the counter, my body writhing in pleasure I couldn't feel.

I screamed into the void of my own mind, paralysed inside myself.

That was three years ago.

And I'm nothing but a Peeping Tom, peering through the open windows of my own eyes, forced to watch everyday intimate moments, while never being a part of them.

I watched as time moved forward without me, and everything changed. I don't even look like myself anymore. It started slowly at first. A new haircut, much shorter than I'd normally go, and a new colour; blonde. Then, my whole wardrobe was new, and my makeup was different. It was a new me. A different person altogether.

I wept while my body smiled.

If Ryan noticed a change in my personality, he never confronted me on it. In truth, I think he was just glad to have me back. He forgave the little things I forgot, was even pleased I was taking up an old passion again: painting. He seemed undisturbed at my new talent for drawing horses and meadows.

I had resigned myself to this misery of nothingness, this void of existence, until recently. I found something new. I *felt* something new —a small fluttering. At first, it was so minuscule I thought I'd imagined it, but it was there, deep within me.

A new heartbeat.

I revelled in that feeling, of the little movements that quickly became kicks and stretches. I exulted in the oneness of it all while I could, knowing it would be over too soon and I would be alone again. Trapped in nothingness.

But then I felt it. *Really* felt it. Right there.

A small crack. A little space, just big enough to squeeze into.

Right next to the little heart.

MICHELLE RIVER
ABOUT THE AUTHOR

Michelle has always had a creative spirit and has a passion for painting, photography, pottery and writing. To her husband's dismay, she is happiest when she has three projects on the go, revelling in the chaos around her.

Michelle hails from Ontario, Canada where she is lives with her wonderful husband, fearless daughter and newborn son. A lover of hot black coffee and everything dark and terrifying, she spends her nights writing horror and dreaming about all things that go bump in the night.

She runs Eerie River Publishing, focusing on promoting indie authors and publishing high-quality dark fiction.

Follow her adventures in publishing and writing here:
Twitter: MRiver_Writes
Facebook: www.Facebook.com/EerieRiver/
Facebook: www.Facebook.com/MichelleRiverAuthor/

A HOUSE FOR THE AGES
BY JOHN H. DROMEY

*T*he house on Mulberry Street had a long, colourful past. Barring a natural disaster or a manmade catastrophe, the house would also have a long, bright future—except, of course, during recurring periods of darkness when the house either sat vacant or was occupied by beings (human or otherwise) with sinister intentions.

Despite occasional superficial cosmetic alterations to the exterior, the core of the house remained basically unchanged through the years. In sharp contrast, the grounds were—more often than not—in a state of flux. A lush, green lawn might be replaced by a vegetable garden, a flower garden, or a witch's garden of delight—the latter filled with deadly nightshade, toadstools, and the like. Sometimes there was statuary, sometimes not. Seldom were the open spaces overgrown with weeds from benign neglect. The use and maintenance of the property was subject to the whims of the owner.

In the recent past, for instance, ownership was acquired by a holding company, Gretel Enterprises. Who, exactly, was behind the purchase was not readily apparent. No breadcrumbs were strewn along the paper trail that wound its way through a maze of corporate offices on its way to the ocean's shore and beyond.

With perennially closed shutters on the outside of the house and—on the inside—opaque curtains, likewise closed at all times, the structure itself was shrouded in mystery.

Privacy fences further obscured any activity around the property. Visitors could come and go through a hinged section of the backyard fence, which opened into an alley that lacked the benefit of street lamps. Consequently, at night, even heavy foot traffic was virtually anonymous.

During that stretch of time, much of the after-sundown activity was restricted to a single room.

The décor of the spacious chamber reflected the designer's fascination with blood sports. Some items on display were animal-related. Spurs for cockfighting. A picador's lance, darts for banderilleros, and a matador's sword. Oil paintings depicted bear-baiting, rat-baiting, and fox hunting.

In addition, weapons associated with gladiators filled most of one wall and several glass-topped display cases.

In a nod to more modern combative customs, a montage of photographs captured the spirit of the times when bare-knuckle fights were in fashion, plus the *Zeitgeist* when men adept in the use of bladed weapons considered a Heidelberg scar a badge of honour.

Against that backdrop of potential violence, six individuals in long, flowing unisex robes stood submissively in a more or less straight line. Their gender was further disguised by pillowcase-sized hoods that concealed their hair and facial features. The colour of the participants' eyes—peering out from the shadowy depths behind the slits cut in their head-covers— was anybody's guess. Gloves covered their fingernails, whether bitten, manicured, or polished. Anonymous from head to toe, they wore plush booties over their regular footgear. Although silent at the moment, each was outfitted with a device to electronically alter his or her voice. Presumably, they were first-time guests in the house.

An arm's-length away, an equal number of masked hosts stood in line, facing the newbies.

Standing apart from the others, the wearer of a crimson mask addressed the assembly. He spoke in his normal voice—a rich baritone.

"Good evening, everyone. Upfront, I'd like to clear up some misconceptions some of you may have. If you think you're pledging a co-ed fraternity, you're mistaken. There are no Greek letters over our front door. Although we are situated in relatively close proximity to an institute of higher learning, we have no affiliation with the university. That means hazing of pledges is permitted, and our initiation rites are unregulated. We are a secret society with our own set of rules. Welcome to the Club. If you can pass a few simple tests, you'll be invited to join. Nevertheless, membership is voluntary. You were brought here blindfolded. If you choose, you may leave the same way and henceforth have nothing more to do with us. All we ask is that, before you go, you participate wholeheartedly and without reservation in our initial test. After that, if you decide to leave, you are enjoined to protect our privacy at all costs. In future, you must not even hint of our existence. Failure to comply with this simple request will result in dire consequences for you and for anyone you take into your confidence. Are there any questions?"

A mechanical growl emerged from one of the newcomers. "Is this a Fight Club?"

"I'm not going to waste time pondering what prompted you to ask that question. I'm not going to answer it either."

Someone got the giggles. With the tension broken, others joined in. Chuckles, chortles, snorts, and guffaws ensued. Because of auditory alteration, however, it was impossible to sort out which was which. Had the preceding remarks genuinely tickled their funny bones, or was there a spontaneous outburst of nervous laughter? It was difficult to say. Instead of an obvious expression of merriment, the distorted cacophony more closely resembled the sounds one might imagine being generated by an artificially intelligent robot undergoing torture.

"Now, the real fun begins," the moderator said. "To be a good leader, you must first be a good follower. We've devised a taste test that will determine how well you follow instructions. Rather than go the namby-pamby route of having you consume —sight unseen—overcooked pasta dipped in mayonnaise; we're going to offer you real, honest-to-goodness worms to eat with your eyes wide open. Grubs, actually. Hold out your dominant hand, palm upward."

The potential inductees complied.

"Please wait until everyone has been served before you indulge."

An additional masked figure entered the room. Her form-fitting robe revealed her curves. The bowl she carried, and the chef's hat she wore, confirmed her purpose for being there.

She used salad tongs to transfer the grubs, one at a time, to the outstretched hands.

"It tickles," someone remarked.

"Save your comments for later," the moderator said. "A word of advice. To prevent the tickling from continuing down your oesophagus, chew thoroughly before swallowing."

The chef reached the end of the line. She nodded to the moderator.

"Altogether, now. Start eating."

Half a dozen closed hands simultaneously snaked their way upward under an equal number of hoods. By design—to prevent the pledges from holding whispered conversations with each other—the voice filters amplified any utterance they made, no matter how softly spoken. The mildly distorted sounds of chewing and swallowing that followed were, for the most part, unremarkable. The only disruption was the sound of two people gagging on separate occasions or one person gagging twice.

"All done? Please spread out."

With his eyes downcast, the moderator walked around the recruits.

"I don't see any grub carcases lying on the floor. That's a good sign. Next, I'm going to inspect the pockets on your robes. Before I start, does anyone have something to tell me?"

Silence.

"Raise your hands and keep them up until I finish." He began his search. "What have we here?" he said a short time later. He held up a motionless white lump in front of the face of the shortest pledge.

"That's not mine. I ate my grub."

"I believe him or her," another pledge said. "He accepted his grub with his right hand. You took that one from his left pocket. You might want to question the pledge to his right."

"I'm not accustomed to taking orders from pledges."

"I was merely making a suggestion. I meant no disrespect."

"Fair enough," the moderator said. He turned to the pledge on the right. "What did your grub taste like?"

"It was bitter."

"And yours?" he asked the pledge to the left.

"A little like chicken, I suppose, without any seasoning. It was bland, anyway."

"That is the correct answer. Fetch us a replacement grub, will you, Chef? Bring a bitter one this time. We don't want to spoil our guest's expectations."

Two hosts, one on each side, secured the pledge's arms. The red-masked moderator slowly raised the hem of the hood high enough to reveal a moustache on the pledge's upper lip.

"Looks like we have a gender reveal here. It's a boy! I won't be passing out cigars, though. He's yet to prove his worth to the family."

The chef returned with a small dark grub which was wriggling non-stop in a futile attempt to free itself from the firm grip of the tongs.

"Open your mouth."

The pledge refused.

Without hesitation, Red Mask reached out and pinched the pledge's nose. When the man involuntarily opened his mouth extra-wide to gasp for breath, he presented a perfect target for the chef. She dropped the grubworm in place.

While maintaining pressure on the pledge's nostrils, Red used his other hand to lift the man's chin and force him to close his mouth. "Chew and swallow. Otherwise, with your next big breath, you'll likely inhale your organic snack food. Believe me, you don't want that little critter alive and kicking in your windpipe."

The man's jaws began to grind. He swallowed hard a couple of times.

Red released his grip on the man's chin.

The man drew a deep breath.

"Was it bitter?"

The man shook his head.

"Oh, oh! I'm afraid the chef may have given you the wrong variety of grub. It's an easy mistake to make. With the light out in our refrigerator, it's hard to read the labels on the storage trays."

The man began to shiver. His initial shudders soon escalated into full-blown spasms. Then, just as suddenly as they'd started, his erratic movements ceased. His head flopped, and his entire body sagged. Only the continuing support of the hosts on either side kept him from falling. A pledge tried to step forward, but a host put a restraining hand on his chest.

"Let me get to him. I'm pre-med. I'll administer the Heimlich manoeuvre. If that doesn't work, we can try CPR."

Red gave permission with a wave of his hand.

The remaining hosts crowded around to watch. Most of the pledges followed suit.

The falsely-accused pledge hung back on the fringe of the gawkers. So did the pledge who'd spoken up earlier.

The short pledge raised an open hand to lip or chin level and then moved it outward—the sign for 'thank you.' The quixotic rescuer responded by holding up and hooking index fingers, inverting them and hooking them again to signal 'friend.' Afterwards, deliberately sliding up the cuff of his robe, he showed off a small, red, heart-shaped tattoo on the inside of his wrist.

The other pledge mirrored his action. That prompt response resulted in the revelation of a distinctive silver bracelet encircling a delicate feminine wrist. Next, she used a forward waving motion of her hand to sign 'fish.'

Her observer, hanging on every word, nodded his head in acknowledgement. He thrust both of his gloved hands forward with his fingers spread wide. Then he circled the fingers of his right hand to form an O. Lastly, he held up three fingers. He looked up in anticipation and was rewarded with a nod.

Their silent exchange had taken only moments, but there was no point in pressing their luck. The young man held up his extended index finger in front of his temporarily invisible lips. They both turned their attention to the stricken pledge.

The pre-med pledge's efforts at revival were in vain.

"That's enough," Red said. He pointed to a pledge whose robe could not disguise his muscular build. "Help him get rid of the body. One of the transporters will give you detailed instructions."

Other than to insert an index finger under his red mask to scratch his chin, the moderator waited quietly until the designated pledges carried the corpse out of the room.

"Because of this little incident caused by a lack of discipline on the part of a pledge, all of us are now complicit in the commission of at least one felony. Therefore, there's been a change of plans. No more hazing. All of you remaining pledges are eligible for immediate induction into the Club. Do any of you want to turn down the invitation?" Red barely paused before adding, "I didn't think so."

"What about the two pledges who left with the body?" someone asked. "What if they decide to go to the police?"

"Don't worry. That won't happen. Only one of them was an actual pledge. The other was a host with a double disguise. The pre-med pledge broke a cardinal rule by revealing personal information prior to his induction into the society. He'll be given a final evaluation by the host. If he passes, he'll become a colleague. If not, there will be two bodies discovered in time for the morning news. Any other questions?"

There were probably many unspoken ones, but no one dared to express them out loud.

"Since none of you has a need to know the street address of this house, you'll again be blindfolded, and the transporters will drop you off individually in neutral locations.

*T*he following morning, at precisely 10.03 am, a young man entered the seafood restaurant nearest the main campus of the university. He wore a long-sleeved shirt.

As he walked to the buffet, he noticed a young woman wearing a short-sleeved blouse. She was seated at a two-top, facing the entrance. A book bag was at her feet. Her left arm rested on the table, putting a silver bracelet on full display. She half-heartedly picked at a salad with her right hand. The co-ed looked up briefly as the man walked by but did not try to catch his eye. She appeared to lose interest as soon as he passed. He got in line at the self-serve buffet.

As he assembled a salad for himself, the man surreptitiously studied the other diners. He returned to the co-ed's table and sat down. He set his plate on the edge of the tabletop, then pushed up his sleeve. "I like your bracelet."

"I like your tattoo."

"It's temporary." He peeled off the adhesive-backed red heart. "You can have it if you want."

"No, thanks." She leaned forward and whispered, "Are we safe here?"

He leaned forward until their foreheads almost touched and whispered back, "I think so."

"I'm Emily."

"Winston. At least that's the name I'm going by at the moment. What's your story, Emily?"

"I don't have one."

"Everybody has a story."

"Not me. I was adopted by a childless couple and led a pampered existence until my late teens when they were killed in a plane crash. I inherited lots of money. So much, I'll never have to work another day in my life if I don't choose to. I thought enrolling in college and meeting new people might broaden my horizons. I'm sorry to say I exaggerated my limited life experiences in the essay I submitted to the admissions board. I wanted to seem more adventurous than I really am. For example, despite having a fear of heights, I somehow turned a one-time abortive attempt at rock climbing into an expressed desire to scale Mount Everest. Joining a society to meet new friends seemed like a good idea, too, but the Club is way more than I bargained for. What can I do?"

"Fortunately for you, I'm in a unique position to offer you two clear choices. First, you can walk away from this mess, free and clear. I have contacts who not only can arrange for you to disappear overnight but they'll also help you with the paperwork to establish a new identity. The result would be similar to participating in a witness protection program, except this ones off the books. Afterwards, you'd be completely on your own."

"What's my second choice?"

"You can stay here and fight to expose the criminal organisation behind the secret society you were coerced into joining."

"I'm leaning toward the second option. Something needs to be done about the Club."

"I agree, but it could be dangerous."

"Will you stick around to protect me?"

"I will. To the best of my ability."

Winston gave Emily a burner phone. "You may be the key to identifying someone higher up in the Club's chain of command. Contact me with full details as soon as you're given an assignment."

"*I*t's awful, Winston. I've been asked to set up a faculty member for blackmail for having improper contact with a student. The first part of the plan is already underway. Professor Bates invited me to his cabin on a lake this weekend for a private tutoring session."

"Will you be riding to the cabin with him?"

"No, he told me to rent a car."

"That's an ominous sign. We've suspected all along there was a recruiter on campus. Someone with access to students' records. Rumour has it the man preys on young women as a reward for the work he does for the Club. If so, at the end of the weekend, the professor probably plans to dump the rental car in the lake with you in it."

Emily let out an involuntary gasp.

"We won't let that happen. Just let us know what route you're taking to the cabin, and we'll intercept you along the way.

We'll give you some electronic gadgets to facilitate a safe encounter."

*E*mily wore a wire when she approached the remote cabin. Winston was among the anxious out-of-sight listeners waiting nearby.

In response to her knock on the door, there was an audible "Come in".

Outlined in the doorway by a flickering light, the professor wore a pale blue robe.

"I put lots of wood in the fireplace, so it's rather warm in here. Make yourself comfortable. Take off your clothes."

"What?"

"You heard me. Strip."

A brief silence was followed by a staccato sound.

"Now!"

"Was that a slap?" Winston asked. No one answered. The response team—armed and wearing masks—was already on the move. They swarmed into the cabin through its unlocked door.

Once inside, two men pinioned the professor's arms. A third put a hood over his head.

Winston gently took hold of Emily's arm. "Let's go. Our work is done."

"Won't I… we have to testify?"

"No. These proceedings will never go to court. Members of the Club did irreparable harm to many people. Some of their victims had powerful friends. It's payback time."

"How did you get involved?"

"I was just a hired hand. A lone-wolf private detective with no local connections."

"Why do you describe yourself as a lone wolf?"

"I don't have a caring significant other trying to talk me out of taking on risky undercover assignments."

They walked arm-in-arm to the car Emily had rented.

"What will happen to the Clubhouse?" she wondered.

"My guess is it will have a 'For Sale' sign in front of it quite soon. By that time, the initiation room will be an empty shell with all the fighting paraphernalia removed."

"Is there any way we can find out where it's located?"

"We could look for newspaper or online real-estate ads with photos, I suppose. Don't tell me you're feeling nostalgic."

She turned to face him.

"Well, it *is* where we first met. I'll admit I have strong feelings, but I don't think it's nostalgia as much as it is propinquity. What do you think?"

"I think the feeling is mutual." He leaned forward and kissed her. "I'm going back home. It's half a continent away. Why don't you come with me?"

"Okay."

JOHN H. DROMEY
ABOUT THE AUTHOR

John H. Dromey was born in northeast Missouri, USA. He grew up on a farm, but likes the conveniences of city life. John enjoys reading—mysteries in particular—and writing in a variety of genres. His short fiction has appeared in *Alfred Hitchcock's Mystery Magazine, Flame Tree Fiction Newsletter, The J. J. Outré Review, Mystery Weekly Magazine, The Sirens Call eZine, Stupefying Stories Showcase,* and elsewhere, as well as in numerous anthologies, including *Chilling Horror Short Stories* (Flame Tree Publishing, 2015) and *Beyond the Realm: Sword & Sorcery Volume 2* (Black Hare Press, 2020).

THE HOUSE AT THE BEND IN THE ROAD
BY SCOTT DYSON

The mansion appeared deserted. It was an old structure, set in the middle of nowhere, or so it seemed to me. Only the reflection of our headlights, winking at us off of the unbroken windows, had drawn Annie and me to it when our car stalled on the country road which passed in front of it.

When our cell phones showed no reception, I had wanted Annie to remain in the car for a few minutes while I went to the door. It was late, and I half expected some old gentleman with a shotgun to answer the door with a threat to blow my head off. I didn't want Annie exposed to that.

Or to something even worse.

But she insisted on going to the door with me. So, with some trepidation, we walked a short distance to the bend in the road. Then up the long driveway, which almost seemed to be an extension of the road itself. I encircled Annie's waist with my arm and felt her shiver. A chill was in the air, but that wasn't the cause of Annie's tremor. I felt it too. It was the house.

I rejected the thought as soon as it entered my mind.

"Some shortcut, huh?" I whispered. Annie shook her head. "It looked like an easy way to shave some miles off our trip."

"It didn't work out that way, did it?"

"Are you mad at me?" I asked. Annie hadn't been in favour of getting off the interstate in an area we were unfamiliar with.

She didn't answer. "Sorry," I muttered under my breath.

We stared at the house from the broken-down front gate. The darkness behind the windows was intimidating. We scaled the stairs on to the porch and approached the oversized front door. I searched for a buzzer or a doorbell, but I didn't see one. Instead, I pulled on the large ornamental door knocker and let it fall.

"It's open," Annie pointed out. I looked at the crack between the door and its frame; she was right. It was indeed open. "What should we do?"

I knocked again, longer and harder. No one answered. "Go in, I guess." Images of Jason and Freddy flashed through my mind. But that was the movies. So, I pushed away the thoughts.

"We can't just barge in," Annie said. "Can we?"

"We have to. Have you seen a car go past here since we stalled?"

Annie shivered visibly, again. I pushed the door, and it swung open, creaking. The sound was unnerving.

The house's interior was dark, stagnant. A musty, vaguely floral scent wafted to greet us. The foyer was a black hole. I couldn't see a thing.

"Hello!" I yelled. No answer. "Anyone home?"

Annie called, "Can we please use your phone?" Silence answered her.

My eyes were slowly becoming acclimated to the level of light in the foyer. Shapes became apparent. I could make out a table of some sort to my left. Ahead of me, on the right side of the entrance hall, a staircase up to the second story. I stepped through the doorway; Annie followed closely.

"Hello!" I called again—the same result. "Let's find a phone," I said to Annie. "I don't think anyone is here."

"Where is a light switch?" Annie asked. I went around the door and tried to locate a switch, but I couldn't find one.

"No lights," said Annie, pointing toward the ceiling. "But there's a candle." She indicated towards the table on our left.

I felt around my pockets for matches, but I didn't have any. Annie pulled a lighter from her purse and handed it to me. I looked at her quizzically. "*You* have a lighter?"

"Habit, I guess." Annie had quit smoking at my request almost a year ago. For the first time, I wondered if she had really quit. *Now is not the time to get into that,* I thought.

I lit the candle, and its flickering glow illuminated the foyer. The dancing flame cast eerie shadows up the walls toward the two-story vaulted ceiling. I picked it up, ignoring the hot candle wax that dripped onto my hand, and started down the hallway toward the rear of the house. I felt Annie's hand on my shoulder, grasping, as she followed.

I thought that there should be a kitchen somewhere back there, down the hallway. A kitchen might be a logical place for a telephone. "There's gotta be a phone here somewhere." I hoped I sounded more confident than I felt.

"Maybe no one lives here," Annie offered. "No electric lights? That's weird, wouldn't you say?"

I had to admit it was strange. And the lack of electricity didn't bode well for the presence of a phone. I pointed to the walls. "Looks pretty well preserved if no one lives here," I observed.

"Maybe they're on vacation."

"Yeah," I said. "Probably stalled on some deserted highway, just like us." I tried to laugh, but it didn't sound very jolly.

"Well, they don't seem to have any electricity. No switches or light fixtures anywhere I can see." Annie tugged at my shoulder.

"What's through there?" she asked, indicating a closed door to our right.

"Should we check it out?" I asked, looking back at her. Candle wax seared the flesh of my hand again, and I grimaced. The pain passed quickly. Annie pointed at the door again and nodded.

I opened the door slowly. I don't know what I expected to see, but images from *The People Under the Stairs*, a horror movie we had seen on Netflix recently, came to me. Once again, I pushed them away.

I wasn't far off. It was a stairway, and it apparently descended to a basement. "I'm not going down there. How about you?" I joked to Annie.

"Not a chance." She managed a weak smile.

"Through there," I said, shutting the basement door and indicating an archway to our left, just ahead.

The archway proved to be the entrance to a sort of den or study. The candlelight seemed to be swallowed up in the room. Annie indicated a candelabra resting on a desk in the middle of the room, which held five short candles. "Light those," she said. "It's dark in here."

I did, and the room brightened considerably. Still no phone or electric lighting. "Well, it looks as if these folks live in the Stone Age."

"Maybe upstairs," Annie suggested.

"This looks like an office to me. If there was a phone in this house, I would imagine there would be one here." I looked around. The shelves were filled with books; the volumes appeared ancient. Strange artwork and sculptures adorned the room; some were hideous, and some were oddly attractive. "Maybe they're cell phone people. No landlines," I speculated.

Annie slowly walked out of the study while I blew out the candles. "Let's find the staircase," she said.

"You really want to go up?" I asked.

She shook her head. "I don't want to, but I guess we should." She wrapped her arms around herself protectively.

"Let's look around down here a bit more," I suggested. "We have all night, or so it appears. What's through there?" I crossed the room and flung open the door, revealing a large dining room. The table was long, twelve feet at least. "Shall we?" I asked, gesturing into the room.

"Not me," said Annie. "I'm just about ready to go back out to the car and sleep there tonight." She tremored visibly, again. "The longer we're here, the more this place gives me the creeps."

I shut the door. "Lemme look around in here a bit. Then we'll run upstairs, check things out, and if we don't find a phone or something, we'll do exactly that."

"Do exactly what?" she asked.

"Go sleep in the car. Some first night of our vacation, huh?" I looked at Annie. The candlelight reflected off her making her look tragically beautiful.

Tragically beautiful? Where did *that* one come from?

"Better than spending the night in here," she said. "All these statues and stuff look like gargoyles to me. They're creepy."

"Gargoyles ward off evil spirits... I think," I said. "If these are gargoyles, we should be safe here." I smiled, but Annie didn't. "You know what, hon? You look magnificent in candlelight," I complimented. That got a smile from her.

"Tell you what," she said. "We'll buy a whole bunch of candles and put them around the jacuzzi at the resort when we get there."

It sounded good to me.

I went to light a candle that rested on a small table near the dining room entrance. By accident, I knocked a small book on the floor. I bent to pick it up.

The book was old; the pages crumbled in my hands. I tried in vain to see what was contained within the covers of the volume, which was titled "Journal". The paper turned to dust in my fingers.

"Look at this, hon. It's a journal. Really old, too."

"It's falling apart," she commented as she came to stand beside me. "You should put it down. You'll wreck it."

I turned to a page which was intact and saw the strange words there. "This is in some weird language," I said. I struggled to pronounce the words. *"Omratta Ascaroth Ipwess Riotta Trafles,"* I intoned, trying to come as close as I could, phonetically.

The look in Annie's eyes was one of pure fear. "Honey, don't..." She backed away from me.

"Moldarinos Cethula Drarvonat," I finished, and suddenly, for just a moment, I felt a rage the intensity of which I had never felt before.

After a moment, the rage passed within me. But something was in the room with Annie and me. It headed toward Annie, and I heard her scream. I tried to rush to her aid but found I could not move. It felt as if my legs were gone.

I could only watch as the thing grabbed her, hit her once with a backhand. I heard her screams stop. Something dripped to the rug from Annie's limp form, and the thing hauled her around the corner, back toward the front door. I followed; it felt as though I was floating in my pursuit.

The thing flung open the basement door and descended the stairway, dragging my wife with it. There was light emanating from the depths of the cellar now, and I glided downward, not really wanting to see what was down there but helpless to resist whatever drew me. I watched with horror as the being began to dismember Annie. I couldn't even scream with horror; I could only watch, helpless. Presently the unearthly light in the basement faded, and I could see nothing as it extinguished completely.

I awoke with the damp cold feel of the stone cellar floor

against my cheek. In my hand was a hacksaw. The candelabra from the study rested on a shelf; its candles burned down to nubs. I was covered with something slick and viscous. I stood, unsteady on wobbly legs.

My wife, Annie, lay on the floor. She was no longer in one piece. Here was an arm; there was a leg. Her head stared sightlessly at me. I cried.

Some pieces seemed to be *missing*. Some appeared to be *gnawed*.

I looked down at myself. Illuminated by candlelight, the slick viscous fluid coating my clothing and my skin appeared coppery. I recognised it. Blood. Annie's blood.

The hacksaw in my hand was also covered with blood. I had done this. I didn't know how, but it had been me. How could I live with that knowledge?

Or had something used my body to kill my wife? I couldn't have done it. I loved Annie. She was my world, the only thing that mattered to me.

The words in the book... What had they meant? What had they summoned? And, was it still in me? I thought that maybe it was.

But who would ever believe me?

I cowered in the corner of the basement, unmoving. Where could I go? I just wanted to be dead.

Then I felt the rage, followed by the hunger. As I floated to the ceiling, I heard a voice. *Is it in my head, or are the words spoken aloud?* I didn't know. But I knew what was said.

"*I haven't eaten in so long...*"

SCOTT DYSON
ABOUT THE AUTHOR

By day Scott Dyson works as a healthcare professional, and is a
husband and a father to two boys. In his spare time, he writes
and self-publishes his tales of horror, mystery and science
fiction/fantasy. He has been writing since grade school but it
wasn't until the mid 1990's, when he was helping to host a book
and writing forum on Delphi Internet Services called "The Book
And Candle Pub," that he got more serious about creating works
of fiction. He is the author of four novellas, one novel and three
short story collections.

Website : www.scottdyson.com
Amazon Author Page: https://www.amazon.com/Scott-
Dyson/e/B00FK493K4/

THE WRETCHED HOUSE
BY NICHOLAS WILKINSON

*T*he house itself was unremarkable. Nothing more than a rather garish replica of homes you would see dotted up and down the New England coast.

Lumps of congealed paint hanging from the corners of a green slab door that's been kicked in a time or two added drama to the bright yellow tape showing this was the scene of a recent crime.

The inside would be almost quaint if the papered walls weren't still dripping with arterial spray. The retro shag carpet was an inspired neutral cream, one hundred per cent unsalvageable. It stunk of gunpowder and putrefied tissue.

Similar carnage played out room after room.

A blood-soaked duvet rested haphazardly over a wooden cradle in the master suite. A loose bulb in the hall bathroom flickered, calling attention to the fat maggots stuffing themselves on the entrails that spilled out into the common areas.

The clawing stink of death permeated every square inch of the ram-shackle estate. Dried urine and rotting flesh wafted through the air. Her eyes stinging and watery as she watched a multitude of bugs and insects crawl in and out of the twisted carnage fanned out on the kitchen table.

Pleased with herself, Becca turns around, her mouth contorting into a toothy, wide-eyed grin.

"How much for the dollhouse?"

NICHOLAS WILKINSON
ABOUT THE AUTHOR

Nicholas Wilkinson is a writer and father living in Kearny, AZ by way of Philadelphia, PA. He enjoys taking unusual points of view and new interpretations. Everything he writes is in the hope that he's remembered, and possibly even understood, after he's gone.

RUTHERFORD MANOR
BY NICOLE LITTLE

*D*arcy pulled to the side of the dusty back road and consulted her hastily scrawled directions once again; she squinted in the gathering dusk and cursed expressively. Leaning in through the open window, she hauled a bedraggled pack of emergency cigarettes from the glove compartment. She wondered, briefly, if cigarettes had an expiry date, then shrugged. She'd take the risk. Stepping out of the car, she inhaled deeply and blew the smoke out forcefully, hoping to exhale her frustrations with it. She needed this job. Badly.

The crunch of gravel and flash of headlights signalled an approaching vehicle. Darcy crushed the cigarette beneath her heel and raised a hand to flag it down.

"Darcy Bridgewater?" rasped the voice within.

"Yes! I'm looking for … "

"A-yup. Rutherford Manor. Groundskeeper here. You missed a turn 'bout 2 miles back. Turn 'round. Follow me."

Darcy climbed back behind the wheel and did as she was told. The old guy in the beat-up Ford seemed like the lesser of evils as darkness descended on the abandoned stretch of road.

The path to Rutherford Manor was winding, narrow and

rutted; trees grew unfettered, malignant, bowing towards the car, forging a claustrophobic canopy of murky writhing shadows. The shocks in the car straining audibly, Darcy issued a sigh of relief as the path began to open and then gasped in surprise when the house came into view.

Rutherford Manor - stark and grandiose - rose an impressive three stories high. Its crumbling bell tower, jutting from the very top, was bereft of its bell and near collapse. It's scorched wood soot-stained and water-warped. The rest of the house was not much better. It was in urgent need of a facelift, a coat of paint and a new roof. The single lightbulb beneath the sagging porch did little to dispel the impenetrable darkness that cloaked the facade.

Darcy shivered involuntarily as she exited the car. She retrieved her suitcase from the trunk and walked briskly up the front steps. The rotting boards moaned and groaned beneath her feet; she raised a shaky hand to knock at the door – unnecessarily, it seemed. It creaked open of its own volition, and a voice inside called: "Please come in!"

Darcy entered, and the door swung shut behind her.

Margaret Rutherford was a charming throwback to a bygone era. Dressed in a high-necked ankle-length burgundy dress, an antique cameo pinned to the lace at her throat, she met Darcy in the foyer. She held out a wrinkled, paper-dry hand for Darcy to shake and gestured for her to follow. Her manners were impeccable. She graciously offered refreshments – a tray of tea and cookies were placed on a side table in the parlour – before getting down to business.

"My niece – Alice – well, her condition necessitates constant confinement to the manor, I'm afraid." She frowned and wrung her hands. "My sister recently passed. I travel often for my humanitarian work... we felt Alice would do well with a live-in companion."

Darcy swallowed anxiously. She'd no medical training other than Basic First Aid.

"You needn't worry, Ms Bridgewater." Margaret smiled, sensing her unspoken concerns. "Your main duty is to keep Alice company. She loves being read to. You will find a wide selection of books in our library on the main floor. Sometimes she just likes to chat."

"That sounds great!" Darcy exclaimed, a voracious reader – and talker – herself. "When do I get to meet her?"

An unidentifiable emotion flickered darkly across Margaret's face. "She's resting at the moment, I believe. And it's getting late. You must be tired from your trip! Please let me show you to your rooms. You are just down the hall from Alice, so you can hear if she calls at night."

Margaret led Darcy through an expansive hallway and up what had once been a stately mahogany staircase. Darcy's third-floor accommodations were large, airy and bore evidence of having recently been cleaned. It did not harbour the same aura of neglect or the same musty smell as most other parts of the house.

Weariness from the long drive quickly overcame her, and she succumbed to sleep within minutes.

A bell rang. Darcy jolted awake, suddenly aware that the room had grown very, very cold as she'd slept. She was chilled to the bone, her teeth chattering a staccato rhythm in the quiet.

What was that? She pulled the blankets up to her neck and groped sleepily in the pitch black for her phone. As she dangled her arm off the side of the bed, swiping the floor in search of it, her mind conjured unpleasant memories from her childhood of *The Boogeyman* and things that go bump in the night. Stretching further, she mentally scolded her foolishness. Then, another sound. The soft tread of a barefoot, the creak of a loose floorboard, a stifled giggle.

"Alice?" Darcy whispered.

Abruptly, a hand shot out from beneath the bed, clamping tightly around her wrist. Darcy twisted and tugged, desperate for release from the icy grip. High-pitched laughter fractured the silence. Darcy, struggling fiercely now, felt herself being pulled from the bed as it reached a punishing crescendo. She hit the floor in a heap, and something started to drag her under.

The overhead light turned on with a blinding flash.

Darcy screamed.

*C*radling the cup of tea in her chilled hands, Darcy glanced toward Margaret, seated across from her in front of the fire.

"I'm so sorry, dear," Margaret murmured, distressed as she eyed the bruising on Darcy's arm. "She just wanted to play. I'm sure she didn't mean to frighten you!"

"I don't understand," Darcy breathed, afraid that she actually *did* understand.

"Oh, Darcy, we really should have told you from the beginning. Alice was only twelve when she died in 1894. Then, she… lingered. Our family's greatest tragedy became our greatest secret. We thought, perhaps, a companion—someone open-minded like yourself—could keep her company. She's very lonely while I'm gone."

Darcy's eyes widened.

"Please, would you consider staying? She really is a lovely child!"

Well, Darcy thought, *the salary is quite good. And I certainly need the money.*

"Ok, but no more hide and seek?"

Margaret arched an eyebrow and nodded approvingly at Darcy. "I'm sure that can be arranged."

ALICE, IN WAIT
BY NICOLE LITTLE

*T*here is a man outside my house.

He is out there at the end of the driveway, standing beside the battered old oak tree. Mired in shadow, his face is hidden; he is married to the night. From time to time, I glimpse the glow of a cigarette as he takes a long, slow drag. He has been there for thirty minutes now.

I wonder if there is a method to this madness if there is a reason why he stands there still and stares. Why he has come tonight, of all nights. I glance away, just for a moment, and when I look back, he has moved. It is so subtle that, had I not been staring at the exact spot for this past half an hour, I might not even have noticed. I cannot see his eyes, but I know this has been done to improve his line of sight. All the better to see you, my dear.

Briefly, I allow my mind to surrender to the panic. It takes me to a hellish place where this man is not a man at all but a ghastly, beastly thing that writhes and hungers, inching its grotesque bloat across the asphalt, slithering up the side of the house to leer at me through the glass. Its mottled face pressed against the pane while I scream myself hoarse. No help comes. And I am devoured whole.

I have been told I have an active imagination.

The streetlight at the end of our road has been broken for weeks, and I wonder now, have there been other nights when this grim spectre has paid me a visit? Nights when I have not noticed, but he has been watching, lying in wait. So now *I* watch, and *I* wait. A standoff... as midnight grows ever closer.

There is a deafening crash below me; my attention wavers for a split second, but it is just long enough. When I whip my head back to the window... he is gone. I hear it then: the squeal of rusty hinges on the front door, the same door that Father had sworn he would fix but never did. And at once, there is the thunder of footsteps across the foyer. No subtleties now.

Sound carries well in this old place, and I can easily picture him pausing at the bottom of the steps, gathering himself— supping the air; savouring and anticipating. But I shall not succumb to the fear. I will stand my ground.

He is taking his time now, thump thumping up the steps, a leisurely pace. He is toying with me, that wretched man.

Thump. Thump. He's at the landing, and he pauses for a moment. Listens.

Thump. Thump. I hear him breathe his fetid breath just outside my door. He clears his throat, and I squeeze my eyes shut and brace myself for the denouement –

"Let me help you," he drawls. "You linger here, but there is much that awaits you beyond the veil. I can show you the way to Glory."

"Leave!" I shriek. The house shudders and moans around me, the glass rattling in its frame. "You are not welcome here!"

"It is time, Alice."

And I know it is. But I will not go. I am sure of what awaits

me on the other side, and there will be nothing glorious
about it.

NICOLE LITTLE
ABOUT THE AUTHOR

Nicole Little lives in St. John's, Newfoundland, Canada. Her short stories have appeared in sixteen anthologies thus far and her first novella, The Lotus Fountain: A Slipstreamers Adventure, was released in November 2020. She has won several competitions including the June 2018 Kit Sora prize from Engen Books for her flash fiction piece "Sweet Sixteen;" her short story "Doxxed" placed 3rd in the Writers Alliance of Newfoundland and Labrador's "A Nightmare on Water Street: Scary Story Reading" in October 2018 and her three-sentence horror story, "Tasty Babies" earned her the much-coveted Hell Hare award from Black Hare Press in January 2020. In her spare time, Nicole has either a pen in her hand or her nose in a book. She is married with two daughters.

https://www.facebook.com/NLitNon
https://twitter.com/beez_mom

THE HOARDER
BY GREGG CUNNINGHAM

"What you say, Boss?"

"I said, I bet it still smells like shit in there!"

"Uh?"

"Nothin', just keep moving; I think we'll have to go around the back!" I fixed my mask back over my face again, realising this was going to be a bigger job than I had originally quoted for. The streets around here are full of houses like this one; the only difference is this one has a bad history.

This house needs to be cleansed.

Sun-bleached Converse sneakers spin lazily in the breeze hanging from the phone line above us, twisting the knotted shoelaces like ribbons wrapped around a Morris dancers' pole on May Day celebrations.

The garage porch attached to the side of the old house on Maple Street looks like it is ready to fall over, just like its last owner. Clutching its chest and slumping to the left with all the grace of a drunk pissing against an alley wall on a Sunday morning. Even the roof tiles look like a toupee that has slid forward onto the bridge of the nose of a lounge bar singer who had too many free drinks placed on the piano. The car parked under the sunshade hasn't moved in years; the dusty contents inside fill both the back seat and the front seat space all the way up to the roof. Peering inside the car, I can see the same carrier bags full of worthless garbage I witnessed inside the house earlier.

But the house, the house stands as tall and menacing as it always has.

The garden is filled with a lifetime of bagged memories of the now deceased. Although to Trey, it looks like fifty years' worth of rotting garbage the owner couldn't be bothered to trash while they festered inside the four walls. I watch as he picks up an old basketball and pitches it over the roof, raising his arms like Kobe Bryant when he hears the sound of the dunk from the empty skip out front.

"Quit fucking around, dude and grab your shovel; I don't want to be here when it gets dark!"

Yellowing piles of newspapers are stacked high like castle walls corralling the overgrown bushes surrounding the Old Mama Martinez property. Rusting washing machine carcasses housing rat nests and faded cuddly toys piled against the huge gnarled Oak tree planted by the original owners. A tyre swing hangs on a frayed rope. Excited grandchildren now unable to be swung on the bald Firestone because of the bramble branches that now twist their way around the crumbling rubber.

"Why not, you scared boss?" Trey makes the spooky hand gesture and laughs, pulling up his overalls. The kid is a fool, but I don't have to pay him much to put in a hard day's graft, so I let his bullshit slip most of the time, even although he can really piss me off.

"No," I sigh, "they cut the power off yesterday Trey, and I don't want to be shovelling rat shit in torchlight again."

He shrugs, kicking a turf of weeds into the air.

We walk through the garden filled with rusting vehicles poking from the tall dandelion weeds with their wheels immobilised deep in the decades of crawling bindweed. Peering through filthy cracked windshields and inspecting the torn upholstery in disgust, I wonder if the forgotten cars would ever see the tarmac of another Sunday drive down the coast again. The piles of corrugated fencing lying against their once finely turtle waxed panelling suggested any further road trips unlikely.

"Shit, how could anyone let one of these machines die like this man!" Trey shakes his head as he tried to open the door of a '58 Plymouth. It doesn't budge. Instead, I head the banging of the hinges as he pulls harder.

"Fucking sacrilegious!" he curses again, unable to loosen the rusting door.

"Come on, dude, we ain't got all day to weep." I wander on into the weeds.

From the garden at the back of the house, the walls seem to bulge at the seams. Walls bowing out with the weight of the accumulated filth inside. The foul smell only hitting me when the wind turns, and I catch its stench in my throat, reminding me of the smell from running over three-day-old roadkill that had been baking on the side of the freeway all day.

But the house stands tall and menacing, letting us know that the filth accumulated inside its historical walls has nothing to do with it. I stare at its foreboding back door, banging in protest against the fridge half in half out of the kitchen, wondering if my crew of four was enough to handle this job and if coming back to actually **do** the job was a good idea. We both inspect the icebox and realise it's still full of rotten food. When Trey accidentally pulls open the fridge door, the smell of curdled milk makes me gag as he slams it shut again and recoils from the stench.

"Something's died in there for sure, dawg!"

"Grab an end, Trey, quit whining; nobody has died in there. It's just the milk that's gone bad."

"You reckon? I heard the cranky old bitch killed her son and grandkid then buried them out here with his cars!" Trey grunts as we pull the fridge to one side and walk inside the kitchen.

"Hey, maybe she cut off their balls with one of these," he picks up a large rusting carving knife that lay on a pile of crockery in the sink filled with dead roaches and flies. "Then she cooked them hairy Mexican meatballs up and fed them to her cats!" He chuckles, throwing the knife back into the sink with a clatter.

"Yeh? Did she get the recipe from your mother, Trey?" I had to play the game; it's what Trey does to pass the day, mocking my people whenever he gets the chance.

The linoleum floor, or what's left of it, is balding and grey. Cat fur balls are scattered across the lino checkers like Viet-Cong booby traps awaiting the next enemy to tread on them.

"No way, dawg, my mama only uses the finest of homegrown American ingredients, none of that foreign shit you lot eat over the wall!" Trey laughs as he inspects the drawers for anything of value.

I ignore him, most of the time, his jokes are racist as hell and lame, but he is a good worker.

"D'ya think she actually slept in here?" Trey wipes the sweat from his brow with the back of his glove as we barely manage to slide through the stinking hot corridor filled with torn bags of clothing and more newspapers. The heating is off, so I'm not sure why the hell the place is so damn hot. Rat shit is sprinkled everywhere like hundreds and thousands. I guess we must be walking through the filth a good 16 inches off the carpet below —if there even is one now.

"Through there is where they found her," I say, pointing to the bedroom door and making the sign of the crossing across my torso.

"Por La senal de la Santa cruz, de nuestros enemigos libranos senor dios nuestro."

Trey ignores my blessing as always and pipes up, peering

inside over the piles of children's toys and books. "Shit, how'd they get her big ass out of there?"

"They had to take out the window, and dude have a little respect for the dead, will you."

Trey chuckles, "Why? Because the fat bitch had *so* much respect for herself while she lived in this shit shack, didn't she?"

I stop and stare at him for a moment, making sure he feels my disgust at what he has just said, and for a moment... just a moment, I feel the house awaken. "Dude, folks like Old Mama Martinez, are just frightened people who couldn't cope with what's happening around them. Maybe she lost a kid or some other shit. Be cool, bro' and take an end." In my sudden frustration, I nod to the large kitchen dresser blocking the way to the front door where the skip is waiting on the lawn and scowl at Trey.

"Yeh, well, these folks need locking up, I reckon. Something wrong, which if you need to keep shit like this around you. I mean, who the hell wants to keep this kinda shit in their house?" He points to a pile of used crusty diapers in the hall. On it is a scrapbook filled with dog eared photographs and kids' plastic toys.

"They just animals is what they is!" Trey looks on, disgusted as a pile of dusty books and photo albums fall over onto the floor.

"Dude, fuck you!" I snap back.

I pick up the fallen framed photographs of the old lady, pondering over a couple before stacking them in the dresser. Together we walk the antique out to the front yard, followed by the rest of the furniture we could salvage for resale. I place the photo album into my pick-up truck, not wanting to mix it up with the junk that was to be thrown out. I feel I need to keep the pictures, to remind myself that somebody cared about the old lady once upon a time.

The proud house creaks with every shovel full of debris we

clear, every bag of stench we carry away from the corners its once fine décor. At one point, I'm sure I can hear the walls whisper to me, asking me if I remember.

The tales this house could tell.

We pull dead cats like parchment paper curled under the darkness of the worn sofas that's reeked of piss. We drag stained mattresses that look like ancient maps of the continents. Issues of New York Times that look like we have uncovered the dead sea scrolls within the gratings of ovens caked in years of crispy burnt food. We clear bathrooms filled with bags of shit because the toilets were being used as storage.

We clear it all. Trey grumbling his way through every room, every stinking shovel he places into black bin liners.

By the end of the day, the house is empty, and the skips are full. The house stands tall and menacing now that almost all traces of Mama Martinez's sad life has been removed.

The House has been cleansed.

Almost.

Just the water damaged photograph albums remain, those and the whispers in my ears.

The wind has picked up. There seems to be a creak of approval coming from all the doors inside as if the house is stretching away the decades of decay and welcoming in the fresh breeze of life. I must admit I can sense something in the air has changed the mood.

We stand there, allowing the wind to cool us as we listen to the cacophony of groans. Wondering if the house is thanking us for our work and readying itself for the new tenants to harass and terrorise.

Trey hands me a cold one from his truck and yanks the ring pull of his own, chugging back half of the can before I've even opened mine.

"Who'd da fuck would want to move into this nightmare of a fuck-hole?" He points over to the sign on the lawn with his can.

The for-sale sign poking from the overgrown flower bed sits squint, the face of the realtor beaming from the advertisement that said, "Your next dream home."

I stare back at Trey with a sly smile. "There's always some fool who wants to buy cheap."

"Yeh, well, I ain't interested in the Bates motel, no matter how cheap they be selling it for!"

As we watch the last of the cleaners leave the premises, the front door opens slowly, beckoning me inside once more, and I turn to Trey.

"I'm just going to take one more look inside, Trey; you go ahead with the guys, I'll catch up."

"You seriously ain't going back inside, boss?"

"I just want to pay my respects to the old lady is all Trey, shouldn't be too long."

"Yeh, well, don't be too long inside dawg. First-round is on you."

I watch them drive away in the van before I turn and walk to my pickup, pulling out the old photo album I had salvaged and make my way back inside the clutter-free house.

When I crossed the threshold, the front door slowly closed behind me with a click of the lock, but I expected that. It's as if the house was waiting for me to return.

The place stinks of bleach now. Every room washed down and scrubbed so that every surface is disinfected and wet. You can still smell the funk through the detergent, but it is masked by that fresh bottled pine smell. It sticks in your throat, and underneath the sickly-sweet odour, the stench of rotten corpse still remains. But I don't mind it; honestly, I don't.

Now, all that is left in the main room now is a folded chair propped up against the radiator by the torn curtains. And a couple of boxes of cleaning products the cleaners have forgotten. I pick up the picnic chair and make my way through to where she had died, tucking the album under my armpit.

The bedroom seems smaller than I remember from my childhood here. The wallpaper hanging from the dampness in the corners of the ceiling was still the same. The same wooden crosses adorn the far wall next to the large misty mirror, and when I walk over, I catch my blank reflection staring back, still wearing the face mask. When I remove it, I see those steely eyes staring back at me, but they don't feel like my own. I wonder if we truly cleansed the house.

I pull open the seat and sit it down by the window, then walk over and open the curtains to allow the light from the streetlamps to fill the room. The bleach is strong in here, so I open the window and sit down, placing the photo album on my lap.

The house has fallen silent by now. I wonder if it recognises me after all these years and is waiting to see what I am up to.

I smile, pulling out the folded photograph that had been taken in happier times. One of the old lady pushing her grandkid on the Firestone tyre garden swing, flicking through the old photographs of my gran and me. The empty pages tell their own story, and I smile with each turn of the blank sheets. His face has gone from every picture taken, pulled from the photo album as if he was never even there. Him and his sordid lies.

He has been wiped not only from my memory but also by hers.

But not the house.

The house says nothing as I flick my way through the album one last time; it just sighs, remaining the perpetual silent witness, even although it knows my deep secret. It has, after all, kept it quiet for over thirty years.

And now it whispers in my ear; it's *you who need cleansing boy, not me!*

After a while, I stand up, leaving the album on the folded chair and slowly walk over to the wooden cross over by the wall. I place the faded dog-eared picture of my gran and me behind the wooden trinket, crossing myself, then head for the back garden.

The moon lights up the junk hidden in the weeds, showing me the track to where Trey and I had walked through earlier, and I make for the big old Oak tree standing in the middle of the garden.

The house watches its prodigal son approach the Oaktree with eager eyes. I can feel the dark tentacles wrapping around me once more when I get to the swing and stop, scuffing the earth with my boots until I have cleared the weeds from underneath the swinging tyre.

I unzipped my trousers and began pissing on my father's grave. The hot arc of urine pooling in the dry earth as my bladder empties like a leaky drainpipe spilling onto the sidewalk on a stormy night.

I wait until my bladder is done and just stand here, shaking the drips, watching as the moisture is soaked up into the earth completely.

My father had killed my beloved nana, Martinez. He had pushed this once happy lady over the edge with his drugs and his guns and his gangs. First, my mother, God rest her soul. Then my Nana. Slowly turning her insane in her own house as he pushed his drugs and his women from her own porch.

It was me who had put an end to his wicked ways.

"Fuck you, Papa!"

I turn and walk back to the porch without looking back, the gloom of the house enticing me back inside, just like it had when I was a child watching my nana suffer. It had been a long time since the house had lost its grip on me, and now it wants me back. It needs to cleanse my thoughts. The anger I felt towards my father, I thought was long gone, is now rising to the surface once more. I welcome the feeling as it courses through my veins—those bubbling evil thoughts rising again. The darkness shrouding me like a soothing arm around my shoulders as the porch door softly shut behind me and make my way to the living room.

I need to be cleansed, it says.

I can feel the house inside me now, leading me to the front room and guiding me to the box on the floor. I reach inside without thought and unscrew the safety cap, bringing the sloshing bleach to my mouth, and begin drinking.

It needs to cleanse me.

Welcome homeboy.

GREGG CUNNINGHAM
ABOUT THE AUTHOR

GREGG CUNNINGHAM, 49, is a short story writer from Western Australia who has contributed to various genre anthology books since 2014.
He hopes to one day clean off the dust bunnies and find a home for his current Space opera manuscript hidden in a shoebox under his bed since 2017.

Zombie Pirate Publishing 2017-2019
Full Metal Horror, Relationship Add Vice
Phuket Tattoo, World War 4, Grievous Bodily Harm

Black Hare Press, 2019
Angels, Beyond, Deep Space, Monsters, Apocalypse, Storming Area 51, Worlds,

Black Hare Press 2020
Bad Romance, Banned, Passenger 13, School's in, 2113
Raygun Retro Zombie Pirate Publishing 2020

More information is available at:
@GGGcunningham (twitter)
cortlandsdogs.wordpress.com

DEAF HOUSE
BY PHILIP ROGERS

*B*rian was born deaf and blind, which is probably the reason why the killer spared his life. Unfortunately, it wasn't the same for the rest of his family.

Brian's father was first to die. A serrated knife driven into his throat as he answered the door. A brutal death, but at least it came quickly.

His wife, who was stood halfway down the stairs, could do nothing but clench her dressing gown. Her voice was broken in fear, unable to move as the killer charged towards her. The initial stab wound puncturing down through her chest would have proven fatal, but he continued. Clasping the knife with both hands, he penetrated her a further 14 times.

Brian's sister Katie stood a chance. But a creaky floorboard gave away her movement, and she was grabbed at the doorway whilst trying to run into Brian's room. Her fingertips clasping to the frame she screamed. Brian remained asleep. Once Katie's grip was released, the killer wrapped his arms around her neck and threw her to the floor. As she began to lose consciousness, Katie reached out, but there was nothing she could do.

In the morning, Brian made his way downstairs, cursing to himself when he slipped on a wet patch in the hallway. It made him lose count of his steps. It was just a normal morning, and he was oblivious to the dead bodies on the floor, the door wide open or the police approaching the house.

PHILIP ROGERS
ABOUT THE AUTHOR

Award-winning journalist, author and co-creator of the charity
horror anthology book 'It Came From The Darkness' and
Founder of Philip Rogers 101 PR.
His poetry Drabbles and short stories have been printed in
several books

Twitter: https://twitter.com/rogersphilip101
Instagram: https://www.instagram.com/rogersphilip101/

UP IN SMOKE
BY PETER J. FOOTE

*T*he chainsaw sings its deadly song at the entrance of Oakgrove Community Park.

The labouring saw roars and cuts through the shattered and broken sections of the towering oak tree. Heavy limbs fall onto dirty snowbanks and roll away, tearing police tape from the chain-link fence as they come to rest as a tangled mass on frozen ground scarred by rubber tire tracks.

"Lance? You about done trying to drop this damn tree on my skull, I gotta junk up these hunks you're cutting." Perry shouts while wiping a thick coat of sawdust from his goggles, the cigarette in his mouth bouncing in agitation.

His only response is another loud burst of Lance's chainsaw from high above, a crack more resembling a gunshot and the plunge as a colossal tree limb streaks downward. Tossing his idling chainsaw away, Perry dives sideways into the soft snow. Tattered orange safety overalls get a new stain of sap, oil, and sawdust as he rolls away from the bouncing tree branch that seemed determined to seek him out.

Roughly pulling his hard hat off, Perry forces one eye open and sees a frozen puddle of blood inches away from his nose. He scurries to his feet, thick-soled work boots slipping on the crimson ice.

"You damn idiot, I ought to knock you out of that buckle! This cursed tree has already killed one guy; I don't wannabe another." Perry yells, his face flushed and eyes large. A shaking hand pulls the broken cigarette from bloodless lips.

The idling hydraulic motors on the truck speed up and come to life. The cherry-picker hums, and the basket swings away from the great oak and comes back to its cradle on the rear of the town services truck. It bounces, causing a fine layer of sawdust to fluff off like a severe case of dander. Hydraulics shut down, and the man in the cage unclasps his safety harness and hops to the ground beside a pale Perry.

"You ok, buddy?" Lance says, yanking off heavy work gloves before laying a hand on Perry's shoulder, which causes the man to jump. "That one got away from me. So many twisted and intertwined limbs in this old bastard. Honest, I wasn't fooling around." Lance says, his normally boisterous voice subdued.

Perry nods his head, colour coming back to his face. "I'm ok, just more of a scare than I needed." Staring up at the gigantic oak tree, the town worker speaks, his tone muted. "Do you believe the old legends about this being a hanging tree back in the old days? That they hung witches and such? My old Auntie Ruth swore it whispered to her. And look what happened to that linesman, some say it looked like the tree attacked him."

Withdrawing his grip from his co-worker's shoulder, Lance beats off the heaviest layers of sawdust, clinging to his coveralls as he replies. "That's just a bunch of bull. Sure, it's a shame that fellow from the power corp died, but he was in a cherry picker, all alone up there working to repair power lines in a blizzard. It's sad but, no curse, just plain rotten luck."

Staring at the tangle of cut and fallen branches that covered the ground, Lance scratches the stubble on his chin, looks at his shaken co-worker and nods to himself. "Ok, enough for today. We'll come back tomorrow and finish up."

"But Lance, we were supposed to chip the branches and haul off the bigger limbs, Betty said…"

"Enough of the Betty said, Perry. You've had a shock, and my Grandpa always claimed the best thing for a shock was a stiff drink. First rounds on me, it's the least I can do for giving you a scare. Betty and her clipboard and everyone safe and warm back at the office can shove it. Hop into the truck, and with any luck, a lot of that lumber will be gone by morning; people like free firewood when someone else cuts it." Lance says with a broad wink, chuckling at his joke.

With a shaky nod, Perry stares up at the oak tree, its branches swaying in the winter air, the few desiccated leaves still clinging to branches making a hollow rattling. Ears straining, he murmurs. "Kinda like laughter, old woman cackling…" and jumps in fright when Lance toots the truck's horn. Shaking his head, Perry forces his eyes away from the tree and hastens to the work truck and the promise of a stiff drink.

*T*he crescent moon beams its piercing light through the tree branches of the ancient oak tree.

It was the sole illumination to light Oakgrove Community Park until the wavering yellow light of headlights from an old pickup turned onto the park's street.

The battered old ford truck creeps along, the misfiring engine producing a hoarse cough like an elderly lady clearing her throat in the library.

It slows as it passes the dark driveways along the street, snowbanks offering scant protection against the prying eyes of the occupant of the truck.

Grey primer paint, blisters of rust and a thick smear of

frozen mud cover much of the original blue of the truck. It rolls to a stop where Lance and Perry laboured earlier in the day. A plume of oily blue smoke flows out of the leaky exhaust. The driver's window rolls down, the dry seals against the glass akin to nails on a chalkboard. A smouldering cigarette butt flies out the window; it being the herald to the door opening, squeaking hinges loud in the winter night.

With one leg dangling from the driver's seat, Dempsey shakes a fresh cigarette out of the breast pocket of his filthy flannel coat. Sparking it to life with the lighter in his dash, blowing blue smoke against his clouded windshield, the wiry man slides out of the abused truck. Rubber boots with the steel toecaps worn through thud onto the asphalt and the man inhales deeply from his cigarette as he peers up and down the desolate street.

The driver's door is left open. The dome light of the truck illuminates the heap of timber, remnants of caution tape, and battered traffic cones. Grunting to himself, Dempsey pulls a worn pair of work gloves from beneath the drivers' seat, jams his cigarette in the right side of his mouth and sets to work. Tossing chunks of oak onto the back of his truck, their sharp thuds as they meet the metal box of the truck reverberate through the night. It silences the low calls of roosting birds in the surrounding trees.

The ageing springs of the pickup groaning, Dempsey is about to call it quits when he spies the forgotten chainsaw that Perry left in his mad dash from the falling branch.

"Well, lookie here. Christmas has come early to old Dempsey." Fingers reach and yank the chainsaw, pulling it from the broken branches, the tiny oak twigs holding it as if fingers gripped it tight. Swearing, Dempsey yanks it free, twigs snapping, the surviving branches of the oak tree rattle their dead leaves.

Spitting into the remaining tree limbs, Dempsey heaves the

abandoned chainsaw onto the passenger seat and climbs into his truck.

A high-pitched groan issues from the pickup's transmission as it's forced into drive, but with belching blue smoke, the truck rolls down the street, its ill-gotten claims safely on board.

"Time to go home, that was thirsty work, and I need a drink," Dempsey says as he uses his knees to steer the pickup as he gropes to find and light another smoke.

"*H*ome sweet, home," Demsey says, his voice bitter, as he jerks the steering wheel of the abused pick up off of the gravel road and heaves into the unploughed lane. Tires spinning as they drift between the ruts formed by previous trips, the truck makes steady progress up the lane. Silver birches have infringed upon the route. Their snow-laden branches reach out like talons and scratch along the sides of the battered truck until the mansion comes into sight.

"What you must have looked like in your glory days, old girl, before the blight got into you," Demsey says as the weak headlights of the pickup shine against the darkened mansion. Even with crumbling masonry, missing shingles, and peeling paint, the old house is a work of tremendous beauty and craftsmanship. Windows with leaded glass, miraculously unbroken, absorb the scant light against them and pulse as if a living thing. Tall brick chimneys thrust through the roofline. With a grunt of contentment, Demsey sees that the chimney in the study still has a slim wisp of smoke issuing from it.

Driving around the formal gardens, their overgrown shrubbery hidden beneath piles of snow and ice, the old pickup skids to a stop before the formal entrance. The grey stone steps and marble pillars resembling a jagged mouth in the weak moonlight.

Drawing deeply on his cigarette, Dempsey stares at the looming front door and pushes himself deep into the truck seat.

"Sod it. It's just an old house. Better digs than you've had in ages. Be thankful, fool, it was a lucky find." Dempsey mutters to himself as he opens the truck door, worn hinges groaning with the effort.

Sliding out of the truck, Dempsey turns his back to the mansion, clutches the stolen chainsaw, its steel teeth adding fresh scratches to the cracked vinyl seats.

With a deep breath, as if about to dive underwater, Dempsey faces the front door and climbs the stone steps. Standing before the massive oaken door, still strong enough to keep out all but the most determined, even with its peeling varnish and faded brass, Dempsey looks up. Sure enough, the toothpick he wedged between the door and the casing is still there; no one has entered the vacated house since he left.

Likely no one has been inside for decades before I came around. This house just screams, "Leave me alone", but this is more comfort I've had in ages, and these old bones can't sleep rough anymore.

Realising that he's putting off going in, as he does each time he stands before the door, Dempsey shivers, plucks the toothpick and steps into the derelict house.

*B*alancing the stolen chainsaw on his hip, Dempsey leans down, snatches the flashlight from just inside the door and flicks it on.

Panning the weak light through the foyer of the abandoned mansion, Dempsey shivers and from more than just the cold. He can feel the empty house watching him and can't help thinking he's a fly caught in an invisible web.

Like the outside, the home's interior reveals that it was once opulent, though neglected for untold years. Magnificent plaster medallions with crystal chandeliers decorate high ceilings. Gold painted crown moulding ring the walls, stunning tiled floors, and a sweeping staircase made the foyer an entrance to amaze any visitor.

His eyes tracking the ray of light, Dempsey sees his dusty footprints made last fall when he first explored the deserted house. That one trip was adequate to tell him the house didn't want him here. Like a dozing jaguar high in the jungle canopy and a rodent scurrying through fallen leaves, the jaguar has overlooked the rodent thus far since its hunger hasn't peaked. Dempsey has been careful to keep it that way.

Remembering when he first explored the house last autumn, Dempsey shakes. The sweat between his shoulder blades feels like ice. How rooms changed shape and location, doors would appear and disappear, and the undeniable feeling that he was being tested and found wanting. It was only that sense of dismissal that convinced him to risk squatting in the old house for the winter; he'd never been happier to be a disappointment.

With nothing but the tiny footprints of mice crisscrossing the tiled floor, Dempsey tears his eyes away from the foyer and hastens to the study door. The one room that has never played tricks on him.

As if sensing the weight of eyes upon him, Dempsey hurries to open the oak door and slip through, the chainsaw banging and marring the trim in his haste. Inside the study, his makeshift home, Dempsey shuts the door, the latch loud in the oppressive quiet.

Leaning against the closed door, Dempsey exhales the breath he didn't mean to hold and relaxes, snickering at his own irrationality.

"Home sweet home," Dempsey says. Built-in bookshelves line walls, bare except for a stack of flyers, several loose candles, seven cans of beans, and a roll of toilet paper. The other furnishings are a pathetic looking wooden chair, a wire reel serving as a table, and a rumpled sleeping bag atop a thick lay of cardboard. He drops the stolen chainsaw atop a small mountain of pop cans and plastic bottles that shift and sag—bagged up, ready to go to the depot for much-needed drinking money. The recycling bags crinkle as the chainsaw compacts them, but the heaped mass stays in place.

Saw forgotten, Dempsey scurries over to the enormous tiled fireplace and holds his chapped hands to absorb the lingering warmth of the fire he laid hours ago.

Clenching and unclenching arthritic fingers, Dempsey stirs up the coals and tosses several fragments of broken shipping pallet into the glowing embers, which alight and help brighten the room.

"Tomorrow, I'll have proper firewood to keep me warm, not these scraps I've been able to collect from around town. I'll have enough heat to keep me nice and cosy until spring." Dempsey says to himself as he leans closer to the puny flames and wills this thought away from the rest of the house.

*T*he roar of the chainsaw cuts through the tranquil winter morning air. Birds spooked by the abrupt sound flee from their roosts in the neighbouring shrubs, their haste dislodging snow that cascades to the frozen ground.

Oily smoke issues from the stolen chainsaw as Dempsey adjusts the choke until the motor stops sounding like a three-pack a day smoker to a high-pitched whine.

Dropping the pickup's dented tailgate, Dempsey drags the first large branch from the oak tree towards him and gets to work. The country music station playing on the radio fills in the brief moments of quiet.

With the afternoon sun still above the treetops, Dempsey has his stolen firewood cut up. Illustrated by the piles of sawdust staining white snowbanks and the countless broken twigs stomped into the slush.

Heedless of the damage he's causing to the house, Dempsey tosses the firewood through the study window, the delicate hardwood floors receiving further abuse from the man squatting within its walls.

Dempsey has a grin on his sweaty face, his labour completed.

As Pa always said, *wood will heat you three times. When you haul it when you cut and split it, and when you burn it.* About the only wise thing, that old bastard said.

Wiping his brow with a stained handkerchief, Dempsey tugs his flannel coat on over his sticky shirt. His exertion already wearing off as the bite of the winter air causes him to shiver as he lights a fresh cigarette.

Putting the chainsaw on the back of the truck, the few remaining drops of fuel within its tank sloshing, Dempsey closes the abused tailgate with a bang. He then covers the chainsaw with his bagged recyclables, pulls the study window down as best he can from outside, and hops into his much-abused truck.

"Now let's go see if I can find someone who wants to buy that saw in this town. Must be one or two who won't ask questions about where it came from." Dempsey chuckles to himself as he guns the truck's engine, tires throwing up gravel and snow.

The faint wisps of smoke from the chimney in the study waver in the wind as if waving goodbye.

*I*t's nightfall before Dempsey returns to the secluded mansion.

Bobbing headlights flash upon it as the battered pickup bounces between frozen ruts as it snakes up the lane, "Golden

Oldies" heralding its approach. Rolling to a halt in front of the formerly stately home, Dempsey turns off the coughing engine. Opening the door, he tosses an empty beer can over his shoulder to land in the empty truck bed. Sliding out of the truck, Chinese takeout bags in one hand and an open box of beer in the other, the squatter staggers towards the house.

Though fuelled by alcohol, Dempsey forces himself to enter the mansion without creating undue noise. The cold and invisible eyes he can feel upon him sobering him better than a pot of coffee ever could. That burden on him sloughs off as soon as he enters the study, and his good spirits return, though not to their former levels.

Dropping the leaking bag of takeout onto his make-shift table. Dempsey struggles to fish out a beer from his open box and weaves his way to the once beautiful fireplace, its tiles now black with sooty grime.

"Let's get this party started," the dishevelled man declares to the empty room. The forced humour in his voice plain in his own ears but forces it to the back of his mind. As Dempsey takes a large pull from the beer can, he builds a fire up from the pile of firewood dominating the room.

The fresh wood from the oak tree smokes and pops with sparks, but this just makes Dempsey laugh louder and have another drink as he watches the flames grow.

*T*he candle stub jammed into the wine bottle flickers as the spent wax flows down the glass, sending dancing shadows against the naked plaster walls of the study.

Empty beer cans form a lop-sided pyramid in the middle of the battered study floor. Open Styrofoam containers with the remnants of Chinese food lay on the make-shift table. Dempsey is asleep atop his sleeping bag, a half-eaten egg roll in his fist.

The mansion is silent. Other than the wheezing snores of the squatter, and the pop and hiss of the fresh wood in the fireplace, there is no other noise, but something awakens. Comfortable in its slumber, aware but overlooking the insignificant mortal hiding within it, the house senses another evil within its walls, one just as insidious and cunning as itself.

Raising its hackles on alert, the house lets the new evil know that it is aware of its presence. The air temperature drops colder than that outside, doors sways, floorboards creak, and fingers of frost cover every window in an instant. One minute passes, then another, the new evil acquiesces, realising that the evil within the mansion has home-field advantage.

When no attack is forthcoming, the house relaxes but doesn't return to its slumber; instead, it waits and observes this new intruder.

Sensing a reprieve, the malignant evil that had lived within the ancient oak tree reaches out. With far darker deeds behind it than a simple gallows tree, the massive oak has seen and dealt greater malice to the race of man than anybody alive knows.

If the inhabitants of Oakgrove knew the truth, they would have hacked down and burned the ancient oak centuries ago. And scattered the ashes where no innocent souls might encounter them.

But the man squatting here is far from innocent. Trapped within the firewood, the splinter of ancient evil can sense the blight within the man Dempsey. If the residents knew what the shabby man who had drifted into their town last fall had done, they would have strung him up without a second thought. Thanks to Dempsey, evil knows evil, and the malice is no longer trapped but released through the flames.

From the flames, a wisp of rolling smoke escapes the confines of the once ornate fireplace and snakes its way into the study.

Tentative at first, it moves as if testing the air. When no

interference is forthcoming from the house, it picks up speed as it hunts. Through the jumble of oak cut for firewood, the smoke snake slithers. Up and through the gaps between the pieces, it rushes, recognising a part of itself but incapable to touch it. Frustrated, it probes the rest of the room.

Gathering strength as it travels, growing ever more significant as it draws more and more of its smoke-fashioned body from the fireplace, the evil travels through the study.

Snaking its path through the chair legs, up and over the make-shift table, weaving through the pyramid of empty beer cans, causing the topmost to sway, the smoke-snake arrives at Dempsey. It has found the evil it sought.

A slight flick and the smoke-snake reaches out and touches Dempsey's ankle. The old man's snoring pauses and his body shudders, but he settles again into a restless slumber. But one taste was sufficient, and the smoke-snake enjoyed the flavour of the man's corruption.

Quick as lightning, the smoke-snake strikes Dempsey. Coiling up his legs, hugging his hips, and clamping his arms against his sides, it squeezes the man. Jarred out of a nightmare, Dempsey wrestles against the unseen bonds that are crushing him, but his weak struggles are to no avail.

Tighter and stronger, the evil that flourished within the oak takes its malice out upon the life who brought it here. Dempsey, far from feeble, is no match for the smoke-snake as it squeezes his body and soul. Joint's pop and Dempsey gives a blood-curdling scream that gets cut off as the coils constrict around his rib cage, not allowing the man to inhale.

When his frantic gasps get shallow, the smoke-snake finishes the man. Mouth wide, the smoke-snake feeds off Dempsey. It forces the evil within the man out of his broken body. His corrupt soul slips past his protruding tongue, and the smoke-snake consumes without letting a wisp escape.

The man's heels drum against the make-shift mattress of

cardboard, his back arcs until bones fracture, and dirty fingernails gouge furrows into the floor. With every drop of Dempsey's stained soul given up, the smoke-snake releases the body. It collapses, shattered and unmoving.

Fed and content, the smoke-snake slithers back to the fireplace and up the chimney, leaving the house to find an unclaimed hunting ground of its own.

The coals are now exhausted, and with them, the evil brought into the mansion by Dempsey. Content that it is once again alone, the house returns to its slumber, ever vigilant for those who enter it.

The candle flickers and hisses one last time as the wick exhausted, and the study goes black.

*W*arm breath thaws a tiny circle in the frost-covered study window; a rugged face attempts to stare through the dirty glass.

"Are you sure this is a good idea, Lance?" Perry asks, his voice subdued as if fearing discovery.

Stomping his feet and blowing into his hands, Lance replies while standing beside their work truck in front of the old mansion.

"Well, do you want your saw back or not? It makes no matter to me. Ain't coming out of my paycheque."

Turning away from the frosted window, Perry glares at his co-worker.

"If you haven't nearly killed me, I won't have forgotten my chainsaw, and Betty won't be on me about it."

Lance holds up his palms as if to ward off blows. "Easy, buddy. I'm here, aren't I? We'll get the saw back, and Betty can go back to counting paper clips in the office. Don't forget that I'm the one who heard that someone saw the drifter driving outside of town with a load of wood. With your saw missing and half the wood from that cursed oak tree gone, this sounded like a safe bet. And look," Lance waves at the snow-covered ground around them, sawdust and chunks of bark scattered everywhere. "It looks like I was right. Between the two of us, we can get your saw back." Lance slaps his hands together.

Staring at the deserted mansion, Lance shivers. "That drifter must be nuts to shack up in this house, didn't he know its history? There's a reason no one lives here."

"Quit babbling, Lance and help me with this window. It's the only one not frosted over, and I don't want to be inside anymore of this place than I have to." Perry grunts as he struggles to lift the wooden-framed window.

Between the two of them, their struggles pay off, and they get their fingers under the windowsill and forced it up. Knocked backwards by the stench of unwashed bodies, spoiled food, smoke, and the smell of sulphur, the two town workers poke their heads into the study and into a scene of terror. The men scramble back to their work truck as if they were being chased.

"What about your saw?" Lance yells as he struggles to jam the key into the ignition.

"Screw the saw, get us out of here!" Perry shouts as he slams the truck door.

Missing the drifters battered pickup by inches, the tires of the town's work truck fling snow in a high arc as it races out of the driveway, leaving the horror behind.

A thick layer of frost is growing within the study as if it were a walk-in freezer. The frost continues to grow over firewood, walls, and furniture, regaining the room from the man who temporarily lived within it. Dempsey, his body crushed and broken, his lifeless eyes frozen open in terror, stares at the ceiling.

The house can finally rest again.

PETER J. FOOTE
ABOUT THE AUTHOR

Peter J. Foote is a bestselling speculative fiction writer from Nova Scotia, Canada. Most of his stories are within the genres of Science Fiction, Fantasy, and Horror.

Outside of writing, he runs a used bookstore specialising in fantasy & sci-fi, cosplays with his wife, and alternates between red wine and coffee as the mood demands.

Believing that an author should write what he knows, many of Peter's stories reflect his personal life and experiences.

As the founder of the group "Genre Writers of Atlantic Canada", Peter believes that the writing community is stronger when it works together.

More information is available at:
https://www.facebook.com/peterjfooteauthor
https://twitter.com/PeterJFoote1
https://www.subscribepage.com/c3j4h4

WALLS OF ROT AND LOVE
BY HARI NAVARRO

*T*he dark rain beads and slides as it gathers the grease from the roof and rides it across the skylight high above the moan of my lips. Of our lips.

My clawing fingers grip and hoist aloft and slip as they hold up and then let fall this beautiful thing. This carcass that, too, rides and beads and moans at my hips.

I am waiting for it. I am waiting for that glorious instance when both of our bodies tense and knot as one. That transcendent moment that pulls me away from the ancestral sinew that forever tendrils out through time and holds me here and just so.

It arrives in a flurry, and, at once, I scurry to escape my lot in the light-headed zenith of its climax. My skin shudders and quakes, and I grip tight at my sweat-drenched bed. I tumble into the new husk at my side.

I want to know it. I want to be it.

Less than seconds pass before I double over with the pain of the call, and it pulls me back and into reality. They are so delicious, these fleeting diversions, but I do so prefer my destiny. My calling. Between these walls and beneath the great

Gothic beams that arch and flicker in the firelight high above my head, I am at long last content. I want for nothing else. I want to be this monster I am.

"That wasn't bad," the beautiful thing exhales as it rolls from my body and falls to the gentle prickle bite of wet sheets.

"You've had better?" I ask, but I do so through a smile that knows full well that there is no possible way for this to be true. What I deliver is perfection. There is nothing frivolous or hurried nor cheap about the pleasures that I conduct through my body. I am the artist, and sex is but one of my brushes. I am a master.

"I can't believe that I'm here. It's so surreal. To actually be here. In this house. With you," it says.

"I should tell you that you are nothing more to me than one of many," I say as I begin my ritual of testing the resolve of these creatures I so fastidiously choose.

This house. My inheritance, so many years deprived of its true heir. A house with a soul that only I could revive. If my parents were alive, they'd see and be so proud of just how diligently I remembered all that I was taught. The words that were muttered as we all sat, and we dined, and the meat fell away from the bone.

When I returned, these walls were long since cold and dead. But I knew; I remembered just how they were to be fed. I knew that they would embrace me and that they would thrive and breathe when loved. Like all things, I guess. But the paper on the walls is peeling; the window frames creak as the joints of old men and the curtains are curling and staining where their tips reach the floor as if they were long dresses that sweep like a besom through mud. There is so much work that still needs to be done. So many details that need to be tendered. A labour of love, if ever there was.

I do love it. And the house... it truly loves me back.

"I cry every time. Every time I look at you. Every time I've ever looked at you. You smother all of my senses, and I can't breathe... you take away my words..."

My God. What is it going to do... break into fucking song? Oh, how they fawn! How pathetic as they stroke at my skin and fall like the famished to my feet. This one has such beautiful nipples. Sorry, that was random, but there's just something about how the autonomic nervous system functions to regulate the body's unconscious actions that drives me crazy. I think it's also called the sympathetic nervous system, which also beautifully describes these ancient neurons that regulate and control the erectile muscles in our tissues. Nipples don't lie, and I must admit that sometimes, when so much around me is forced and fake, I do so lose myself in the truth of their sympathy.

"You should breathe. I do love to watch as you do. Lips part to draw in the essential molecules. The throat undulates and swallows them down into the swelling bulge and then fall of the chest. It's like watching automation. Each part-integral and relentless in its efforts. Like the finest clock mechanism ticking on and on and on and never once faltering until, then, of course, it does. At my hand. The very best part is the end, you know? When the machine winds down and struggles and with futile gusto tries to grip onto this life. I get off on the power of dictating the end. I do. Toying with those final precious moments and then letting them smash to the ground. Well, all but."

"You are so deliciously strange, but I do not have the slightest fucking clue about what you are talking about," it breathes.

"That's OK. You have no need to fathom my words. But yet, in saying that, did you not grasp at least the essence of what I just said? I am the end."

"I don't care. I feel safe with you. It's refreshing. You are so much more than I imagined."

"And in there lays the lesson. Feelings and instincts... they are nothing more than constructs. They are wish fulfilment. You would do well to ignore them. Now, how about you refresh my glass instead?" I whisper, waving my empty flute in the direction of the Clicquot that chills beneath the fleshy glow of my bedside lamp. I love that lamp; I made it all by myself.

The beautiful thing that has, now officially ascended to the status of muse in my mind, turns at its hips. The naked drip of its form excites my artist eyes as I follow the sheen stretch of its muscles.

My mouth dries, and I hear the ice shift and fall in the bucket as it twists and lifts out the bottle. I bite and rip a strip of my own lip as then, with such seamless fluidity, it turns back toward me, and the bottle drips a trail across my sheets. The muscles again play out through its arm and into the tendons that contract its long fingers into a gentle floating caress across mine. I sigh as they then slide like wisping smoke down the carved bone stalk of my glass. I made that too, you know? Such perfection, such ornate craftsmanship, even if I do say so myself. I am so proud of these works that I forge.

"I want to reach inside you as you move and feel the torque in your meat," I think but accidentally say aloud. My words, for the very first time, sound so ridiculously contrived. What is this? Something is happening to me. I feel off. I feel strange, and I do not like it one fucking bit.

"I'd like that. I'd like you to hold me, to clutch at my true being," it says, and I frown, staring up and into its eyes. This one is so, so very different than the others. Something is missing. What is it? I clear my throat, and I sip from my glass. I prod, and I search for this thing that's not there.

"I have something to say," I announce.

"Say away," it replies.

"At some point before this evening is done, I'm going to savagely attack and then all but kill you."

"All but?"

"You don't believe me. But you should."

"I should believe that I should believe you?"

"Good. You make fun of me. This will most probably help. No need for undue torment. There is so very much of that to come."

"I have no reason not to believe you. I just joke about shit that I don't understand. It's a reflex. I'm sorry."

"Reflex... it is kind of funny, I guess. That you think this all a joke. And yet, the things that I am going to do to you are orchestrated for no other reason than to sate my predilection for cruelty and savagery. I really don't see the humour but chuckle away if indeed it soothes."

"OK. So... so, you are serious? Am I, then, permitted to ask of you why?" it purrs, and it shifts, curling into my pillows. And there it is. That's it. That's what is missing. This thing has no fear. Not one tiny drop. It wants to deceive me. Take all that I have. Is that it? I can't tell, but I'll play along for now. For a few more minutes, at least.

"Why am I going to maim and torture you, in particular? Or, why do I do it in general?"

"Both, I guess."

"It's genetic, a family thing. Legacy shit, and I get off on it like I said."

"Sexually?"

"Yeah. But it's also the rush of destroying something beautiful, you know? It's jealousy, plain and simple. I need to be the most beautiful thing in the mirror. I want to rake my fingers into the blemish-less and tear away all that is more beautiful than I..."

It snorts, and fine champaign splutters and mists through the lamplight. It laughs. It fucking laughs. It's laughing at me. **Me.**

"Nothing is more beautiful than you. No one compares to

you. What happened to you as a child robbed you, didn't it? It made you blind to just how exquisite you are?" it says with a smile.

"You know nothing of me."

"I know that you have suffered. I know you... lost... your parents. I know that you disappeared and that certain forces, perhaps, denied you your fortune. I know you had to shoulder those vile rumours about what happened. I know you were so young. So very young."

"Rumours... You know the truth."

"Look, you don't need to talk about it. All that is real is now."

It is attempting to dictate. To tell me what and how I should feel. I know my reality. I know that reality has nothing whatsoever to do with what it is we want it to be. Skin is truth. Bone is structure, and hair can be spun into lace. That is reality.

"I was young, it is true, but my youth and what happened on that day had nothing to do with this thing that I am. I have always known what I was. We that are monsters. Generation after generation of hunger poured down and into my marrow. The endless hunt for perfection of body. Of immortality."

"All that matters is you. Fuck your family! Fuck what they did! You are nothing but you."

Did it just dishonour my heritage? Really?! Why do I not now tear its throat from its neck? Why do I hesitate? Why?

Fuck your family... Seriously?!

"That day had its purpose. It had nothing to do with who I was but everything to do with what I became. We wanted to be gods, and that day showed us we were but human. I lost everything, but now, I am back. I'm back in this house where I belong. And, within it, I will thrive, and I will dress it in all of your pretty skin. I am not a god. I embrace my mortality, and I reside to live out my days wrapped in the perfection of your flesh."

"If you are looking for perfection, then you found it. You. Nothing else matters. Nothing that you did matters... I understand."

"As you seem now to imply, the rumours were true. When they eventually found me, I was surrounded by what was left of my parents. My midden. The rescue team that blasted through into that foul place found me feasting... gnawing on their gristle. It is what it was, and I am what I am. I am no more and no less."

"You have no need to be more. With me, you can just be you."

Now it's sounding like a fucking campaign pledge, but it is upset. This is still not through fear, though. It's not pity. It is something else again. What? Is this love? Surely not!

"Can you not see? I am telling you that I am literally a cannibal. I eat people; at least, I did eat people. The irony of that day, this aspect of my past that you seem so particularly fascinated with, is that I was an eater well before I ever stepped foot in that place. For generations, my family ate of the living, and the extended irony is that, in the end, I was forced to eat them. My mother tasted the best —such an exquisitely beautiful woman. I tried to absorb her soul. I tried, but I failed. And then I knew the only way to perfection is the house. It was always about the house."

"I remember, that was the first time I saw you. That footage of you being plucked from that hole in the ground. It was the first time anyone had ever seen you —such a radiantly, sad beautiful creature. I, too, was but a child, but in those pools of your eyes, I was bewitched. The world fell hopelessly in love with you. But it is I that loves you the most."

"Love, so that is it," and again, my thoughts unwittingly manifest as words.

"There, you said it. Tread carefully; it is at times such a jagged little word to say."

It's getting to me. I know what it is doing, and I'm letting it. Maybe, I should just get it all over and done with now.

Yes, right now.

Do it. Do it. Rip that lovely tongue from its throat. Stretch and dry it out before the fire. They do make for such strong leather to bind.

"I have love only for these walls. I love this house and nothing more," I stutter and try to steady my keel.

"Where did you go to for all those years? Where did they take you to ruin you so? Some said you had gone insane. Some said that they stole your family's fortune and locked you away in a school in some faraway country. They said you were the only student. Alone and locked away in the trees."

"Some say a lot of things. I was stolen from, and those who stole from me will pay. I have a little place set aside just for them. If you put your ear to the floor, you can hear it. This house holds many different frequencies of energy; what do you feel? Did you feel the eyes of the spectres in the wall as they defiled your privacy and looked down upon us as we fucked? Or do you have other daemons entirely that leach out to you from the woodwork?"

"I do not believe in such things. I believe in things I can touch. You are real. The bed on which we lay and the roof above our heads, they are real. Life is terrifying enough without conjuring fantastical beasts. The food that we eat is real."

This thing is so fascinating, and I run my gaze across the olive tint in its skin. I cannot help but smile.

"Are you happy?" it asks.

"No, I have no idea what that is. But you do make me smile. And you are wrong, you know? There are many fantastical beasts to be had in this world. They are not imagined; they are real, and you can touch them. I have seen them. I am mortal, unfortunately, but real terrors do reign in this world."

Now, it is the thing's turn to smile, and it is radiant and

infectious. Happy? I smile again, and my jaw begins to ache. Damn it.

"When will you start to hurt me?" it asks.

"Not just yet. You said that life terrifies you?"

"Yes, it does, and, honestly, I've never felt the comfort and security that I have tonight in this bed with you. I can't explain it, but this is how I feel, even in the knowledge that you are now about to kill me."

"All but," I correct.

"Ah, yes. Sorry, all but."

It is trying to win my favour, isn't it? This beautiful bone and meat-filled sheath is trying to catch me off guard. It is so calm. So collected. It tells me it's terrified by all in this world but here, alone with me and after everything I have said, it exudes not one single shred or droplet of fear.

"When you emerged from the wilderness after all those years, I consumed every last bit of you that I could—the reclusive artist. I collected prints of every piece of your work— such exquisitely corrupt renderings of beauty. I tried to imagine just what that sad child had grown into so as to create such pain in the paint. I needed to find you. The wide-eyed girl now grown. The artist behind the brush. I had to be with you."

"And here you are."

"I watched when you started doing the interviews. You sat there on the screen with that seasoned old interviewer stuttering and tumbling over his words. Your face. Your body. The pearlescent perfection of your skin. It was if you had, somehow, rendered yourself from the finest tips of your very own brushes."

"You are then just like everyone else. You wish only to consume all that I am."

"Are you not about to consume all of me?" it asks.

"No. I will not be eating you today. I have evolved and moved on from such horrible things, remember?"

"I have always been alone. I have my family, and I love them dearly, but I also have this nothing void, and my loneliness is bitter and endless. I have only ever had you, always. Since that very first moment, I saved myself for you," it whimpers, and tears hang low in its eyes.

"You are a liar. You expect me to believe that someone who looks like you is alone? That no one looks at you? No one cannot help but look at you. I saw you and, believe me; I am very specific in what I see. I saw you tonight at the gallery opening, standing there in your black and whites with a silver tray in your hand. I was drawn to you like a moth to the flame. I saw others as they, too, could not escape your pull. I chose you from a room chock full of perfect faces. I imagined how I'd sketch you and then draw from my library of thick oil pigments as I attempted to capture your beauty. But, in my mind, I failed. You exude and stream tones and hues that, within my art, I have never once been able to conjure. You are very special, and you know it."

"I know people look at me, but they don't see me like you see me. Like I see you."

She is good. She is close. Closer than any other has ever gotten. But she won't get to me. No, she will not—time to up the ante.

"My ancestors were the first to envisage such a masterpiece as yourself. The perfect being and, for generations, they bred and interbred in hope of producing the perfect issue. Then came the cannibalism. Eat the beautiful so as to become it," I say, running the tip of my finger across the gorged veins of its foot.

"You truly cannot see it, can you? You cannot see past what they have driven into you. Ascension into perfection is impossible. But then, here you are, as close to it as I've ever seen. So, your family succeeded. If to them you wish to afford such credit. It is as you said; you are what you are. You are you, not them."

"I am a forgery. I am an overwrought abomination. No matter how perfect, my flesh could never be as naturally flawless as yours. My family came to this realisation many years ago. The very best any of us could hope for was to live within your flesh. Within your souls."

"You want my skin. I get that; I really do."

"I'm talking about the house. It's always the house. It is it that needs of your flesh."

It is starting to understand. It is looking at the walls. It is feeling the beat of the dead.

"My grandparents were mongers of war, you see. They profited greatly from arming whomever it was that paid the premium. They had no allegiance to flags. They would have done it for free. They loved that they had such a defining hand in the tearing down of lives. They truly loved the destruction, and it nearly destroyed them when peace rose up its ugly and inevitable head."

"They built the house?"

"They built this place as an everlasting, constantly transforming, conduit of beauty and grace. You see, the thing with war profiteering is that the same lines of business can flow even during times of peace."

"I don't understand."

"They began to harvest the dead. Crate upon crate of shattered flesh and bone. Purchased on the blackest of markets and shipped from the killing fields that they had, once, so diligently filled."

"Why?"

"They took what remained of the gallant and the brave and ground them into a dust, which was mixed with the cement that formed the foundations of the magnificent edifice in which now you sit."

"The fuck they did!"

Yes. I'm breaking through. Where are you, sweet shuddering fear? Come out! Come out! Come out, if you dare!

"Everything here. Every last nail. The tiles on the roof and the panels on the walls, everything was derived from the bodies they hoarded. My parents were born in this house, and they, too, grew to love and embrace its power."

"Both of your parents were born here... oh... I see."

"I am what I am. I have no shame for this. It is shame to deny that which we are. I accept it. And so, this is why I do what I do."

"You desecrate the fallen because your parents were brother and sister, and your fucked up lineage, rather than eating beauty, thought to build a house made of beautiful flesh so that you could live vicariously through its patchwork power?"

"No, I've moved on. I don't desecrate the dead. I desecrate the living."

"Come again?"

"My grandparents built the skeleton, and my parents fleshed it out. They used hair to laminate and form into the resin boards that spiral and loop beneath our feet. They poured over wrenched teeth and sorted them like diamonds before, then, setting them into wonderfully sculpted fittings. They were artists, too. The sinks in all of the bathrooms are made almost entirely of teeth. It is a perfect symmetry, you see? A perfect cemetery in which the smiles of the dead look up as we brush and check at our smiles in the mirror."

"So, they killed people, and now you do too so as to live within their... auras?"

"All but."

"Oh, that's right, all but. A house built entirely from the dead. That is fucked up. That is fucked right up and all the way down. You know this, right? You know what you are, and this house, isn't it."

"All I wanted when I came back home was to pick up where

my family left off. Nobody knew about this place—this glorious, ever-expanding project. There was never a deed, no records, so after what happened to my parents, it was just sold off as an empty derelict and then lost. I bought it. I clawed my way back here and, when I walked in through the door, I was primed and ready for the kill. It was just something that had always lived in my fingers, you know?"

"Yes, I do know. I feel so sad, not pity, just sadness, for you. Your destiny is not this house."

"I couldn't do it. I couldn't kill. I just couldn't bear to accept the finality. The power of being able to take everything was immense, but the killing, the forcing of that final tick of the clock, I couldn't do it. So, I decided to keep them. I keep them all."

"You keep them?"

"Yes, I relieve them of their beautiful arms and the lithe stretch of their legs, but I keep them. Alive. Well, not entirely dead... stacked in cages... in the basement... with little watering tubes... like chickens."

"Like chickens? Like battery hens?"

"Exactly, there you go, see, now you're picking up what I'm putting down. I am getting very proficient with a scalpel and the stitching and the fighting of infection. I actually love cleaning them. Disgusting as it is. Don't get me wrong; I still love seeing just how much misery I have created from these things that were once so pretty. So handsome and now so not."

"So, you're a doctor?"

"Hells, no. I've always warmed toward the science of medicine, but I picked up most of my skills from tutorial videos and the rest I just kind of makeup as I go along. I'm a bit rough, to be honest—a bit hack and slash. I lack the finesse of the finish. It's not like with my art. I have total control over the brush, but it's those joint sockets that give me the most trouble. I must admit, I do lose a few along the way."

"You hate them that much?"

"No, I love them."

"You love them, yet you keep them in agony?"

"I love the idea of absorbing their beauty. But I love more the rush of slow torture. The look in their eyes as I walk to that table with a blade in my hand. Some of them even get hard, you know. It's just reflex, but it's flattering, and it powers me. It's called the sympathetic nervous system, you know?"

"Are they all the same as me?"

"Gender, you mean? The same as you and I?"

"Yes, as you and I."

"No, I'm an equal opportunity sadist. This is not a diatribe against the opposite sex if that's what you're thinking."

"Why do you take their limbs? There can only be so much you can fashion into doorknobs and novelty swizzle-sticks."

"The limbs? I have stuffed the walls with their limbs. Sealed in plastic, they bloat as they break down and liquefy. It is a most awesomely effective form of insulation. I just dread one of the bags rupturing. The stench would be..." I smile and reach out with trembling fingers to touch its beautiful cheek.

"... horrific. You are shaking. You don't need to," it says.

"Those that came before you begged me for cause. Why? Why? Why me? They bawled for reason in the darkness I laid upon them. I have nothing to offer you but that I am cruel."

"You don't need to explain any more."

"I really don't know why it is that I am explaining. Maybe, I'm trying to see how far I can push you. How far your disbelief will suspend before it breaks you. How far I can push before you try to run."

"Maybe, I don't want to run."

"Maybe. Or maybe, you are just trying to lull me away from my path. Unsettle me. Make me second guess my footing to give you a chance of getting the upper hand."

"Even if I did, I'm sure you would find a way to cleave it off," it smiles.

"Why are you so calm?"

"Perhaps, I'm a cop. Perhaps, the house is surrounded, and your sick family's reign of vile terror is about to unravel for good."

"Perhaps," I say, and I think that I am starting to cry.

"Do you want to hold me?" it asks, and I smother the escaping yelp of a laugh.

"Why are you laughing?"

"I don't have the slightest clue. I'm suddenly so numb. So happy."

"Come here!" it says.

And I do, and it is warm. I feel my body sag, and I try to speak, but I can't. My jaw won't work, but I listen to it as it's does.

"I have loved you for so very, very long, and I'm sorry that you don't see this world as I do. I listened to all that you said, and I get you; I really do. But you have strayed from the path. Tonight, I bow and adhere to the cravings of our ancestors. This house is the abomination, not you. Tonight, dear cousin, I will call the family to conclave. Please, it is futile, so don't try to speak. The poison has rendered all but your eyes and ears as useless. You are now officially the world's most beautiful captive audience."

I can't move. I feel, though, I feel the fear, and it tastes like dripping rot in my throat. I don't want to die. I don't want to die. I don't...

"You are lost and quite deluded, but I do like some of the ideas you mentioned. Not the house. That really is fucked up. But the chickens, there is something in them. So, perhaps, a fusion is possible. Perhaps, I will lay you out on the dining table, a centrepiece, a nakedness of the most exquisite form. And piece by tiny piece, while you still breathe, we will feast on your flesh and taste the succulence of your suffering. I'm not making any promises, dear cousin, but I'll try to restrain them. Though, they are such a ravenous bunch. I'll try to save just enough of you... just enough so that I can keep you alive. Well, all but, right? Like a chicken wedged into its cage. All but..." it says through the moist curled puff of its lips and the most glorious and perfect of smiles.

HARI NAVARRO
ABOUT THE AUTHOR

Hari Navarro has, for many years now, been locked in his neighbour's cellar. He survives due to an intravenous feed of puréed extreme horror and Absinthe-infused sticky-spiced unicorn wings.

His anguished cries for help can be found via Black Hare Press, Raven & Drake Publishing, Black Ink Press, Hellbound Books, 365 Tomorrows, Breachzine, AntipodeanSF and Horror Without Borders.

https://navarrodarkfiction.wordpress.com/
linktr.ee/hari_horror

AGNES HOUSE
BY ALANNAH K. PEARSON

*E*veryone avoided Agnes House. It was not just the overgrown garden, straggly dead grass, peeling paintwork or the rusted iron fence. There was something rotten about the mansion that gave the street its name.

The local kids dared each other to ring the doorbell, but no one ever did. Fear that the dusty net curtains in the front window might twitch. Proof that the monster really did live there.

He had been a rumour, more ghost than reality, a local bogeyman to frighten younger siblings. That all changed when the police arrested him, a wiry, mousey-haired man with spectacles. When the forensic teams arrived, the rumours became evidence, became truth.

Agnes House really was rotten to its core. Many wanted to believe no man could do such things, but those working the forensic scene knew better.

The rot was more than surface blood stains, it went deep: beneath the floorboards, behind the walls, and into the plumbing. Excavations lifted the bodies from the earth. Took decomposing remains from the walls and floors, but they never found all the missing.

The monster did not just create the rot in Agnes House, he fed upon it, consuming lives like the demon many accused him to be.

Everyone still avoids Agnes House. Now, it is for fear of the truth. Fear the rot might spread.

ALANNAH K. PEARSON
ABOUT THE AUTHOR

Alannah K. Pearson lives in Canberra, Australia. A speculative fiction author inspired by mythology, folklore, archaeology, history, and the environment, her short fiction features in anthologies from US, UK and Australian publishers. She is a keen nature and wildlife photographer, bookshop, and Museum devotee. When not writing, she enjoys exploring the Australian wilderness accompanied by her dogs (the canine assistants). In her other life, she is an academic in archaeology and human evolution.

www.alannahkpearson.com
Twitter & Facebook @alannahkpearson
Instagram @alannahk.pearson

THE FORGETFUL DARK
BY G. ALLEN WILBANKS

John Alexander stepped out onto his front porch and peered up at the sky. It was blue and completely clear of clouds. The wild temperature variations of spring had, at last, yielded to the more stable warmth of early summer, and it appeared that today was going to be a beautiful day.

His head was pounding as it did most of the time lately, and the sun hurt his light-sensitive eyes, forcing him to squint and hold a hand up against its white-hot glare.

"God damned migraines are going to be the death of me," he cursed.

The headaches were new. For seventy-two years, John had enjoyed almost perfect health. Sure, there was the occasional cold or minor injury, but otherwise, he had suffered no illness of significance that he could recall—certainly nothing as pervasive and disabling as the migraines that plagued him every day since that stupid accident.

He shook his head and grumbled at his own carelessness. He had been in a hurry, coming down the stairs too quickly when his foot slipped. He missed the next step and tumbled the remaining distance, arms and legs akimbo. The fall was only from a few feet up, but he had not been able to get his hands out in front of him in time to prevent a nasty blow to the head as his face struck the hardwood boards on the first floor of his home.

He remembered the pain and the stunned feeling of dizziness that followed. John had tried to push himself up from the floor, but the vertigo and nausea overwhelmed him, and he collapsed helplessly back down. He thought it was possible he had vomited at some point during the ordeal but could not recall with any certainty. He might have remained like that for hours, days perhaps, trapped helpless in his own home, if not for the fortunate timing of his neighbours' shopping trip.

The couple next door decided at that very moment they were going to make a run to the local grocery store. They asked their son, Pryor, to visit John and ask if there was anything the old man wanted or needed them to pick up for him. Pryor, ever the dutiful child, had marched right over to John's house.

The boy knocked, then let himself in. The front door was never locked. John figured there was nothing worthwhile in the house to steal, so why bother securing it from intruders. Anybody that wanted to come in and take something was welcome to it. They would be doing him a favour, clearing out some of the clutter and trash accumulated around him over seven decades.

Pryor entered and found John lying on the floor. The boy immediately called for help.

That was a month ago. The bruising around John's nose and eyes had faded, but now he had these migraines to contend with. He had hoped early on they would subside with his other injuries, although he now feared they might be here to stay. John occasionally debated calling the doctor and making an appointment to get checked out. The headaches might be warning him of more serious damage underneath the surface, but he decided ultimately to wait a little longer.

He would be fine. Or not. At his age, he figured he may as well leave it in God's hands.

Still shielding his eyes with his hand, John gazed out over his yard at the surrounding neighbourhood. There wasn't much activity today. No one worked in their yard or wandered the street walking their dog. Any kids on the block were either indoors or at school.

Was today a school day? John shook his head, unable to remember. Living alone left him mostly unaware of the passage of time, and he frequently forgot what day it was. That wasn't the head injury's fault; that was merely bored old man forgetfulness. He had been dealing with that particular frailty for a few years already before his unfortunate header down the stairs.

A soft breeze moved through the neighbourhood, rustling leaves in the trees and causing a small ripple of movement over a few of the lawns in more desperate need of mowing. As he visually inspected his surroundings, an unexpected, shapeless lump in the middle of the street caught his eye. Something was lying in the roadway.

John stepped off his porch and walked along the pathway leading from his front door to the sidewalk. His eyesight wasn't keen, and he was trying to get a better look at the object that had grabbed his attention. It was small, orange and white in colour, and it looked like...

"Oh dear," he tsked. "Cat."

John paused at the edge of his lawn. He could see the animal clearly now, and he had no desire to move any closer. It was an orange and white tabby cat lying in the middle of the road. Another gust of wind ruffled the fur along its back, but there was no other noticeable movement. There was also a significant amount of blood on the asphalt around the poor creature.

Although the body did not look badly damaged; it was obviously dead.

John's mouth turned down in sympathetic sorrow. He recognised the cat. It was not simply some stray that had wandered into the neighbourhood before meeting its demise under the wheels of an unidentified hit-and-run driver. This was Pryor's cat, Stevie.

Or Stewie, maybe? John wasn't certain. He never could remember its name. It seemed like every time he thought he had it figured out, Pryor would shake his head, laughing at him as he corrected him. The point was, it was Pryor's cat, and the boy was going to be heartbroken when he found out.

John had no intention of removing the cat from the roadway himself; the thought of touching the bloody corpse with his bare hands repulsed him. He figured he should probably call Pryor's parents and give them notice of what had happened. They could then come claim the animal and bury it or throw it away, or whatever funeral rites they felt were appropriate. He turned, planning to return to his home and call the neighbours immediately about their son's cat, but he froze, startled at the sight that met him on his front porch.

An orange and white tabby cat sat primly at the edge of his porch staring back at him with wide yellow eyes. He craned his head to stare at the dead animal behind him in the street, then back toward the cat on his porch. The two looked identical except for... well, except one was dead, and the other was **very** much alive.

Two cats? Or... something else? John thought but did not dare say aloud.

"Hey, Stevie," he called to the feline on his porch. "Stewie? Whatever your name is. Is that you?"

In response, the cat leapt down from the porch onto the lawn, then prowled lazily along the outer edge of the house, heading for the back yard.

"Wait," John said. "Where are you going?"

He followed as quickly as he could, not running exactly but moving more in a lurching stumble. The cat did not leave with any obvious haste as it rounded the corner of the house, but when John arrived at the same location, the animal was nowhere to be seen. It had seemingly vanished. He continued along the side of his home into the backyard but still found no sign of Pryor's pet cat.

As soon as it was out of John's sight, it might have bolted under the deck or maybe hopped the fence into someone else's yard, he surmised. He considered searching further, but a sudden jolt of pain in his right temple demanded his full attention at that moment. Cupping his hands over his eyes, John tried to breathe through the discomfort. After counting out several long seconds, the pain faded back to its previous dull ache, leaving him with a slight dizziness.

John's stomach flipped as the moment of vertigo left him feeling nauseated. All thoughts of cats, dead or otherwise, fled his thoughts. He returned to the front yard and climbed the steps to his porch. All he could think about right now was getting back inside the house. He needed to escape the light and retreat to the seclusion of his bedroom. He wanted desperately to crawl into bed, pull the blanket over his head and lose himself in the soothing dark. He needed to sleep and forget.

"God damned migraines," he muttered.

*ohn slept through most of the day. When he rose from his bed in the early evening, the pain in his head—the one that had sent him fleeing for the comfort of his room had passed, mostly. He felt almost normal. A slight tension at the back of his skull reminded him that a new migraine was always lurking behind the next corner, so he shouldn't get too cocky about this brief respite.

He had missed lunch, but his stomach wasn't complaining at the skipped meal, so John figured he would wait a couple more hours before dealing with dinner. Instead, he decided to go out onto the back porch to enjoy the fading warmth of the day. Fresh air often helped him feel better.

Exiting the back door, John shuffled along the stained boards of the rear deck toward the porch swing. The swing had been built by the home's previous owner, and the guy had obviously known his way around hammer. The swing was a bench-style contraption, lovingly assembled, sanded and painted until there wasn't a rough edge to be found over its entire surface. Once completed, it had been chained and bolted into the beams supporting the roof overhang. The swing was wide enough and sturdy enough to support four grown adults, and it barely made so much as a creak of acknowledgement as John climbed into it.

He released a small sigh of contentment as he settled against the padded cushions lining the swing's rear boards. The sun was still a few hours from setting, but as the rear porch faced east, John was shaded from the direct light. He could avoid staring into that brightness while still enjoying the view of his backyard.

John was proud of his yard. It was small but neatly manicured and carefully tended. Birds, butterflies, and other industrious creatures frequently visited the flowering plants he had selected to populate the space. He had pleasantly wasted away hundreds of hours observing the bustle of their activity.

He paid Pryor a small salary to mow once a week and keep the weeds under control. John used to tend the flowers himself and had quite enjoyed the task; it relaxed him. But that had been before his fall. Exerting himself now too often led to the onset of a new migraine. So, today, he simply sat in the comfortable swing and enjoyed watching the small signs of life surrounding him.

The warm air and quiet lulled John into a light hypnotic trance. He did not fall asleep, but his senses faded as he let the sensations of colour and motion shift around him. Seeing everything and nothing simultaneously, John existed in the moment. When she had still been alive, his wife, Melissa, used to refer to these times as just being a part of the world. A small smile pulled at John's lips as he thought of her. The pleasant thought was quickly followed by a familiar empty ache in his chest. Eight years later, and he still missed her. Especially during times like this when he was 'being part of the world.'

A sudden movement and blur of colour brought him from his revery back to full alertness. In the corner of the yard, a ball of orange and white crawled from beneath a clump of azaleas.

"You again," he said, watching the cat emerge from the shadows.

The cat sat on the lawn and yawned, displaying tiny, pointed teeth and a long pink tongue. This was followed by an agitated shake of the head and a hard sneeze. The cat licked a paw and began industriously rubbing it across his ear and the side of his face.

John patted the bench next to him with one hand. "Why don't you come on over? Have a seat on the swing."

The cat cocked its head at his voice. It rose to its feet and walked casually in his direction, as if saying, *sure why not? The swing looks as good as any other place.*

Somewhat to John's surprise, but to his utter delight, the cat strolled onto the rear deck and made its way over to him. With a sudden tensing of its hind legs, it leapt onto the swing beside him. It padded in a small circle, getting acclimated to the feel of the cushions under its feet, then settled down to sit. Wide, yellow eyes turned in John's direction, the pupils little more than black slits running the length from top to bottom.

The cat yawned again. *Okay, I'm here. What now?* the expression seemed to say.

"You have to be careful around here," John said. "The streets around this neighbourhood are dangerous. People drive their cars much too fast and don't pay attention to what's in the road in front of them. I saw what happened to your friend this morning. I don't want that to happen to you."

The cat continued to stare at John. There was no acknowledgement of what he was saying, no knowing look that indicated the animal understood his words. It was merely the curious gaze of any house cat.

John reached out a hand to pet the animal. The cat's eyes flicked toward his hand, attracted to the movement, but it did not flinch away as he extended his hand toward its head.

"Good kitty," he whispered. "You're a good kitty."

His hand touched the cat's head, then passed through without resistance.

John snatched his hand back as if he had touched something red hot. He felt an odd tingling sensation in his fingertips like his hand had gone numb from blood loss and was just now beginning to get feeling back. Holding the hand in front of his face, he wiggled his fingers, looking for injury or damage. They were fine. The cat did not react other than to abruptly start purring. It did not seem to mind the odd contact. Or rather, the lack of it.

John slipped out of the swing, moving carefully so as not to move the bench too much and upset the cat. When he reached his feet, he backed away, keeping the purring creature in his sight as he reached blindly for the doorknob of the house's rear entrance behind him. He found the reassuring metal knob, turned it, and scrambled into the house.

Safely inside, John placed his back to the door now between him and the ghost cat on his porch.

Ghost cat? Was that what it was? John could find no other

explanation. His hand had passed right through it. He knew he hadn't missed the animal's head. His balance and depth perception were affected by his head injury, but not so badly that he couldn't pet a cat that was eighteen inches away from him. He had put his hand on its head, and there had been nothing there.

Curiosity began to weigh heavier than fear, and John decided he wanted another look. Rather than open the door and risk letting the spirit of a dead cat into his house, he decided to sneak along the interior of his home to the kitchen. The window over his sink looked out into the backyard. He could see the porch swing from that window. Once he reached the kitchen, he crept to the glass pane, careful not to stand directly in front of it where the cat might see him. He paused and took a few deep breaths to calm himself, then he bent at the waist and peered around the frame of the window until he brought the porch swing into view.

The swing was empty.

He sidled to his right to get a clearer look and confirmed what he seen before. No cat. The swing swayed gently back and forth as though only recently evacuated, but Stevie/Stewie had moved on. John looked desperately right then left, scanning the entirety of the backyard from fence line to fence line. He found nothing. The cat was gone.

He took a step toward the back door, intending to go outside once more to search for Pryor's pet. He paused before taking a second step, reconsidering his actions. Did he really want to find that cat right now? No, he decided. He didn't. Best to let this mystery go for the moment, give himself time to mentally process what had just happened.

"I'll look for him later," he said aloud, trying to bolster his courage. "There's no need to find him tonight. Tomorrow, maybe."

John shuddered, feeling a spidery presence crawl from the

base of his spine all the way up his back. The thought came back to him, unbidden:

Ghost cat.

☠

The next morning, John rose from bed and went downstairs. He hadn't slept much that night. His mind would not stop fixating on Pryor's cat and why the animal's spirit was hanging around his house. This morning, in the light of a new day, he still had no concrete answers. He didn't even have any good questions if he was being honest with himself.

John decided he would look for the cat again today. He felt confused and a little bit in shock over the previous day's incident, but at least the fear had mostly gone away, replaced by wonder and a desire to know more. The cat had shown no malevolence toward him. Even when he had tried to pet it, the fluffy ghost hadn't done anything other than start purring. In hindsight, John was certain—almost certain—the cat was not dangerous and meant him no harm.

Besides, he told himself with a little bit of excitement, how many people could actually claim to have seen a ghost? And a ghost cat, at that. He should be revelling in such a unique opportunity rather than running away from it.

John exited the back door and stepped onto his rear porch, eager to see what he might find. He did not see the cat anywhere in the yard.

"Hey, Stevie. Or Stewie, or whatever. I'm back. You want to come out and say hi?"

Nothing moved. He peered under the azaleas, but he could see nothing stirring in the shadows beneath. Trudging over to the swing, he rapped a knuckle on the wooden armrest.

"Should we have another sit on the swing? I won't run away this time. I promise."

Still, no response was forthcoming. He sat down in the swing.

"Kitty, kitty? I'm sorry about yesterday. I'll just sit here and wait for you to come join me."

John waited. And waited. For half an hour, he sat in the swing and gazed out over his yard. The cat did not reappear and join him. At last, bored and partially defeated, an idea occurred to him. Maybe the cat wasn't avoiding him. Maybe it was gone altogether.

How long would a cat's spirit hang around after its death? He had no idea. That wasn't a fact he had ever stumbled across in any book or television show. Last night may have been his only chance to interact with Stevie/Stewie? Before he wandered off to wherever it was that ghost cats went.

At the same time, he was thinking Pryor's cat might be gone; he realised he had never called Pryor's parents about the animal's remains in the street. He wondered if they had found the cat's body or if it was still there. Pushing himself to his feet, John re-entered the house, walked through the interior hallways and then exited onto his front porch. He stood at the top step leading down to the concrete pathway through his yard and looked toward the street.

The roadway was clear. The hunched, furry body he had noticed the day before was gone. Pryor's parents, or perhaps someone else, had removed the animal and disposed of the remains. That was something, John supposed. He no longer needed to call the boy's parents and tell them the family cat was dead.

Staring at the spot where the corpse had been, John found no signs whatsoever of the accident. It appeared that even the blood spilt when the cat was hit by a car had been cleared away.

Nothing remained that would hint at the tragedy that had occurred.

Perhaps that was why he couldn't find ghost cat. When the body was removed, there was no longer any reason for the spirit to hang around. John decided if this was true, then there was no reason for him to hang around either and turned to go back inside.

Something made him pause, though he wasn't exactly sure what it was. He turned again toward the street. What he saw startled him, but he held his ground, determined not to run away this time.

In the middle of the street, an orange and white tabby cat sat on the asphalt in the exact spot where the dead cat had been the day before. When the cat noticed John looking, it meowed a low moaning sound.

"Okay," John reassured it. "I'm here. I won't go inside. Do you want to come up on the porch?"

The cat rose to its feet and sauntered, almost regally, toward him. John grabbed the porch railing and lowered himself until he was sitting at the top of the porch steps. He waited quietly. Patiently. The cat stepped onto the curb and continued striding toward him, across the sidewalk, down the walkway, and finally to the foot of the steps.

John patted the wooded porch beside him. "C'mon then."

The cat padded up the steps before settling next to him. John could hear the animal begin to purr as it gazed up at him with those round, oddly knowing, yellow eyes.

He held out a hand and stroked it across the cat's head. His hand passed through the animal, down through the head and chest and out between the front feet. Expecting the result, John did not jump to his feet and flee this time. He did not even flinch. Instead, he waved his open hand through the insubstantial feline from left to right, then back again. The cat did not noticeably react; it simply sat next to him and purred. It's eyes partially closed in contentment.

John lowered his hand through the cat's body again, top to bottom, until his palm touched the boards of the porch under the cat's feet. He patted the wood a few times softly.

"Amazing," he breathed. "I can see you so clearly, but you're not really there. How did this happen?"

He withdrew his hand and rested it in his lap. The cat lowered itself until it was lying on the porch, its front paws tucked under its chest. The purring grew slightly louder, and the cat's eyes closed further until it appeared it was about to fall asleep. John watched the tip of its tail occasionally twitch back and forth.

He waved his hand one more time experimentally through the dozing animal.

"Do you know you're dead, little guy?" he asked. The cat's eyes opened a crack when he spoke but closed again after a moment.

"Or do you think you're still alive? Do you remember what it felt like to get hit by that car? Do you remember dying?" He sighed in frustrated contemplation. "I really wish you could talk to me."

Movement pulled John's attention to the sidewalk in front of his house. Pryor had wandered over from his house next door and had just stepped onto John's front lawn. The boy was scanning the grounds around him intently, searching left then right as if he had lost something important. The boy's gaze rose and passed over the porch where John and ghost cat sat.

Pryor froze in place. His eyes went wide, and his mouth popped open in a small 'o' shape. The boy raised a hand and pointed a shaky finger at the porch steps.

John bobbed his head in encouragement, a smile spreading across his face. He pointed toward the cat beside him.

"You see him, too. Don't you?"

Pryor gave a puzzled nod of agreement.

"I'm not going crazy," John said quietly to himself. "I'm not the only one seeing this cat." Then raising his voice again, he said, "Pryor, is this Stevie?"

The boy shook his head in the negative.

"That's Stewie," he said, his voice understandably unsteady.

"Stewie. Damn it. Okay, so Stewie got hit by a car yesterday, right?"

Pryor gave him another shake. "Stevie got hit by a car."

"Wait a minute. I thought you just said his name was Stewie."

Pryor's nose crinkled, and he appeared deeply confused, as though he wasn't certain he was awake and having a real conversation.

"Stevie got hit by a car. That's Stewie on the porch with you."

Stevie *and* Stewie. Two different names and two different cats. It was John's turn to grow confused.

Two cats, he thought. *Two cats, not one. What does that mean?*

"What are you doing here, Mr Alexander?"

"Where else would I be? This is my house. I live here."

Pryor took a quick step backwards as if frightened by John's words.

"Yes, sir. It's your house. But how are you...? I saw you... They put you in that van. They took you away."

John lurched to his feet. "Van? What van? Who took me away?"

A sudden blinding pain filled his head, like an ice-pick driving through his right eye and piercing deep into his brain. It was too much, too fast. He clapped a hand over his eye as if he could locate the source of the pain and draw it out. He screamed in agony and confusion.

"I can't," he shouted at Pryor, partly in apology and partly in explanation. "I have to go inside."

At his feet, the cat called Stewie leapt off the porch, darted across the lawn, and disappeared around the side of the house. *Two cats. What van?* John wondered before another jolt of pain blasted through his brain, shutting down any further rational thought.

"I have to … I have to…" John muttered. He staggered into the house, not bothering to pretend to open the door.

The shaded interior offered little relief. He continued to lurch forward like a drunk at the end of a long evening in the pub, trying to reach the bartender for last call. He needed to get to his room. He needed to close his eyes and rest.

John stumbled as he approached the staircase, stepping around the large bloodstain on the floor and catching himself on the polished wooden bannister.

Where did all that blood come from? he thought. More pain pulsed through him, pushing that question aside. It would have to wait with all the others. John climbed the stairs, pulling himself along the railings with his hands as his feet sluggishly lifted and fell, step after step.

He needed his bed. He needed to lie down. He wanted desperately to lose himself in the dark and forget.

G. ALLEN WILBANKS
ABOUT THE AUTHOR

G. Allen Wilbanks is a member of the Horror Writers Association (HWA) and has published over 200 short stories in Deep Magic, Daily Science Fiction, The Talisman, and other magazines, as well as featuring in best-selling anthologies from all over the world. He has published two short story collections of his own, and two novels. His most recent book, A Life of Adventure, was an Amazon U.S. top 100 release, and he has a short horror novella, "They," due out in May, 2021.

For more information, please visit www.gallenwilbanks.com, or check out his weekly blog at www.DeepDarkThoughts.com.

TRICKERY
BY CHISTO HEALY

*T*he door was locked.

Of course, it was. It made perfect sense. Cody didn't know why he was surprised. The moment Allie Hernandez said she wanted to go on a date with him, he should have assumed it was a trick and not a treat. He had been pining for her since middle school, and she didn't even know that he existed until last night—apparently.

They were from very different social circles. Right now, she was probably outside laughing at him with some narcissistic jerks who were ready to go play community college football and who believed they were rock stars.

Happy Halloween, he thought.

When he ran into her at Gino's pizzeria during lunch with his brother, she had seemed different. She seemed like she had grown up. She was no longer someone who saw life as a popularity contest. She was friendly and sweet. They were about to embark on college journeys that would take them to the opposite ends of the country. Still, she invited him out on a proper date anyway, and on Halloween night, his favourite day of the year.

To his surprise, she said that she had always liked him, and she didn't want to leave without dating him at least once. Cody had played it cool, but he was more excited about tonight than he had ever been about anything in his life. He thought it was going to be the best Halloween ever.

It had started off great too. They went out to eat at an Asian buffet where he got to see that the petite cheerleader was not bashful about food. She packed it away, although he didn't know where she put it. It felt good to see her so natural and comfortable.

After dinner, they went to the movies. In true Halloween fashion, they saw a horror film, which made a lot more sense now that he thought about it. It was probably all part of the plan, to get him frightened before bringing him here. He shook his head and cursed as he tugged at the door again. He couldn't wait to be away from this town and all the people he went to high school with, including Allie.

After the movie, she didn't want to go home. She wanted to take a walk. She chose the cemetery, another game piece that he was too wrapped up in her to see. As they walked through the tombstones, they talked. They reminisced about old times. She recalled moments with him. Moments he didn't think she ever realised had happened, never mind remembered. At that moment, Cody would have gone to the moon if she had asked him to.

The moon wasn't what Allie had in mind though. There was an old, abandoned house by the cemetery. It was supposed to be haunted. All of the kids had been telling stories about it for as long as he could remember. It was a Halloween favourite.

The woman who lived in the house long ago, Veronica Stack, was said to be a witch. The townsfolk had hanged her from the chandelier in her own foyer. Then they cut her down and buried her bones in the basement, but not before burning them. Legend had it that anyone who entered the house was taken by old Ms Stack, taken, killed and buried in the basement. The local kids claimed that the basement of this old house was a cemetery for children and adults alike who were foolish enough to enter.

Even after all the years that kids like himself told the stories about this house, Cody hadn't thought it was a bad idea when Allie said she wanted to go in with him. Everything was going so perfectly. She said it would be a great send-off before they left town. To visit the local haunt and share their first kiss there. The kiss part was all Cody really heard or thought about. Sixth grade was the first time he had thought about kissing her. She had been picking his brain about a science project they were both working on, and he watched her lips form the words. He had wondered what it would be like to kiss those lips. He ended up doing her project for her, which looking back now, had been the start of a long line of manipulations that ended here. He was really kicking himself.

She didn't lead the way. The windows were boarded up and nailed shut long ago. Allie told him to open the door. It opened right away without any trouble which should have seemed strange to him. It would have if he had been thinking clearly, but he had never thought clearly around Allie Hernandez. She did something to his mind. It wasn't just her beauty which was definitely apparent, but something more than that. She had this magic about her, this charm. It was irresistible.

He didn't know her mother. Maybe her last name was Stack. Wouldn't that be the plot to a thousand movies he'd seen? He never expected to star in one. He would have preferred an actual romance.

The door had probably been unlocked already, set up and waiting for him. It was all just part of the big master plan, the final trick to play on Cody, the loser, before college. Thank you, society for being so disgustingly predictable and annoyingly habitual.

They could have at least left me with some candy, he thought.

Allie had asked Cody to lead the way, to go in and make sure that there was no witches or ghosts hanging around waiting to kill them. She asked him to protect her and kissed him on the cheek, making him swoon. He felt like Hercules marching up into that house. Then the door slammed shut behind him. Allie hadn't come in yet. Big surprise. Immediately, he turned around and grabbed the knob to open the door and let her in, only to find it locked.

There was no lock on the knob for him to turn or any way that he could see to unlock it. There was a keyhole. Allie must have locked it from the outside, locked him in. He banged on the door and yelled for her to open it, but he couldn't hear any response. She was probably already gone. She did her part of the going away prank. She got him inside the scary house on Halloween night.

Maybe they intended to let him out in the morning after he had spent the night inside. Maybe they wanted him to find his own way out, and they had no intention of coming back for him. Maybe Allie's real boyfriend was waiting somewhere inside, prepared to pounce on him.

He didn't like any of those options. He tried to peer out of the filthy glass between the boards on the windows. He couldn't see anything. He sighed then and turned around. It was time to find a way out of this place. At this point, he just wanted the day to be over. He wanted to get home and get on with his life.

He walked through the old house, choking on the dust that covered everything. He didn't know if there were ghosts in this house or hiding football players, but there were definitely spiders, and a **lot** of them at that. There was a fireplace with a painting above it. *Was that Veronica Stack?* She didn't look like an old witch. She was young and beautiful, with long auburn hair in two braids draped over her tan shoulders.

"Are you in here?" he said. Maybe I can still end this night with a kiss, he thought. "You were gorgeous, Ms Stack."

There was no response, and truthfully he was glad for that. If she had actually spoken, beautiful or not, he probably would have run screaming through the house.

The house is actually kind of cool, Cody thought. The old-fashioned wood stove. The rotary telephone. The candelabras and paintings. This place was like a museum. He used his cellphone to light his way, though, rather than the candles or gas lanterns that the house provided. He considered calling somebody for help, but he really didn't want to explain how he got into this predicament. He would have felt like a fool.

He opened a door in the kitchen and saw a flight of stairs going down.

The infamous basement, he thought. There could be a door to the outside down there. He took the old wooden steps carefully and shivered as they creaked and squealed under his weight. There was no denying the creep factor of the old place.

When he got to the bottom, he sighed. The bad news was that there didn't seem to be any exit down there. There wasn't so much as a window. The good news was that there also didn't seem to be a cemetery of Veronica's victims. It looked very much like a basement. The floor was concrete, not dirt. If anyone had been buried, it had been long ago and filled in with cement. He went back up the groaning stairs and back around to the front of the house.

He tried once more to bang on the door and call to Allie. He didn't actually expect to get a response, but he felt it didn't hurt to try. At least he hadn't been beat up by jocks yet. There was always an upside. You just had to be willing to find it.

He found a study full of old books. He didn't want to look through them just yet, mainly because he didn't want to compete with the dust and spiders, but he was sure that there had to be some gems on those shelves. A collection that old had to be full of classics. He made a mental note to come back to it during daylight hours.

The only other room on the first floor was behind the staircase to the second floor. It was a creepy place to find a room, and Cody doubted it held a way out of the house, but he couldn't conquer the curiosity that nagged at him. Part of him hoped the strange door would be locked.

It wasn't, of course.

He stepped inside the room and found shelves and shelves of mason jars. Some of them had shrivelled flowers in them. Others had dead rodents. Some had what looked to be organs of some kind. If this was something the other kids set up to scare him, they did a really good job. The jars were old. They were dusty. The liquid inside them looked rancid. Could these have been spell ingredients? Was this the hidden witch's pantry? If somebody had found something like this all those years ago when people were superstitious and afraid, it wouldn't surprise him if they had hung her.

When he exited the strange room and walked around to the front of the staircase, he looked at the enormous chandelier that hung from the high ceiling beside the stairs. He tried to imagine the beautiful girl from the painting hanging there, grasping at her throat, terrified and not wanting to die. Fear was such a dangerous thing in the hearts of men.

He'd already checked the basement and the entire first floor. The only place left to go was up. When he got to the top, more old paintings lined the walls. Maybe they were Veronica's parents or grandparents. They looked pretty high society. It made him wonder who the Stacks were before the last descendant was dubbed a witch and murdered if, of course, any of that were even real.

Cody went into a room that looked to be a guest bedroom. The lone window was boarded up just like those downstairs. He thought maybe the old wood would be rotted and easy to remove, but he tugged on it to no avail.

The next room was also a bedroom, but he was pretty sure

that this one belonged to Veronica herself. The bed was enormous and had a canopy over it. It was a lavish red that matched the bed spread and pillows. The four posts were made of gold and were etched with intricate patterns and designs. There was so much of value in here. Cody couldn't believe that this stuff had been here for so many years without anyone stealing it. Were people so afraid of the legends surrounding this house that they wouldn't even take the gold from it? That was a pretty powerful fear.

The window was boarded up just like the other, so he went back to the landing. He sighed and put his palms on the dusty banister. There was nowhere left to go in this old house. He was either going to have to wait until morning and hope Allie came back for him or man up and figure out how to get the boards off of one of these windows.

As he stood there contemplating, something hit him over the head. He went tumbling over the railing, but he didn't hit the floor. Something was around his neck. He couldn't breathe, but he could see the front door. He immediately knew where he was. He was hanging from the chandelier, grabbing at his throat, afraid and not wanting to die. Just as he had pictured Veronica Stack earlier. This prank had gone too far. They were going to kill him. What had seemed like the makings for a fine Halloween was quickly becoming the worst one of his life.

Then he was cut loose.

He fell hard to the wooden floor below, landing with a bang and an eruption of dust. He moaned in pain. His body hurt, bad. He felt broken, and he was pretty sure in some ways he was. The fall was loud.

Surely, someone heard it, he thought. Then he coughed and rolled his eyes at his own stupidity. Who was going to hear him? The dead? The only thing nearby was the cemetery.

That was why they brought him here, wasn't it? It was the perfect place to torment or kill someone and get away with it.

There was no one to see or hear anything. For the first time since sixth grade, Cody felt like he was finally over Allie Hernandez. He was actually feeling quite hateful.

Screw her. Screw all of them.

Then something started dragging him. He wanted to fight back, but he couldn't. He thought his back might be broken. He yelled at them to let go. He told them they were taking this too far. He said that he was really hurt and needed help. He told them to call an ambulance —all he got back was silence.

Then he was going down. No. This was too much. This was way too much. He was in the basement then. There was a hole behind the staircase that he hadn't seen when he was down here earlier. "What are you doing?" he asked. "Please stop this."

Then he was thrown into the hole. He couldn't imagine anything he had done to deserve this. His crime was having a crush on a cheerleader. Was that really worth killing him over? High school was over. They were all about to move on to college. Why do this to him now? Was this their last hoorah? Let's kill the loser from high school before we go away? It was insane. No one would ever find him here. His mother and father would have no idea what happened to him. It was the perfect crime. He just wished someone would speak to him, at least tell him why.

He thought about the legend. The way the tale went, he was to be buried down here. Were they going to bury him alive? His eyes widened with horror as he remembered; not before being burned. As if on cue, he burst into flames.

He screamed in agony as the flames seared his flesh. He screamed in terror as death came for him. Then they were snuffed out by shovel loads of dirt being dropped down upon him.

He had never known pain like this, never even imagined it in his life. Who was up there? Which one of them was doing this to him? He wished he could see, but he couldn't. All he could do was scream until he couldn't do that either. The dirt filled his mouth and his lungs. Once the hole was filled, and Cody was gone from the world, the earth was covered with wet cement.

At the front of the house, the door opened. Allie Hernandez stood on the porch looking in. "It's about time, you jerk!" she yelled. "You locked me out. Did you think that was funny? I thought you were being killed in there or something. Was this your idea of a going away trick? Scare the cheerleader for not noticing you in high school? What a jerk move! Cody?"

When she got no response, Allie realised the trick wasn't over yet. He was ruining her last Halloween before leaving for college. It made her angry. She was done with this date, but she wasn't going home without finding Cody and slapping the crap out of him. She stepped into the house, and the door slammed shut behind her.

Seriously? Had he gotten outside somehow? She was growing angrier by the second. Allie turned around and grasped the knob.

The door was locked.

CHISTO HEALY
ABOUT THE AUTHOR

Chisto has been writing full-time for one year and in that year he has had almost 200 published works. He lives in NC with his equally wacky fiancee, her mom, his two brilliant teenage daughters who have proven to be incredible muses, and his son Boe who keeps them all on their toes.

You can follow him on Amazon or check his badly maintained blog at https://chistohealy.blogspot.com

CONTROL
BY RACHEL C. PENDRAGON

She never allowed us to leave.

If we behaved, did as the whispers asked, we were well taken care of. Dinner was on the table every night, by candlelight on silver trays. Dishes were washed, carpets were cleaned. All was beautiful.

But God forbid we tried to escape.

She knew our thoughts. Every time an attempt was formulated, she knew. Wallpaper began to peel, pipes burst. Dinner was served rotten, rife with maggots and slime. Rats escaped from the walls, crawling, scratching. Biting.

Father tried to escape once, without thinking. He ran down the hall, tearing open the front door. Crying for help. But she knew. A gargling liquid scream was all we heard; a foul-smelling pile of flesh and crushed bone in the threshold was all that remained. Mother cried for days. We begged for forgiveness.

But she never listened. She was just as controlling in death as she was in life. Keeping us prisoners at her beck and call–day and night.

And now, the house belonged to her.

RACHEL C. PENDRAGON
ABOUT THE AUTHOR

Rachel C. Pendragon is a California native and single mother, currently living in Kansas City. She developed a love for storytelling from a young age, and now shares that love with her daughter. She has been published in Season of the Moon online magazine, and is a featured author for both Black Ink Fiction and Breaking Rules Europe Publishing. When Rachel is not writing, she works at a busy orthopedic hospital, mending broken bones.

THE HOUSE IN THE MIDDLE OF THE STREET
BY SCARLETT LAKE

*Y*ou know the house. The one at the end of the road down the long driveway that seems to have a permanent shadow hanging over its head. The one that sends shivers up the spines of people who pass as they quicken their pace and bow their head in the hopes nothing will happen to them. The one that is the gossip of the water-cooler, yet no one really knows why.

This house, though, wasn't at the end of the road beyond the long gravel path. This house sat in the middle of the street, in the middle of a bright family suburb. A grand old house that has been passed down generation after generation. It was a stunning house to look at from the outside, with red wooden panelling accentuated by white Victorian beams. With neatly trimmed bushes and a few steps up to the front door, nestled in amongst a street lined with similar houses, each containing two point four children. Family homes.

Children rode bicycles and kicked balls up and down the street, passing the house time and time again. Mothers pushed strollers while fathers washed their cars in the driveways opposite. And there the house sat, day after day. Night after night, sending shivers down the spines of those who dared to look upon the red wooden house in the middle of the street.

Isn't it a conundrum then that no one ever comes or goes? No person has been seen to cross the threshold in years. Yet lights come on at night, and shadows can be seen moving in the windows by those brave enough to risk a look. Post gets delivered to the little letterbox on the edge of the sidewalk, and the postman will tell you it's gone come the next time he delivers. Ms S Lake, the letters say through that small cellophane window, but no one on the street could tell you what she looked like, or even her age.

No friends or family come and go. No delivery men (besides the postman) and no servicemen. No decorators, no electricians, no gardeners—yet still the garden stays impeccably trimmed. No carers, no nurses, not even a car comes and goes. Yet the lights still come on at night, and a shadow moves within.

Maryann walks past that house every day on her way to and from school. The one rumoured to be belong to a reclusive witch. Her house only a few doors up with a boring brick exterior instead of the beautifully clad red and white. Every day she stands outside on the sidewalk right on the boundary line. She stares up at the building, not feeling those shivers she's heard her parents speak of. Maybe it's something to do with her age; at only 10-years-old one tends to not have the worry of adults. At 10-years-old one tends to still believe in fairies and Santa Clause. The Easter bunny and monster that lurks under the bed. Witches and wizards, dragon wielding warlords and princesses locked up in towers waiting for their prince charming to come and save them.

Her mind races as she stares at that house, wondering whether the occupant within fits into one of those categories. Whether she is some damsel in distress who needs help from a charming knight in shining armour. Or maybe she's...

"Maryann Krakowski!" her wild daydreams are interrupted

by the screeching tone of her mother standing in the road several doors up with her hands on her flour-covered apron-clad hips.

"Coming," Maryann replies with one quick glance back at the house as she runs up the road and into her boring brick house.

The next day Maryann is back, standing outside that red house in the middle of a suburban street. Last night she decided she was going in. She was going to walk up that path, climb the couple of steps to the front door and knock. If no one answered, she would knock again. Maybe even try a little turn of the doorknob and see what happens.

Maryann believed that not everything needed to be solved by a man in shining armour. Sometimes a 10-year-old girl might be just what's needed. After all, she slays dragons and fights vampires in her sleep, so this should be a piece of cake.

She sways back and forth on her heels, excitement and a little bit of fear running through her veins. Taking a deep breath, she steps over the boundary line and onto the path beyond. She stops and closes her eyes as though waiting to be struck down. Opening them again, she steels herself and strides towards that front door with the look of a stubborn child unwilling to back down. She walks up the small steps, raises a little fist and knocks.

KNOCK.

KNOCK.

KNOCK.

Maryann stands and waits, nervously chewing her lip as she sucks it into her mouth.

After several long minutes—she timed them with her pink sparkly watch—Maryann raises a fist and knocks once more.

KNOCK.

KNOCK.

KNOCK.

Still nothing. No one comes to the door. No one shouts from the other side. No footsteps are heard—just silence from within. Maryann reaches out for the brass round knob and turns, expecting resistance but not finding any. The knob shifts with a clunk and turns to the left as she opens the door to a house that no one has ever seen open.

Her eyes go wide, and her heartbeat picks up speed as she steps over the threshold and into the mysterious house in the middle of the street.

💀

*M*onday, April 13th 1987
Local girl goes missing

10-year-old Maryann Krakowski was last seen leaving school on April Friday, the 10th, 1987. She regularly walked the few block trip from St. Helena's Primary on her own and was accustomed to the route.

She was last seen in a pair of blue jeans, a yellow t-shirt and a blue jacket with a red satchel which she wore over her shoulder.

If you have any information, please call the San Diego police department.

💀

*M*onday, April 4th 1988
Local girl still missing

Nearly a year ago, then 10-year-old Maryann Krakowski, went missing on her way home from school. Police and family are still appealing for any information on her whereabouts or movements on Friday, April 13th 1987.

If you have any information, please call the San Diego police department.

*D*ay after day, night after night, people pass that house. Yet on a sunny day in April 1987, no one saw a little girl with a red satchel enter the red-clad building. Families have come and gone. Neighbours have changed, yet the street and that house, the one that sits in the middle, has remained the same.

No one comes and goes from the house, yet the lights still come on at night, and the shadows still move within. People still get shivers up their spine as they pass, but the house prices still rise as they are considered prime real estate. The world seemingly forgot about the little girl that went missing thirty years ago who lived a few doors down.

Post still gets delivered, the only thing that does. Only there is one thing different now. The name seen through that cellophane window that once read Ms S Lake now reads Ms M Krakowski. But no one has noticed.

SCARLETT LAKE
ABOUT THE AUTHOR

Scarlett Lake is a horror, fantasy and romance author from Dorset, UK who enjoys delving into the dark. She loves to stretch the imagination and turn well-known tales into something new and terrifying. Her love of classic horror movies and monsters can often be found in her writing.

When she isn't typing away on her laptop and living in imaginary worlds, she can usually be found walking her dogs or tending to her vegetable patch.
She has had several short stories published by Red Cape Publishing, WPC Press, Ghost Orchid Press, Macabre Ladies, Black Ink Fiction, Paramour Ink, Breaking Rules Europe and Iron Faerie Publishing.

More information is available at:
https://www.facebook.com/ScarlettLakeAuthor

NARCISSUS IN EXILE
BY KIMBERLEY REI

"*B*y the pricking of my thumbs, something... damn it!"

Brianna Sinclair, of Sinclair's Circle, slapped the pause button on her recording and shoved her chair back to answer the door. It was a package she had ordered. It couldn't be anything else. The entire world had been under some form of lockdown for nearly a year now. Televised celebrations/memorials were currently being planned for the anniversary—as if such things should be lauded.

Her journey to the front door took her down the oddly mirrored hallway that came with the house. Every inch of wall was covered, right down to mirrored moulding on the corners. And there were many corners. Much like hotels, each room was tucked back into the wall a foot or so. The sides were covered in mirrors. With so many surfaces coated, Brianna saw several versions of herself from all angles as she walked to the door. She didn't mind. In fact, she often paused to admire the view.

She had been taught, growing up, that vanity was a sin. Her mother only allowed mirrors in the bathrooms so that her brothers could shave properly and a smaller version in bedrooms for applying makeup. She wasn't a cruel woman. No horror tales would be written about her, no therapists would be taking notes. She was loving and supportive, but she refused to raise overly proud and overly privileged adults.

Well... she tried.

Brianna, never ever Bri, realised she would be stunningly beautiful when she was barely in elementary school. Everyone told her how cute she was, with those perfect blonde curls and those bright, intelligent eyes. By high school, she had learned how to use that beauty to her benefit. She graduated with a solid 4.0 she hadn't earned and a yearbook full of compliments and promises to stay in touch. The yearbook was buried in a box in the attic.

College was more of the same, but with the addition of rich frat boys. Her 4.0 slipped to a 3.8. Too many female professors who weren't impressed by her fluttering lashes. But she emerged with a degree and a closet full of clothes to enhance her curves. Boys were so easy.

A string of wealthy lovers allowed her to live the life she wanted—in a large house suitable for extravagant parties, entertaining who and when she chose. Every weekend, her home was filled with people who simply adored her. She was charming and warm, funny and sensual. She practically fed off the worship.

These days, all she had was her own face, thrown back at her again and again. She was glad it was a perfect face.

Brianna opened the door, hoping to catch the delivery man, just to have someone to flirt with for a few minutes. He was gone.

She sighed and dropped the package on a small table. Shopping had lost its allure once there was no one to show off for. Her purchases were smaller now, items that could be seen on camera.

Once a week, she produced a video for her online followers.

Subscribers paid to watch her talk about how she spent her days in isolation. It was all fantasy, of course. They thought she'd escaped to a fabulous tropical location where she lounged on fabulous beaches and sipped fabulous drinks brought to her by fabulously oiled up men. Every couple of days, she held an unboxing, revealing her latest eccentric and expensive purchase. She started every episode the same way, with a creepy opening line and a spin of wit. "By the pricking of my thumbs, something luxurious this way comes." She would have to redo today's video from the start.

She paused in front of one of the mirrors and leaned in, scowling. She was starting to look pale. Haggard. Life under a pandemic was trying in more ways than one. Yes, she felt for those getting ill and dying. Of course, she did. Her mother raised an arrogant woman, not a monstrous one. She'd stopped watching the news because it was giving her nightmares and making her cry. Neither are good for the skin. Her intake now came in the form of social media feeds and videographers she followed. They all told her the same thing—it still wasn't safe for most people to venture out. There were those who had to work, but Brianna wasn't one of them, and she wasn't about to put herself at risk. She barely dared going into her backyard for a little sun during the day.

She tugged one eyelid down and looked closely. Maybe she could do with just a bit more sunlight.

Still, it would be nice to see her friends. To hug and press against the ones she wanted in her bed, to air kiss and giggle with the ones she didn't. She felt as if she were wilting. Fading away without the sustenance of others. She hadn't realised how much she revelled in their energy until it was gone.

Her finger was still holding her eyelid when her reflection blinked. She stumbled back, startled. The second Brianna grinned and waved, then flickered. For the space between one pounding heartbeat and the next, there was no reflection at all.

And then Brianna saw herself, as she should be, paler than ever, eyes wide and terrified.

It was all getting to her. The isolation. The inability to thrive around others. She should call her therapist. If she whined prettily and promised him she'd do that thing he liked when she could see him again, he'd have effective narcotics hand-delivered to her. Maybe she'd take a break from the vlog. Tell her viewers she was ill and taking to a gorgeous bed for a few days. That might do the trick. Let their worry feed her a little. She smiled at the thought of all those concerned messages streaming in.

Her reflection smiled, too, but it was off. Too wide. Too many teeth.

Brianna backed away until she bumped into the mirror behind her. She spun and yelped at the sight of herself.

A laugh, then. Of course, she was there, too. The whole damned hallway was a mirror.

By the time she crawled into bed that night, she could barely keep her eyes open. The entire afternoon and evening had been a waste. She posted her brief message about being unwell, not needing to embellish at all. For the first time since she moved into the house, she regretted the hall. Her reflection, over and over, bouncing back and forth, pallid and worn thin. Her last action before falling asleep was to text her therapist and ask him to send her meds.

She never "asked."

The next morning, she woke refreshed and happy. Yesterday was a lark. An aberration. A blip in her perfect life. The full-length mirror in the bathroom told her so. When she put on her makeup, the face looking back at her was smiling and beautiful.

The morning went exactly as planned. As it always did lately. Breakfast, social media, her favourite shows. The concern for her health was invigorating, and she considered laying low for a few more days—just enough time to let them seriously worry.

Surely, gifts and monetary thoughtfulness would be sent her way.

It was evening before she needed to venture down her hall of mirrors. The lights were lowered, and shadows skittered with every step. For a moment, for that strange space that seemed to hang between breaths, she was scared of her own home. She hesitated to take the next step. Her skin chilled, goosebumps raising. Her heart beat painfully and she felt weak again. Tired.

She paused halfway to the front door and leaned on one wall. Her gaze flickered to the mirrors and away, fear ratcheting higher. This was a mistake. She should check the mail in the morning when the sun was out. When the shadows were thinner. They were climbing higher now as clouds passed over the moon and played with the little light filtering through the front doors. She should have flipped the switch on the overhead, but now she was equal distance from both ends. No way out but through.

Brianna braced herself and stood a little taller. This was ridiculous. She was scaring herself for no reason. Too much time alone and too much bad TV was rotting her senses. She didn't believe in monsters.

Until she looked up and saw her face staring back at her. Her face, but not hers. Her body, but not hers. Certainly not her stylish lounge-wear. The face looking back was old. And sad. It carried the weight of too many years and not enough laughter.

Brianna froze. Her heart had ceased pounding and now ached. She reached out for the woman, some odd need to comfort this stranger overwhelming her.

A hand reached back, wrapped around her wrist, and dragged her into the mirror.

She couldn't breathe. Shards of glass tore her clothes and ripped her flesh as she slid unwillingly from one side to the other. It was an eternity. It was no time at all.

She found herself standing in pitch black. There was no

definition to the space. No wall, no ceiling, no floor. Only obsidian and the mirror. She stared out at her home. One step forward would take her back, right? She took that step. And didn't move. She held out her hand, feeling for a hard surface. Nothing. Her clothes were no longer shredded, her flesh no longer bleeding.

Slowly, she began to realise she was not alone. She turned carefully and faced a sea of herself. Infant Brianna, sleeping eternally in a bassinet. Toddler Brianna, wobbling on chubby legs. Through the years, it seemed every iteration of her waited. For what, she could not fathom. They didn't speak. They didn't move. They simply stared out into the hallway.

There were future Briannas as well. The old woman who pulled her in, and every age between now, then, and beyond. They stood slightly apart from the others as if knowing they didn't yet belong.

Panic rose, choking her. Brianna spun, again and again, seeking a way out. She pushed aside a gathering of pouting teenagers and ran deeper into the 'Other Side'. She ran with wild terror until she had to bend over, hands on knees as she panted and gasped for air.

She hadn't moved an inch.

Tears welled up. This had to be a nightmare. There was no way this was her reality. Another turn. Another strain for the mirror.

An exasperated voice pulled her attention, and she looked over her shoulder to see an elegant, well-dressed version of her current self step out of the darkness.

"You're wasting us."

She pushed Brianna backward and stepped through the mirror, straightening her tailored jacket as she briefly vanished. Brianna tumbled into the elderly women, crying out in surprise and then in horror as the arms that caught her began to melt. She looked up, watching their faces liquefy and slide off their skulls. Their eyes lingered, accusing her before they fell. As one rolled down her shoulder, she pulled away, slipping in what was left of her future.

Sobs tore free, and she tried to throw herself at the mirror, to follow her doppelgänger. To get away. She was unable to move further forward, to venture back through the mirror. She was trapped.

Time didn't pass for the catatonic horde. Other small hints spoke to her of moments rising and dying. The older versions dried, their skulls eventually turning to dust. There was no sunrise and no sunset on their 'Side'. They could watch time-shift through the mirror, but it didn't impact them.

As her imposter lived her life, new future selves appeared, with hungry eyes and malice-painted lips. They smiled at her, knowing the secret to it all but not telling. Words were not exchanged in this place. Brianna had heard nothing since the pretender left.

That was when she gave up. She'd been trying to find an answer—a reason for this sudden shift in her fortunes. But there was no lesson to be learned, no higher power trying to change her ways. She was there, and the why didn't matter.

Her mimic didn't appear to age. They watched her move through life, watched her live while they were held in limbo. And every time her mirror self passed, every time she walked by, that bitch winked.

KIMBERLEY REI
ABOUT THE AUTHOR

Kimberly Rei does her best work in the places that can't exist...
the in-between places where imagination defies reality. With a
penchant for dark corners and hooks that leave readers looking
over their shoulder, she is always on the lookout for new ideas,
new projects, and new ways to make words dance

Her debut novelette, *Chrysalis*, is available on Amazon (https://
readerlinks.com/l/1416028).

Kim is happiest behind a keyboard or doing anything at all with
her beautiful wife.

studio-rei.mailchimpsites.com

THE CREAKY DOOR
BY EVAN BAUGHFMAN

*D*ave closes his laptop, snuffing out the blank white document glaring from its screen. He places the computer onto the wooden floor beside him. The huge house is soundless, undisturbed, alone beside a dusty road. It provides the perfect reading environment.

Dave trades the laptop for an anthology of spooky stories he purchased at a yard sale long ago. Perhaps inspiration lurks somewhere within the book's yellowed pages.

Under lamplight, he examines the table of contents. His imagination takes hold and starts to shake him free of rust.

Is "A Maid and Her Madness" the tale of a beleaguered hotel employee driven to murder? Is "The Roar from the Trees" about a Sasquatch infuriated by deforestation? Well, "Rain of Terror" surely describes a sudden downpour of flesh-eating acid marring some poor family's afternoon picnic.

No longer rigid in his moth-eaten recliner, Dave drapes his legs over an arm of the chair. He smiles and turns to page 66 to see if the titular "Smile in the Dark" belongs to a hungry, sabre-toothed Cheshire tiger.

Behind him, the basement door slowly creaks open.

Dave peers over the top of his seat. Shadows seem to creep up the basement steps and inch their way across the living room.

Dave walks to the door, grabs its knob. He peers into the basement's black maw.

When he moved into the old place two weeks ago, he'd gone into the basement and seen it was empty. No boxes. No shelves. Yes, his flashlight had revealed some cobwebs, but there weren't any other signs of life. No tiny paw-prints or droppings on the hard-packed earth floor. Not even a small window to the outside. The air had been stale and hot below the house, trapped inside a prison of cinderblock walls.

Now, holding the knob, Dave moves the door slightly. It creaks on corroded hinges. He'll have to find a hardware store this weekend. Does the little town off the highway even have one?

And how could the door have opened? No window in the basement means no draft to push upstairs. Besides, the night is calm. Wind's not whistling around the house. Storm shutters sit still.

Dave shrugs. He's no expert on the behaviour of old houses.

As he shuts the basement door, its hinges squeal, whining in protest.

He returns to the recliner, re-opens the book, and gets comfortable once more. Within moments, he's lost in a fictional world. From it, he seeks no escape.

It's been three months since the divorce, and Dave welcomes a bit of fantasy.

Moving into a paint-chipped house that no one wanted, far from others' happiness and laughter had been a fine idea at first. He thought the change in location would jumpstart a bit of creativity in his brain. Force him to finally get to work on another novel. Something eerie and profound. But all he's been able to create thus far is a collection of embarrassing high school poetry about heartbreak, infidelity, and how much he hates, loves, and loves to hate his ex-wife.

Plus, he's gone eight days without conversing with anyone but himself. Sometimes, he doesn't bother to move his tongue at all.

The cardboard box marked 'Books' is the only one he's felt compelled to open. Others are precariously stacked around the living room, monuments to his slug-like state. The house's second story is virtually empty, save for toiletries forgotten by a stained bathroom sink and a lumpy mattress lying on a dusty bedroom floor.

As Dave reads and matches the sinister 'Smile in the Dark' with his own grin, the basement door creaks open behind him once more.

This time, the hinges shriek louder, shriller. Dave cups his hands over his ears, trying to dull the noise. The sound is painful and pierces like a wasp's sting.

He races to the door and attempts to shut it tight.

However... it resists.

In fact, instead of closing, the door pushes against Dave's weight and opens further, creaking. Squealing. Screaming.

Dave grunts and strains as he is driven backward. He slides along on sweaty socks. The door won't budge, but it does a great job of budging Dave as he struggles to stand tall.

Eventually, Dave sees it. A thick, black tendril wrapped around the edge of the door. A tentacle made of shadow.

The darkness in the basement wants out.

Dave runs over to the lamp beside the recliner. He removes the lampshade and angles the bulb, so it burns bright in the direction of the basement door.

Darkness retreats down the steps. Good thing, too, because its tentacles have tripled.

Dave springs into action and slams the door shut. He turns the lock and prays that it actually works.

The house is silent. For a moment, Dave thinks he's okay.

But then the lamp flickers and dies.

The lock on the basement door rotates to the left.

And the door creaks ajar even louder than before.

Dave moves for his laptop. He flips it open, holding it out in front of him like it's a cross with the power to deflect demons. Its weak glow slows his heart rate a beat or two.

He backs up to the window, parts wilted floral curtains, and welcomes in some of the full moon's light.

Dave warns the darkness to stay away, though he has difficulty seeing what it's doing at the top of the stairs.

However, he has no trouble hearing it slowly open and close the basement door over and over again.

Creeeeeeeeeeeeeeeeeeak, the door moans.

Creeeeeeeeeeeeeeeeeeeeeak.

CREEEEEEEEEEEEEEEEEEEEEEEEEEEEEEEEEEEEEEEEEEEEAK.

Why?

Why hasn't the mass of shadows come for him?

Why is it playing such grating night music?

Why is the sentient gloom messing with the door?

In the distance: a howl.

Dave looks out the window. Crouched on the dirt road in front of the house is a gigantic dog.

Scratch that. A wolf. A monster the size of a refrigerator, it raises its snout to the sky and howls again.

Behind Dave, the basement door creeeeeeeeeeeeeeeeeaks.

The wolf's ears perk up like dual antennae. It steps onto his property, easing over a fallen fence, stepping through overgrown weeds on the neglected lawn.

Dave looks at the unopened boxes to his right. Which one contains the block of butcher's knives? Probably the one marked 'Kitchen'.

He tears open the box, but there are no kitchen utensils inside. Instead, there's his framed college diploma, a bobblehead of Edgar Allan Poe, and other knick-knacks from his study back home.

No, no. This is home now—this horrible place with the living darkness and the werewolf approaching the front door.

Oh, God, oh, God, oh, God.

How could he have mislabelled the boxes?

How? How? How?

Wait. His coin collection is in this box, too. And some of the coins are silver. Horror films suggest weaponising the precious metal against various creatures of the night.

He shakes his head. What's he going to do? Throw an American Silver Eagle at the beast like a miniature discus?

The basement door creaks louder, LOUDER. Dave whispers harshly at the darkness to stop; PLEASE, STOP, because the sound is drawing the impossible animal closer, CLOSER.

But that seems to be what the darkness wants. To lure in the horrible beast.

To bring it inside the house.

A huge, black arm snakes out of the basement. Dave shrieks and falls away from the box, certain that the darkness is coming for him. He backs up to the window once more. The room seems to fill with even more shadow, ready to strangle him free of breath.

But the darkness moves past him toward the front door.

The wolf is on the porch, growling.

Dave is frozen. He knows he should flee, hide.

But where is there to go?

He can't remember where he left his car keys. His nearest neighbour is half a mile away. If he makes a break for it, he doubts he can outrun a giant wolf in the expanse of open fields outside the house.

The dark arm turns the front doorknob. The wolf pushes against the door.

The monster enters.

The darkness gestures for the wolf to follow it, and so the creature does.

The wolf lopes into the basement and disappears from view, but not before nodding at Dave, as if to say, *Thank you, sorry for the intrusion.*

The basement door continues to creak back and forth, back and forth.

In the distance: a chainsaw whirs to life.

The creaky door guides into the house a masked psychopath wearing bloodstained overalls. The humongous man kills the motor on his weapon and tells Dave, "Too scary out there. Need a place to stay."

He, too, ventures into the basement.

Dave listens for a struggle between psycho killer and werewolf, but there isn't one.

He only hears the irritating hinges of the creaky door.

Next, the noise brings in a vampire seeking shelter. He explains that recently in his neighbourhood, an arsonist has sent a pair of children to the burn ward. Another drive-by has claimed the life of a mother of five.

"Don't vant to be around that anymore," the creature explains, then flips his cape and floats down into darkness.

After that, a scaly fiend displaced by the latest hurricane steps into Dave's home on razor-tipped flippers the size of rake heads.

A scarecrow defeated by drought puts down its scythe for a moment to shake Dave's trembling hand.

A mummy tagged with Islamophobic epithets expresses its gratitude with unintelligible sobs. It cries so hard that its jaw snaps off and falls to the floor.

All manner of monsters are brought to the basement the creaky siren's call.

A ghost, a ghoul, a goblin.

A Chupacabra afraid to be sent back to its world of

A cyclops, a clown, a chimaera.

Dozens of creepy, crawly, growly things, all in the basement. One by one by one.

How can they possibly fit inside such a cramped space?

There must be other gateways down there, invisible to the human eye. The walls are strictly optional.

The house's last guest is a possessed ventriloquist's dummy who tips his little hat to Dave and then descends the basement steps with a toddler's grace.

The darkness finally closes the creaky door for good.

The lamp turns on, and, aside from an open front door, it's like nothing has happened at all.

Dave goes to the recliner and turns it around, so it now faces the basement. He checks for any straggling lost souls before closing the front door, but there's no movement on the quiet road.

Dave returns to his chair and sits. He bookmarks his spot in the short story anthology and then puts it aside. There'll be time for reading later.

A blank white document beckons from the laptop in his hands. Dave extinguishes the lamplight.

He glances at the basement door. He smiles in the dark.

It's time to write.

EVAN BAUGHFMAN
ABOUT THE AUTHOR

Much of Evan Baughfman's writing success has been as a playwright, his original plays finding homes in theaters worldwide. A number of his scripts are published through Heuer Publishing, YouthPLAYS, Next Stage Press, and Drama Notebook. A resident of Southern California, Evan is a member of PlayGround-L.A. as well as Force of Nature Productions.

Evan has also found success writing horror fiction, his work found most recently in anthologies by Black Hare Press, Blood Song Books, and Grinning Skull Press. Additionally, Evan's adapted a number of his short stories into screenplays, of which "The Tell-Tale Art," "A Perfect Circle," and "The Creaky Door" have won awards in various film festival competitions. Evan's first short story collection, *The Emaciated Man and Other Terrifying Tales from Poe Middle School*, is published through Thurston Howl Publications.

More information is available at
amazon.com/author/evanbaughfman

CPSIA information can be obtained
at www.ICGtesting.com
Printed in the USA
BVHW092047190421
605311BV00002B/209